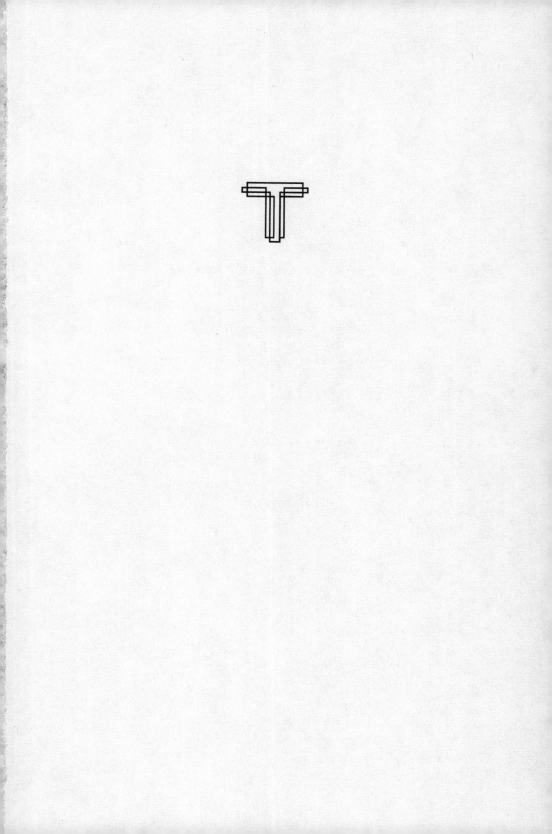

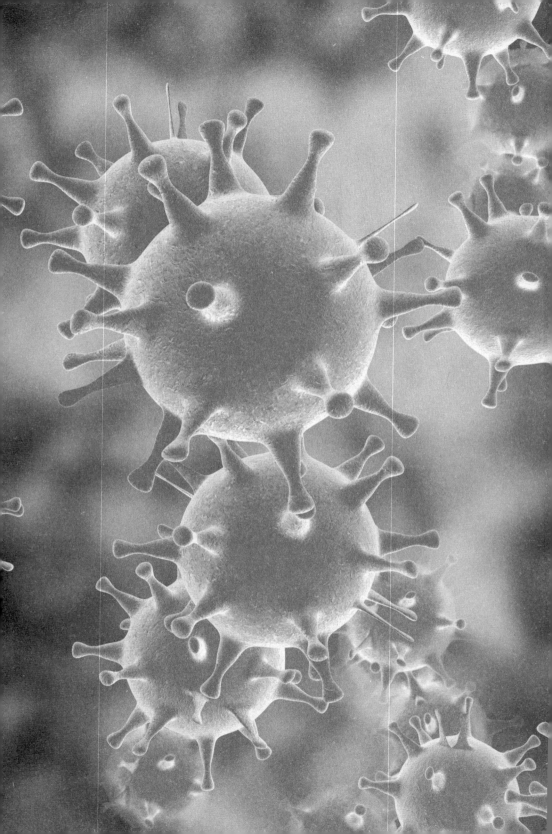

CONTAINMENT

HANK PARKER

TOUCHSTONE

New York   London   Toronto   Sydney   New Delhi

This book is dedicated to all scientists and public health professionals who work tirelessly and often in obscurity to protect the world from emerging infectious diseases

CHAPTER ONE

JULY 29
LANCASTER COUNTY, PENNSYLVANIA

Amos Lapp moved slowly but purposefully on this late-summer day in Amish-country Pennsylvania. He had thirty head of Holsteins to milk before supper, and acres of fields to harvest in the coming days, but he'd completed both of these tasks often enough over the past forty years that he knew exactly how much time it took to do them.

He angled toward the barn doors that, like the rest of the building, needed a fresh coat of paint. The cows were there already, milling around outside the entrance, lowing softly, impatient for the feed that they knew awaited them inside. Amos leaned into the heavy doors. Slowly they slid open, steel wheels squeaking on the rusty tracks. He stepped aside as the cows filed in and instinctively took up stations at the individual stalls that were arrayed in rows along both sides of the barn's length. As he waited by the open doors, Amos noted a dark band of clouds on the western horizon. He sniffed the air—heavy, damp, with a faint, electric odor. He watched the clouds for a moment. It looked like the storm would miss them, but another could crop up at any time. Even so, he wouldn't rush the work. The cows always seemed to sense it when he was anxious and tended to produce less milk.

With the herd in place, Amos moved along the stalls and fastened steel locking stanchions around the cows' thick, sweaty necks. He spoke softly to the animals and gently stroked their heads. He could distinguish them individually, and had given a name to each: Molly, Bessy, and all the rest.

He reached the last stall and swung the stanchion lever into place. As he snapped it shut he pinched his right index finger in the locking mechanism. Dime-sized drops of blood spattered onto the concrete floor. Suppressing an oath, he dabbed at the finger with his bandanna and told himself he'd put some mercurochrome on the wound when he got back to the house. Lord knows he'd seen worse.

With the cows secure, Amos shoveled feed from a large cart into feeding troughs in front of the stalls. He varied the amounts; he knew just how much to give each cow. He then moved to the first cow to begin milking.

Amos dipped a clean rag into a bucket of sudsy disinfectant, swabbed the cow's udder, and directed a steady stream of rich white milk into a waiting bucket. Amos milked by hand. Many of his Amish peers still generally shunned electricity, but most of them had taken to using automatic milking machines, powered by diesel, propane, or natural gas. Amos couldn't afford these aids, and he preferred using his hands. He liked the direct contact with his animals. When the bucket was full, he carried it to an adjacent shed and dumped the contents into a stainless-steel, thousand-gallon tank with an attached chilling unit to retard the growth of bacteria. This was Amos's one concession to modernity: the apparatus was powered by a rack of propane bottles.

Ninety minutes later he'd worked through two thirds of the herd. He paused after milking a stout, eight-year-old cow. "Not too productive today are we, Bounty?" he asked. A healthy milker in her prime should produce seven or eight gallons per milking, but today Bounty had yielded only half that amount. Amos ran his hand along the cow's neck and head, slippery with perspiration. A little warm, maybe. He looked in her nose and eyes. No watery discharge. Grasping the animal's muzzle with his left hand, he rolled back the cow's lips from her teeth and exposed the gums. No rawness or signs of bleeding. He probed gingerly with the fingers of his injured right hand, feeling for roughness or blistering. Everything seemed okay. If Bounty was under the weather—cows, like humans, suffered innumerable mild infections from time to time—she'd be back to normal soon.

Amos finished the milking by six fifteen. He'd leave the cows in the barn overnight. They'd be ready to milk again at first light. He washed out the utensils and hung them on wooden pegs, experiencing, now and again, a twinge of pain from the cut in his hand, but he continued on with his chores. He shoveled manure from concrete retaining troughs behind the cows and tossed it into a nearby manure spreader. When he finished, he closed the barn doors and began the slow walk toward home and a waiting supper.

Three mornings later Charity Lapp awoke to the sound of her husband's racking cough. It had started the previous evening but had now become much worse. She rose from their wooden-framed, Shaker rope bed and groped through the darkness to the small, adjoining bathroom. She turned up the gas in a dimmed lantern, drew a glass of water, and returned to the bedroom.

She handed the glass to Amos. He tilted it toward his mouth and swallowed. With a groan and a suppressed cough, he settled back down on the sheets. Charity positioned her own pillow under her husband's head. Maybe the extra elevation would make him feel better, help the mucus slide down instead of pooling in his throat and causing him to cough.

She felt his forehead: warm and slick with sweat. It reminded her of when her firstborn had been sick, almost forty years ago now. The baby girl had only been two, and her skin had somehow felt both hot and clammy at the same time. Charity had sat up with her all night while Amos brought in a steady supply of cool, damp cloths to mop the girl's forehead. But the child's fever had ticked upward with every hour that went by. She'd died just before dawn.

Charity and Amos had had two healthy sons soon afterward, but the loss of her firstborn left an emptiness in her heart that had never been filled. Amos was a grown, healthy man, hardly sick a day in his life. The grippe must have gotten him, Charity thought. She'd heard that something was going around. But Amos would be fine in a couple of days, with her nursing. No need for a doctor. And anyway, like many of the Amish, the Lapps didn't have health insurance and didn't put a lot of stock in the medical profession.

In the meantime, there was still the milking to do and other farm chores that couldn't wait. She wouldn't ask for help from her two sons, who were living and working in town. As teenagers, they had defied Amos and left the farm and the faith, and they had their own lives now, and seldom even visited.

Her husband coughed again and tried to sit up. Charity put a gentle hand on his shoulders and eased him back down. Amos pushed her arm away. "Leave me alone, woman!" he yelled at her. He wrenched himself out of bed and started toward the wooden freestanding clothes rack in the corner of the bedroom.

Charity rubbed her arm and watched. What had gotten into Amos? Was he planning to get dressed, to head out into the murky dawn, fever and all? She moved between her husband and the clothes rack in the dim, shadowy light, trying to make out the expression on his bearded face.

With a guttural growl Amos grabbed his wife by the shoulders and flung her aside. Charity fell against the edge of the bed, cracking her left elbow against the frame, and toppled to the floor. She lay there in pain but remained silent as her husband pulled his coveralls on, not bothering to remove his nightshirt. Still in his bare feet, he lurched out of the room.

Seconds later, Charity heard a door slam. Did she dare go after him? What choice did she have?

She found him a hundred yards from the house, sitting in the cold mud of the rutted driveway, clutching his sides in a spasm of coughing. "I'm sorry," he croaked. "Don't know what got over me." He struggled to his feet, and Charity took his arm and led him back to the house.

Four nights later, Charity was frantic with worry and fear. Amos's condition had steadily gotten worse. Small, reddish rashlike spots had appeared on his arms and chest, and now many of these had merged into large purple-brown bruises. His gums were starting to bleed and he was passing blood in his urine. His stool now looked like tar balls and the coughing had given way to frequent vomiting. His violent behavior had ceased, but Charity suspected that this had more to do with a lack of energy than any kind of improvement in his health.

She was doing all she could to comfort him, but when she finally admitted to herself that she had to get him to a doctor, it was past midnight and too late. She had no phone to call for an ambulance and didn't dare to leave her husband to walk to her nearest neighbor's house, over a half mile away, in darkness.

Amos was mumbling to her. He needed to use the bathroom again. She pulled the rough wool blanket off his torso, wrapped her arms around his lower legs, and swiveled them over the edge of the bed. Bending low, she grasped her husband under his armpits, braced her knees against the side of the bed, and began to pull him upright. "Amos, you're going to have to help me some," she muttered. Her face was next to his. It looked as if he was trying to say something. She leaned closer to hear his low words.

He vomited, spraying her face with stomach contents the color and consistency of used coffee grounds.

Charity hastily wiped herself off with the sleeve of her nightgown, raised her husband's limp body, and half dragged him into the bathroom. She positioned him on a stool in front of the toilet, then went to the sink and splashed cold water onto her face until it was clean again. She turned back to the toilet.

Amos was lying on the floor, on his left side. His right hand dangled over the lid of the toilet. He was perfectly still. Blood and vomitus trickled out of the corner of his mouth. His eyes were open but blank.

Charity Lapp screamed.

CHAPTER TWO

AUGUST 7
CHESTER COUNTY, PENNSYLVANIA

A stocky, broad-shouldered man drove slowly down a cornfield-bordered lane and rolled to a stop in front of a weathered farmhouse. He eased out of his late-model sedan, stretched, and looked around. Frayed curtains looped across the house windows. No fresh tire tracks other than his own. Green plastic chair still propped against the front door. Beware of Dog sign tacked to a leaning post in the overgrown front yard. He glanced back down the lane. No sign he was followed. No one else knew what went on here, but you could never be too careful.

Satisfied that he was alone, the man strode to a large, free-standing garage of whitewashed cinder block, which made it decades newer than the house, but the paint was faded and stained gray-green with mold.

He reached the front of the garage, ignored the heavy over-head door, and inserted a sturdy key into the lock of a smaller, adjacent metal door.

The space that greeted him inside was in stark contrast to the garage's decrepit exterior. Built and fitted out to his personal design and specifications, it was brightly lit and spotless—floors, walls, ceiling, even the long, stainless-steel lab bench in the center. The room housed state-of-the-art scientific instrumentation. A large machine that resembled an oversized refrigerator stood against the far wall. It was a thirty-three-cubic-foot Caron Insect Growth Chamber, a potential terrorist weapon more powerful than an army of soldiers. He peered through the clear glass at shelves holding metal trays filled with small capsules with perforated caps.

The capsules contained ticks. Most people found ticks to be abhorrent creatures, but the man considered them his pets. Not that he blamed others for detesting them. They harbored a rogues' gallery of bacteria, viruses, and parasites, and transmitted some of the nastiest diseases known—Rocky Mountain spotted fever, tularemia, Lyme disease, and a host of others. That made them vectors—organisms that transmitted diseases between species. He had given himself the name *Doctor Vector.* He had read a number of comic books as a kid, and even though he believed he was doing something for the greater good, he also got a certain thrill from imagining himself as a comic-book villain. Except this time, the evil scientist was going to prevail.

Doctor Vector admired ticks. They'd been around for three hundred million years and more than eight hundred species inhabited the world. You didn't get to be that successful unless you were good at surviving—and ticks were exceedingly good at that. They fed on blood, lying in wait by clinging to grass blades or leaves, forelegs outstretched. When an animal brushed by, they climbed aboard and sought a suitable patch of skin. Once settled, they'd cut a tiny hole in the skin, secrete an anticoagulating chemical, insert a feeding appendage, and engorge themselves. A well-nourished female tick could produce thousands of eggs at a time. Even the larvae were bloodsuckers, feeding on birds and small mammals. As they molted, first to the nymph stage and then to adults, they dined on increasingly larger creatures. And at every stage, on every host, the germs they carried were passed along.

Doctor Vector checked the gauges on the growth chamber, confirmed that temperature and humidity were within pre-scribed limits, and recorded the readings. After a last look at his charges he turned and headed toward the exit. His work was done for now. He would be busier tomorrow. Tomorrow was feeding day.

The next day, Doctor Vector donned a white lab coat with stockinette cuffs, pulled on a pair of gloves, securing sticky tape around the wrists, and walked over to the insect growth chamber. He retrieved a small plastic capsule and carried it to the lab table in the center of the room. The table was equipped with a small moat around the perimeter, filled with an inch or so of water, which would trap any ticks that tried to escape. As an additional precaution, he smeared a layer of petroleum jelly around the edge of the table and placed the capsule into a petri dish with a layer of water on the bottom. Multiple defenses were in place so that no tick escaped. Each was infected with a deadly virus, a pathogen that would not affect the tick but would almost certainly kill any human that it bit. Every tick had to be accounted for at every stage of the procedure.

He gently removed the screened lid of the capsule, placed the petri dish and capsule on the stage of a stereo microscope on the table, and examined the contents.

Each capsule held ten black-legged or deer ticks, *Ixodes scapularis*, the species that carried and transmitted Lyme dis-ease in North America and was also an excellent carrier of the deadly virus that Vector was working with. The growth cham-ber held a hundred labeled capsules. A thousand infected ticks were more than enough to establish a widespread epidemic, as healthy ticks in the wild would breed prolifically, provided there were adequate hosts for their blood meal. And in the days ahead, the population of the lab ticks would multiply several times, especially since each capsule contained a mix of male and female ticks to facilitate mating. Even a single gravid female could spawn a large population.

An hour later, the scientist had worked through all the capsules, counting all healthy ticks, removing and disposing of the few dead or unhealthy ones, and placing the capsules into a container. He then carried the container to the far side of the room, where a number of small cages were arrayed on broad shelves.

The cages contained laboratory mice. Doctor Vector's experiments had revealed that the mice were suitable hosts and blood sources for his pet ticks. He'd tried a number of small mammals and had initially been leaning toward white lab rabbits. Easier to handle, gentle, and passive. All in all an appealing animal to work with. But they'd turned out to be highly susceptible to the virus and lived only a few days after exposure to it. He'd found that mice were resistant to the disease even though they hosted the pathogen and could pass it along. They took up a lot less space and there was never a supply shortage. But the problem with mice was they were difficult to work with. Fast, unpredictable movements, and they'd bite. Handling them required uninterrupted concentration and great care, especially once they were carrying the virus.

He retrieved one of the mouse cages, opened the door, and reached inside with a gloved hand. This was the tricky part. He'd devised a method to securely attach each capsule of ticks to a corresponding mouse to enable the ticks to feed, but the procedure demanded absolutely focused attention. He grasped the mouse with his left hand, pinching it behind the head between thumb and forefinger to reduce the chances of being bitten. With his right hand, which was ungloved for improved dexterity, he picked up a capsule, uncapped it, and quickly attached its open end to the mouse. When he was satisfied that the attachment was secure and that the contained ticks were free to feed, he moved on to the next mouse and capsule.

He'd give the ticks a couple of days to feed to repletion and then return them to the growth chamber. Doctor Vector smiled to himself. Soon his soldiers would be ready for battle.

CHAPTER THREE

Fifty feet above the limestone floor of a tropical forest, Curt Kennedy braced himself as a gust of wind nearly dislodged him from his perch on the limb of a Pacific banyan tree. Kennedy had worn a few titles in his life, not all of which he was permitted to divulge, and arborist was not one of them. But Marianas fruit bats often roosted in the branches of banyan trees, and Kennedy's mission was to capture a few of these "flying foxes."

He rubbed the two-day stubble on his lined, tanned face. He'd settled into the tree the previous night while the bats were off foraging, and had secured himself to the trunk with a harness and rope. At first he'd slept well, but as the large bats—eight to ten inches long from head to rump—returned to the tree with the first graying of the dawn, seeking perches, they often crashed into the branches, disturbing other roosting bats, sometimes causing noisy fights. So Kennedy had given up on sleep and concentrated on capturing some specimens.

He could see dozens of bats hanging upside down on nearby branches, wings wrapped around their bodies. He reached for a fine-mesh net that was secured to a telescoping aluminum pole, extended it to a nearby bat, and gently dislodged the animal into the net. He didn't want to risk a bite from one of these creatures—bats carried some pretty nasty diseases, even beyond rabies, which was what most people associated with them, so he wore heavy-duty leather gloves that extended above his wrists. There was no rabies in the Marianas, but if Kennedy's hunch was correct, these bats might be harboring something far more dangerous, something for which no vaccine existed, something that could lead to an agonizing, painful death.

He eased the captured bat into a burlap sack and extended the net to a second, but instead of nudging the sleeping bat into the net, he bumped its side—too soon and too hard. With a shrill cry, the bat exploded from its roost and flew at Kennedy's face, wings stretched out in a three-foot span, mouth open, revealing sharp teeth. Kennedy ducked, swiped at the bat with a gloved hand, and lost his perch on the branch.

The harness and rope held. The bat returned to its roost. Swaying from the rope, Kennedy took several seconds to catch his breath, and then slowly pulled himself back to his branch. He willed himself to be more patient.

Kennedy figured that most people would have considered this kind of work to be tedious, lonely, and potentially dangerous, but he couldn't imagine doing anything else. That his work might benefit humanity was a bonus, but he loved the intellectual task of trying to solve a vexing medical mystery and the physical and mental challenge of tackling a difficult job.

He'd soon bagged a half-dozen bats without further incident. He tightly secured the drawstring around the sack and lowered himself and his equipment to the ground.

He carried the bats to a nearby van and carefully shooed them into a steel-mesh cage on the floor. As he snapped the cage shut, one of the more alert bats shot toward the door and nearly caught Kennedy's finger in his teeth. Kennedy yanked his hand back and slammed his elbow into one of the doors. *Gloves,* he reminded himself, rubbing the elbow, his heart pounding. *You have gloves on, you idiot.*

The next day, Kennedy was driving along Kalakaua Avenue in Honolulu in a rented Jeep Wrangler. This was only a short layover, but he had enough time before his next flight to Philadelphia for a quick meeting with a colleague. He passed by Waikiki Beach and saw tanned bodies frolicking in the waves. *Someday,* he thought. Someday he'd finally clear his schedule enough to spend some time here. And not just for the sand and the surf.

He pressed a buzzer below a large, flat panel on a nondescript building next to a strip mall.

"Pacific Enterprises," said a voice at the other end.

"Kennedy here."

"Look straight into the panel."

The retinal scan panel above the buzzer confirmed his identity and the door clicked softly. Kennedy pushed it open. He pressed another buzzer on a door at the end of the hall. The door opened and a tall, skinny African American man extended his hand to Kennedy.

"Welcome to paradise," said Bill Cothran, grinning.

"Good to see you, Bill," Kennedy said, gripping Cothran's hand and returning the grin. Kennedy was always happy to see his old friend and colleague, who was not a businessman, as the name Pacific Enterprises suggested, but rather an undercover agent with the CIA who specialized in detecting and tracking terrorist threats emanating from Southeast Asia and the western Pacific. Kennedy knew Cothran to be intelligent and resourceful, two traits that Kennedy held in the highest regard, but he'd also gotten to know the man behind the professional mask. They'd met in early 2003 in Iraq when they were part of a survey group, tasked to find caches of biological weapons reputedly hidden by Saddam Hussein before the U.S. invasion. As they were approaching a suspicious building just outside of Tikrit, a squad of Iraqi Republican Guard troops had ambushed their lightly armored vehicle. The driver and the Marine guard were killed instantly and Kennedy took a bullet in his thigh.

Cothran had retrieved the dead soldier's assault rifle, and managed to take out the insurgents single-handedly and carry the wounded Kennedy to the pickup zone two miles away. Kennedy would always owe the man his life and considered him a trusted colleague and a friend, something he couldn't say about anyone else he knew.

Cothran led Kennedy into a small office and motioned toward a young man slouched in a chair. "Meet my new intern, Angus. Angus, this is Curt Kennedy."

To Kennedy's surprise Angus leaped out of his chair in what seemed to be shock.

The young man didn't quite fall over, but seemed pretty shaken all the same. "Hello, sir, I've been looking forward to meeting you," he managed to sputter.

Kennedy gave Cothran a questioning look. Cothran just shrugged. Kennedy took in Angus's appearance: dark, curly hair spilling over his ears. Jeans, sneakers, and a ridiculous Hawaiian shirt with pens stuffed into the pocket. Kennedy wondered who'd told him he was appropriately dressed to leave his house, let alone spend the day at a high-level internship. But the boy did look bright. If Cothran had hired him, he must be. And there was something else, something familiar that Kennedy felt oddly compelled to look closer at. But he was always doing this, thinking he recognized someone he didn't know from Adam, so he simply nodded again and turned away from Angus.

Cothran motioned to a small conference table and they all sat down. "Angus has been assigned to this office for a few months," said Cothran. "Kind of a training assignment and he'll give us some technical support. MIT graduate, but he's at home here—grew up in Hawaii."

Angus nodded, his eyes never straying from Kennedy. It was obvious to Kennedy that the young man was dying to say something. Practically bursting, but whatever it was he was keeping it to himself. At least for now.

"Curt," Cothran said, "what did you learn in Saipan?"

Kennedy glanced at Angus, who was making him a little uneasy, then back to Cothran, and said nothing.

"Don't worry," Cothran said. "Angus is cleared, and he needs to be brought up to speed."

Kennedy stiffened but tried to dispel his discomfort at Angus's strange behavior, which didn't seem in keeping with an agent. Angus must have sensed it.

He looked at Kennedy and smiled. "Hey, we're good, okay?" he said, in what sounded to Kennedy like a forced attempt at normalcy. "I understand you're with something called the Biological Investigative Service. Never heard of that one."

"It's a pretty obscure outfit," Kennedy said, relaxing slightly. "Our job is to track biothreats."

"But you work for Agriculture?"

Kennedy smiled. Angus didn't have to know everything. "USDA pays my salary and gives me lab space."

Angus frowned and looked like he was going to ask another question, but Kennedy cut him off. "So, Saipan," he said to Cothran. "I confirmed Nipah virus in the bats. The strain matches that of the '99 Malaysia outbreak in swine that killed over a hundred people. So far—"

"What's the Nipah virus?" Angus asked.

Kennedy raised an eyebrow in thinly veiled annoyance. Angus met his gaze but Kennedy thought he saw a bit of deference in the intern's eyes. Kennedy couldn't guess what was going on with the strange kid, and decided to cut him some slack.

"It's a rare disease that we haven't seen in a while," Kennedy said, "but that, it turns out, is carried by these bats and transmitted to pigs—and humans."

"So, zoonotic," Angus said. "Transmitted from animals to humans, with bats as the vector. Like rabies."

"Not really like rabies," Kennedy said. "Rabies affects humans and animals pretty much in the same way, but a zoonotic disease like this Nipah virus might be dormant in animals, like it seems to be in these bats, but still be harmful to humans."

Angus nodded. He reminded Kennedy of a computer downloading a large file.

"So in Saipan," Kennedy began again, turning back to Cothran. "We have three dead and six hospital cases—all pig farmers or family members. First time the disease has ever cropped up outside Southeast Asia. Saipan's got about a dozen small pig operations, and based on what I told the local vets and hospitals about Nipah, they've quarantined the swine facilities and contained the animals. USDA's on its way."

"To Saipan?" Angus asked. "To do what?"

"Sacrifice any animals that have been infected or exposed," Kennedy said. *Have to give the kid credit*, he thought, and found himself warming to the young man. *He's not shy about asking questions. Kind of like me.*

"I assume you got with our guy there," said Cothran.

"Monahan," said Kennedy, nodding. "He's been keeping an eye on the Marianas offshoot of the Animal Rights League. No confirmation yet that they had anything to do with the outbreak, but it's the working assumption."

"But why would animal lovers want to harm pigs?" Angus asked.

"Actually, it's about protecting the bats," Kennedy said. "They're endangered because of overharvesting for food. If I had to guess, I'd say the Animal Rights League is trying to stop the bat harvest by sickening bat hunters. And pig farmers as a side benefit."

"So basically bioterrorism?" Angus asked. "We've been chasing terrorists all over the world since 9/11 and it turns out we need to focus on home-grown crazies? Have these animal rights groups ever used biological weapons?"

"Not yet," said Kennedy. "At least not on a large scale." He had the vague sense that Angus was showing off for him, but he was mildly impressed nonetheless. He wished the kid would just come out with whatever it was that he seemed to be suppressing, but it would have to wait for another day. He had a plane to catch.

On his way out the door, with the young man still staring at Kennedy, Cothran gave Kennedy a hearty handshake and said, "Glad you and Angus were able to meet. Maybe next time we can all take some time and catch up a little more."

Very curious, Kennedy thought. Cothran seemed to be in on whatever it was that Angus was bottling up. Not like Cothran at all to keep secrets from him.

He still couldn't shake the feeling that, somehow, Angus seemed familiar, like someone he'd known before, or seen somewhere. TV, movies, a public person? Kennedy racked his brains. He prided himself on his memory, on never forgetting a name or a face, but he was coming up blank with Angus.

CHAPTER FOUR

AUGUST 14
KENNETT SQUARE, PENNSYLVANIA

Jennifer Kelly stood beside a stainless-steel table in a veterinarian's office in suburban Philadelphia and gazed at the inert form of her golden retriever. The vet, Dr. Fernando Ferreira, knew the woman was worried and tried to project his own calm onto her. She brushed back a lock of auburn hair. "He's so still," she said shakily.

Dr. Ferreira slowly withdrew a rectal thermometer. "Asleep," he told Mrs. Kelly. "Sedative's working." He'd administered twenty milligrams of acepromazine when the dog had first come in, which had made a full exam much easier, especially with a dog this size. Calvert was his name. Ferreira had treated him before, throughout the four years he'd been the Kelly family's vet. He held the thermometer to the light in a gloved hand. "A hundred six. Above normal. I'll get a blood sample."

As Mrs. Kelly looked on, Ferreira shaved the dog's left forelimb, swabbed the area with alcohol, and drew two tubes of blood. He pressed a piece of gauze against the needle stick area, retrieved a notepad, and jotted down the symptoms: lethargy, recent weight loss, swollen glands, clear, watery discharge from nose and eyes, and painful joints. Bare patches on the torso where the dog's fur had come off in clumps exposing reddish, bruiselike splotches on the bare skin. Minor hemorrhaging around the gums. "I need to do a full blood workup," he told Mrs. Kelly. "But I'm thinking canine ehrlichiosis—canine hemorrhagic fever. Not too common around here but I've seen a few cases. Looks like we caught it early enough to treat it. I'll write a prescription."

She looked closely at him, her brow deeply furrowed. "How did he get it?"

"Tick, probably." The vet probed with his fingers under the retriever's thick coat and waited for Mrs. Kelly's next question. There was never just one.

"Could people get this thing?" she asked.

"Maybe from a tick. Not likely from a dog." Now she'd start asking him about ticks, he thought. Ferreira sympathized with her concern, but he didn't have time for a long Q&A. "Ticks carry all kinds of nasty bugs," he said. "They're all over the place and feed on blood. When they bite an animal or human they can transmit bacteria or virus. You want to always check after a walk, get in the habit of using a repellent." Ferreira's fingers paused on the nape of Calvert's neck. *Bingo.* He parted the straw-colored fur, exposed a tiny insect, and scrutinized it through a magnifying glass.

He picked up a pair of fine-tipped tweezers, swabbed them with alcohol, and firmly clasped the tick at the point where its mouth was attached to the dog's skin. He pulled steadily, taking care not to crush the insect's body, detached it, dropped it into an alcohol-filled vial, and capped and labeled the vial. He cleaned the spot on the dog's skin with a disinfectant and swabbed on antibiotic ointment. "Okay, big boy," he said. "Ready to go?"

As Ferreira slid his arms under Calvert and started to lift, the dog awoke, looked up at him with bloodshot eyes, and issued a low, menacing growl. Mrs. Kelly gasped.

Slowly, very slowly, Ferreira laid the dog back on the table and edged away. His mind raced. *Pretty early for the anesthetic to wear off*, he thought. And why would the dog be coming out of it so hostile, especially considering how gentle and loving Calvert had always been? He turned to Mrs. Kelly and asked her to wait outside. Dogs sometimes became protective of their owners in a vet's office.

When she'd left, Ferreira approached the dog again, carefully, with reassuring words and sounds. Calvert continued to growl and his eyes tracked Ferreira's movements. His lips drew back over his teeth. As the vet watched, foamy, reddish saliva began to bubble from the dog's mouth and then his eyes rolled back in his head. Calvert continued to growl, like, Ferreira thought, a creature possessed. *No way this is ehrlichiosis*, he concluded. *Rabies? Impossible.* Calvert's shots were up-to-date. Ferreira needed backup.

He edged toward the door as the dog continued to growl and snarl and, now, to stir. Blood had begun to drip from his mouth. Ferreira groped for the door handle.

The dog struggled to his feet, stood on the steel table, and crouched.

Ferreira's hand found the handle, but he didn't want to move for fear of making the big dog lunge. He gave the door a tiny push, and immediately it squeaked on its hinges.

With a snarl the dog sprang forward, covering the distance to Ferreira in the air, knocking him back against the door, and sinking his teeth deep into Ferreira's left wrist.

Ferreira screamed, not in pain—he couldn't yet feel the wound—but in fear. Would the dog stop at his wrist, or move in on his throat? Just what kind of disease was this animal carrying? Was it transmissible to humans? *This is how I'm going to die*, he thought.

CHAPTER FIVE

AUGUST 17
NEAR PHILADELPHIA, PENNSYLVANIA

Mariah Rossi fired up her five-year-old Subaru Outback and asked herself, as she did every morning, what had possessed her to buy such a car. The roughest road it had seen so far was the Schuylkill Expressway during pothole season. Her main incentive, she knew, had been those ads that had been *everywhere* just when she'd been looking to trade in her old Honda Civic. The open spaces stretching toward snowcapped peaks, the kayak riding the car-top carrier, the hiking and camping gear filling the trunk—she'd been unable to resist, but now here she was driving the same paved highway to and from her office every day, when the Outback was probably longing for a major road trip.

In the parking lot at her office building, she smoothed a few strands of hair into her ponytail and glanced at herself in her rearview mirror. She spotted the dark circles under her eyes and—*what was that? Had she had that wrinkle last night? Oh, stop it*, she scolded herself, grabbing her briefcase from the passenger seat and heading into work.

At her desk, she powered up her clunky computer and opened the file she'd been working on the night before. She checked her notes, punched in a number, and watched an animated diagram of a regional map on the monitor. A small blue dot near Wichita, Kansas, represented a hypothetical case of an animal disease, and it was slowly but steadily ballooning into a large blob that stretched toward the north and west. A digital readout at the bottom of the screen ticked off the cumulative time.

T + 12 hours: The blob had engulfed the entire state of Kansas and was oozing toward Colorado and western Nebraska.

T + 24: Wyoming and parts of South Dakota were turning blue. It was just a matter of time before the stain spread over Montana and Idaho, and then Canada.

As a veterinary epidemiologist working in a government lab operated by the U.S. Department of Agriculture, she specialized in modeling the spread of livestock diseases. The model on her monitor was of foot-and-mouth disease, a highly contagious and economically devastating viral affliction that sickened cloven-hoofed animals like cattle, sheep, and pigs, but didn't harm people. Her expertise was widely recognized and she'd proved invaluable in helping stop a number of potential epidemics of various animal diseases, but in reality hers was a desk job. She had once found comfort within the safe, sterile confines of the lab, but lately it had started to depress her. This morning she was plugging meteorological data into her model to determine how weather conditions would affect the direction and spread of the disease.

Mariah had a strong personal interest in—some coworkers called it an obsession with—foot-and-mouth disease. She'd been in England during the 2001 FMD outbreak there, as a second-year veterinary student who'd volunteered to help out. She'd thought it would be good training. The virus had spread quickly from the first diagnosed case in southeastern England. They'd made concerted efforts to contain the disease, including killing every susceptible animal, every cow, pig, and sheep, in a designated area around each new confirmed case. Nothing had worked. Within two weeks, the outbreak had become a nationwide epidemic, overwhelming the animal health system, shutting down the countryside. In the end, six million livestock were slaughtered.

The outbreak had continued to haunt her and was the main reason she had so willingly taken the desk job. She just couldn't imagine experiencing something like that again: soldiers shooting heirloom cattle in front of their owners, holding the farmers back so that they couldn't interfere. Some farmers committing suicide. Mounds of dead cattle in pits, heads, legs, hooves, horns jumbled together, the earth stained dark red-brown. Burning funeral pyres of animal carcasses, oily black smoke everywhere, the smell . . .

Mariah had wanted to be a vet since she was a teenager. After the UK experience she'd resolved to devote her life to fighting foot-and-mouth disease.

She forced her mind back to her current work, studying the results of her latest model simulation, entering data into a separate program on her computer, making additional notations in a green lab notebook she kept on her desk. Her colleagues occasionally teased her about the notebook. Old-fashioned, they called it, but the notes like the desk provided Mariah comfort and a sense of purpose.

She heard an awkward clearing of the throat behind her and swiveled in her chair to find her boss, Dr. Frank Hoffman, standing above her. Hoffman was the director of the National Laboratory for Foreign Animal Diseases—better known as the Barn. Mariah couldn't remember him ever coming by her office before. He was a summoner; he summoned you to his office, and you showed up at the appointed time.

"Sorry to barge in," Hoffman said hurriedly. "A couple of things have come up and I need you on them. Can you join me in my office?"

Hoffman bent toward the computer monitor. This was just like the man. Even though he had just asked her to his office, he was now going to get himself distracted by Mariah's work. It would be funny, if it didn't happen so often.

He was now scrutinizing the computer screen.

"So this is your FMD model," he said. "Weather factors, right?"

Mariah nodded. "Wind speed and direction, precipitation, that sort of thing."

"What about wildlife hosts?" asked Hoffman.

"That'll be part of the model," said Mariah, trying not to sound dismissive, or condescending. She was beginning to feel like she was undergoing some sort of interrogation. It was well known that some wildlife could be carriers of the virus.

"Insect vectors?" said Hoffman.

He's asking about another obvious factor, thought Mariah. Her model would incorporate the role of vectors in transmitting the disease, but that would also come later. What was with this guy inserting himself into her work like this? She didn't have a sense that he was genuinely interested. Was he just showing off? "Good thinking," she said politely. "That's another parameter that we'll be including."

Now, finally, Hoffman seemed to remember that he hadn't come to her to ask about the model.

"Right," he said. "As soon as you can break free, come on down to my office."

Curt Kennedy leaned back in his chair and rubbed his temple in a futile attempt to clear out the cobwebs in his brain. After nearly two full days of exhausting travel, he'd arrived back in Philadelphia on Saturday morning hoping to have the weekend to catch up on some sleep, but he'd made the mistake of stopping by his office on the way back from the airport. Big mistake. The work had piled up in his absence and he still had a trip report to write. And now Hoffman was demanding a meeting, ASAP.

Kennedy figured Hoffman wanted a briefing on the Saipan work, but why couldn't he wait a day or two? No immediate action was needed and Kennedy already knew what had to be done, and when. He didn't take well to being managed by others. He preferred to work alone, at his own pace, making his own decisions. Thanks to his actions and Cothran's help, the Nipah situation was under control and at this point all it required was close monitoring. But Hoffman was his nominal boss and Kennedy knew he could be volatile. He told himself to suck it up.

He pulled some notes from his briefcase and began to review them. No time for a formal write-up; he'd have to wing it, something he was normally good at, but right now his mind was pretty fuzzy. It was going to be a long day.

Mariah was always slightly caught off guard by her boss's office. She could never dismiss the notion that the director of a national laboratory would, or should, have a larger space. Or maybe the office just looked small because of the crammed bookshelves and piles of papers on the desk and floor.

She eased into a chair on one side of a small, rectangular conference table, feeling cramped. Hoffman was on the phone, and he nodded as he met her eye, but she didn't know whether he was acknowledging her or agreeing with whoever was on the other end of the call. A man sat across from Mariah, a guy she'd seen around the lab but had never actually spoken to. Kendrick? Keener? Something with a *K*. She pretended, awkwardly, not to notice him because he hadn't made any move to introduce himself when she'd arrived. She looked intently at the framed pictures of the president and the secretary of agriculture on the wall behind him.

Hoffman finished his phone call and moved to the head of the conference table. Mariah tried to get a read on his mood. She noticed the fine lines around his eyes. Probably tension, she thought. He held himself erect, with a kind of military bearing that she assumed was the product of his decade as a research scientist at the U.S. Army Medical Research Institute for Infectious Diseases—USAMRIID—at Fort Detrick, Maryland. Hoffman had always come across to Mariah as a consummate professional, totally dedicated to his work. And he was also extremely patriotic. At a conference he'd organized at the Barn a year before, he'd insisted that everyone recite the Pledge of Allegiance when the conference convened, even though several of the attendees were foreigners. It had been the equivalent of a corporate CEO opening a morning meeting with the national anthem, and people still joked about it behind his back.

Maria knew his feelings were tied to losing his wife, Karen, in the 2005 transit attacks in London. Karen had been a passenger on a double-decker bus that was bombed by Islamic extremists with ties to al-Qaeda. Everyone knew Hoffman still wore his wedding band. Mariah glanced at it now and thought about the fact that the couple never had children and that Hoffman now lived alone. A thought flashed in her mind: *I bet he still has his wife's clothes in his closet.*

"Okay, let's get started," Hoffman said, startling Mariah back into the present. "Curt Kennedy, meet Mariah Rossi. Mariah, Curt."

Mariah and Curt barely had time to nod at each other before Hoffman was barreling on. "Welcome back from Saipan, Curt. Gather you made some progress. Why don't you brief Mariah. I'd like you two to work together on the project."

Mariah made a point of maintaining her composure and

watched for Kennedy's reaction. She had seen him around the building off and on for a while, but they hadn't met before now. From his fit and upright appearance, she'd already guessed that he was ex-military. Up close she could see his nose had likely been broken, at least once, and he had a small scar on his right cheek. Both injuries added character to his looks. And he had the most piercing blue-gray eyes she'd ever seen. They gave no impression that he cared that his introduction to his new co-worker had been so offhand. *Okay*, Mariah thought. *You want to play it cool? I'll play it cool.* But now Kennedy was turning toward her, his eyes boring into hers as if daring her to look away.

Mariah listened to his report. He'd been in the Marianas researching some disease—Nipah virus. Mariah knew of it but only vaguely—and now he was explaining that it was infecting pigs and pig farmers and that an animal rights group was suspected of deliberately releasing the virus. He was terse and efficient and Mariah imagined that he wouldn't take kindly to being asked to repeat something. She began a mental list of things she'd research in more depth when she got back to her office: Nipah, flying foxes, Animal Rights League . . . and Saipan. When Kennedy finished, he leaned toward her, his forearms resting on the table, his eyes fixed on hers. She wanted to look away, but forced herself not to. She began to twist a lock of her hair, then caught herself and stopped. Was he expecting questions? She had many but decided to ask only one, the one she didn't think she could answer on her own time. "What's my role in this?" she asked Hoffman.

"Pretty much standard epidemiology," Hoffman said. "We need to nail down the origin of this particular Nipah strain and trace its spread to and within the Marianas. Hopefully the outbreak is confined to Saipan. It'll require a little travel—to Saipan and Malaysia, for starters. The plan is for you two to head out to the western Pacific next week."

Mariah sat back in her chair, trying to keep her mouth from dropping open. *You two? Next week?* She hadn't been out of the country for several years. How could she get ready in only a few days? What about her FMD work? She'd need to make arrangements for her dog. What should she pack? She assumed a limited wardrobe for a working trip to a tropical climate. But what about scientific gear? Was her government passport even up-to-date? Did she need a visa?

Hoffman was speaking again, oblivious to her worries. "One other thing, Mariah. I have a small assignment before you leave. I know you're a whiz at necropsies. Local vet called. Just treated a dog that had canine ehrlichiosis symptoms, but the dog started to hemorrhage and got aggressive. Bit the vet, then had a seizure and died."

"Doesn't sound like ehrlichiosis to me," said Mariah, trying to put Saipan out of her mind.

"That's why I'm bringing you in on this," said Hoffman. "You're a vet, you know the diseases. Plus your necropsy skills."

Kennedy had leaned toward Hoffman, eyebrows raised in question. Mariah felt as if she were auditioning for something, and a wave of resentment swelled in her chest. This was just like Hoffman, she thought. He was a decidedly hands-off boss, and sometimes she'd go weeks without seeing him at the Barn. Brilliant as he might have been, he was also extremely eccentric, and though most of his subordinates would have said they were honored to work with and for him, everyone had a story about Frank Hoffman being off. It was just like him to call Mariah in here, toss her onto an assignment with someone she'd just met, and then grill her in front of this guy, who clearly had some kind of strong-silent-type complex. She pressed her lips together and willed the meeting to end.

"If the vet called the Barn, he must have suspected something dangerous," Kennedy said. "Is he okay?"

"So far," said Hoffman. "But I told him to get checked out by a doctor. We don't know what we're dealing with. Not rabies. Dog's shots were up-to-date and the vet said the symptoms didn't match." He turned to Mariah. "I want you to work in Level Four," he said. "Just to be on the safe side. The cadaver's already in there. Double-bagged. Anyway, good practice for you." He paused. "It's been a while since you've worked in the MCL, right?"

Mariah knew he wasn't implying that she was rusty. He was just careless sometimes with what he said. But Level 4—the maximum containment lab? Space suits and all. *Must be suspecting a zoonotic disease, a hot one*, she thought. Did he have an idea of what it might be? She looked at Kennedy. Still no expression on his face. She kept her mouth shut. If she asked too many questions, they might think she was nervous. She simply nodded to Hoffman: yes, it had been a while since she'd worked in maximum containment.

"You'll need a partner, of course," Hoffman said. "Curt, you work with her. Give you guys a chance to get to know each other a bit before you head out to the Pacific together."

CHAPTER SIX

Four days after her dog, Calvert, had died, Jennifer Kelly awoke from a deep sleep, opened her eyes, and looked at the clock radio: 7:00 a.m. Her husband had left well before six to judge livestock at the Chester County Fair over in Brandywine Heights.

The livestock pavilion always drew a large crowd, and Jenny had planned to take her kids this morning, but she wasn't feeling well. She had a throbbing headache, her nose was running, and she felt exhausted. But she owed it to the kids. They'd be so disappointed to miss the fair, and it would help take their minds off the dog for a little while. They'd taken it so hard when she'd come home from Dr. Ferreira's office and stammered through an explanation of why Calvert wasn't going to live with them anymore and how he'd "gone to sleep forever."

She sat up and started to lift herself off the mattress. God, her head hurt. Like someone had stuck a hot hypodermic needle into her brain. Surely this wasn't the two glasses of wine last night, she thought. She must be getting a summer cold.

She stood and staggered to the bathroom sink. Waves of dizziness rolled over her. She looked in the mirror. Her eyes were bloodshot. She looked like she'd aged a decade overnight.

Now the waves were pushing something up from deep in her abdomen. She gagged and lurched toward the toilet.

She retched, over and over, first vomiting partly digested food, tinged with red—old pizza and wine turned to vinegar—then a brownish liquid, and finally nothing, just dry heaves that seemed to have no end. She gripped the sides of the toilet as if to keep from being swept away into a maelstrom.

Then she noticed the mottled red rash on her forearms.

That same morning, at the Barn, Mariah sipped from a plastic cup of water. Her mouth was dry but she could feel her T-shirt dampening with a cold sweat. She was about to enter a Biosafety Level 4 maximum containment laboratory—MCL—a highly secure facility where well-trained scientists worked with the world's most dangerous microbes. *But anxiety isn't a bad thing*, she reminded herself. As a former professor once said to her, "Lose your fear, lose your life."

Though she was a little out of practice, Mariah had extensive training and experience working in BSL-4 labs. She knew there was no vaccine or treatment for most of the diseases researched in these spaces, and that some of the agents presented significant risk for airborne infection, but access was strictly controlled and limited to highly qualified personnel, who all wore full protective gear and adhered to rigorous protocols. Still, you had to be psychologically up to it too, willing to work with some of the most dangerous human pathogens in existence, knowing that one mistake, one slip of a knife, one errant jab of a needle could sentence you to a horrific death. Mariah considered herself grimly fortunate that she was unmarried, no kids, no close family. Or at least she told herself she was grateful for those reasons.

She entered an outer change room, closed the door, and

turned on the "Occupied" sign. She removed all of her clothing and placed it in a locker along with her watch and a pair of sterling hook earrings, each in the shape of a terrier. Shivering in the cool air, she passed through a shower room and entered another room just beyond. There she put on a set of baggy green surgical scrubs, cotton socks, and latex gloves.

After signing in on a register and placing her right palm on a scanner, she planted her feet and pulled hard on a self-closing door. It was heavy and slow moving because of the negative air pressure sucking it closed. This prevented pathogens from escaping the lab without passing through a secure ventilation system equipped with high-efficiency particulate air filters. Mariah stepped into another room—the suit room. Curt Kennedy was waiting for her, dressed in identical garb.

"Dr. Rossi, I presume," Kennedy said. The quick joke surprised Mariah. "Ready for the operation?" he asked.

"Ready when you are. Have you done this before?"

"Not unless you count the frog I dissected in high school. I prefer to study microscopic things. Less blood and all." Kennedy smiled—another surprise. So he'd just been tight-lipped because of Hoffman?

Mariah turned to a row of blue polyethylene one-piece biohazard suits hanging from ceiling hooks in the room and flicked through them until she found one she thought might fit—or at least that wouldn't be baggy enough to get in her way: standard issue, blue Chemturion encapsulating biological/chemical protective gear—a.k.a. a moon suit or blue suit—that would serve as a self-contained environment in a surrounding sea of biohazards.

She selected a pair of thick rubber gloves and secured the gloves to the suit's wrist cuffs, making a tight seal with the rubber wrist rings. She sealed all the exhaust valves with vinyl tape, closed the suit's zipper, and retrieved an air line—called an umbilical—from an overhead holder. She attached the line to a brass fitting on the back of the suit, turned on the air, and inflated the suit. She glanced over at Kennedy and was satisfied to see that he was keeping up with her with his own suit. As soon as hers was full, she turned off the air and uncoupled the line. She leaned close to the suit and listened for any telltale hiss of escaping air and ran her bare hand around the suit. No leaks. Kennedy signaled that he was ready.

After donning headsets for two-way communication, Mariah and Kennedy helped each other into their suits, pulled on protective booties, and hooked up their umbilicals. For the thousandth time in her career, Mariah thanked God that she wasn't susceptible to claustrophobia. She remembered the young trainee who'd accompanied her into the MCL on an earlier assignment. As soon as his suit was zipped up he'd panicked because of the confinement and started screaming. Coming from inside the sealed suit, his muffled shrieks had sounded far away. But the terror in his eyes had been unmistakable, and Mariah thought about it every time she suited up.

She and Kennedy proceeded to the necropsy area.

A sealed, four-foot, stainless-steel box—an animal coffin—rested on the floor, next to a stainless-steel bench that looked like a surgery table.

Mariah opened the coffin. A dog's body lay inside, enclosed in transparent polyethylene. She could make out dark straw-colored fur. A label taped to the plastic read *Calvert. Four-year-old Golden Retriever, male.* She made out the vet's name on the label.

With Kennedy's help, she lifted the carcass out of the coffin, noting that it had almost completely thawed since its removal from the freezer the night before. She cut the plastic away, using dull scissors to minimize chances of cutting her suit or herself, and saw two labeled test tubes lying next to the corpse. The labels identified the contents as Calvert's blood.

The whooshing sound of umbilical air flowing into the helmet pounded in Mariah's head. Even with the cooling ventilation, she began to perspire. The dog itself didn't make her nervous, but the vials of blood reminded her of what she could be dealing with. She took a deep breath, steadied herself, and looked at the carcass on the table. This had been a beautiful dog. Even in death his fur still shone, and she could see that he had been well groomed.

"Good-looking animal," said Kennedy, beside her. His voice sounded as if it was coming through a wind tunnel. Mariah had forgotten for a moment that she wasn't alone.

She stepped on a scale near the table and weighed herself. Then she picked up the dog, stepped back on the scale, read the result, and calculated that the dog's weight was fifty-two pounds. She guessed that Calvert had probably lost at least 20 percent of his body weight after dying.

For the necropsy she'd have to use incision instruments—known as sharps in the trade—and this would increase the risk of accidental cuts or contamination. She opened a white medical cabinet and pulled out a collection of supplies and tools, including a six-inch, molybdenum-hardened, stainless-steel necropsy knife with a yellow "no-slip grip" handle and a razor-sharp blade. This was her personal knife, stored in its own case, with her name on it. It was her most important tool and she didn't share it. She kept an identical knife back in her lab; this one was reserved for work in the MCL.

Mariah also retrieved battery-operated hair clippers from the cabinet. She began to shave the retriever, and as she watched the fur fall to the floor, she felt sadness and regret, as if she were removing the last of the dog's dignity. When the dog was completely hairless, he looked much smaller, almost like a large newborn puppy.

She next conducted a complete external examination. She

made notes on a pad: postmortem rigidity; limited external decomposition; skin showing extensive petechiae and purpura, latter up to two inches diameter; extensive subconjunctival hemorrhaging in eyes; minor bleeding from gums. *What on earth did this dog get into?* she wondered.

Time to start the dissection. Kennedy held the dog while Mariah cut, using the necropsy knife. She worked carefully, knowing an errant move or slip of the blade could breach her suit and slice through all protective layers, all the way to the bone. She laid back the skin from the dog's thorax, abdomen, and cervix, clamped it in place, and examined the exposed tissue. There were no obvious major problems. The diaphragm was intact and there had been no evident bleeding into the chest cavity. Organs also seemed intact, and surrounding tissue and muscle mass seemed normal and healthy, though there were signs of swelling in the lymph nodes. She removed the abdominal viscera, sectioned it lengthwise, and removed a mass of partially digested material. The digestive matter was tinged with red. She placed it into a polyethylene bag and sealed and labeled the bag.

She cut away the tissue surrounding the hip joints. With a sterile swab, she collected synovial fluid from around the joints and swabbed it onto clean microscope slides.

Soon her shoulders were getting sore and her neck started to ache, but she knew it was more from tension than exertion. She glanced over at Kennedy. Was he impatient or restless, having nothing to do except observe? She saw him raise his gloved right hand and give it a little pump. Thumbs-up?

After a short rest, Mariah collected bone marrow samples. She painted the soft, spongy material onto microscope slides with a fine, camel's-hair brush, added fixative, placed the slides in a holder for later viewing, and sealed the assemblage in a ziplock bag. She removed the major organs and placed each into a separate, labeled plastic bag.

Time to remove the brain. She first severed the head from the dog's body, then made three careful cuts through the skull with a bone saw. With a bone chisel she delicately removed the skull sections from around the brain. To free the brain she'd next have to cut through the cranial nerves and pituitary stalk with a scalpel, but the work with the bone chisel had been tiring, and now her visor was starting to fog up. She paused and slowed her breathing. After resting again, she picked up the scalpel and began to cut, working slowly and methodically.

She soon freed the brain and gently placed it into a 10 percent formalin solution in a large plastic specimen jar. She then removed the spinal cord and radial and sciatic nerves and deposited these into separate jars of formalin.

With that, she'd finally finished the necropsy. When she looked at what was left of the dog, she felt sadness. A once beautiful, healthy creature had been reduced to an empty sack. Mariah felt as if she'd violated the dog. She imagined having to perform this gruesome dissection on her own dog—Dancer, a little West Highland terrier she'd had for five years and loved like a child—and had to pinch her eyes shut to block out the picture. She sensed Kennedy's gaze on her and willed herself to keep moving.

If they were dealing with a virus, Mariah would need living cells to get a good look at it. One source of the cells would be laboratory research animals, mice and monkeys, maintained by the USDA research facility. Tomorrow she'd inject Calvert's blood directly into the animals and wait for replication and symptoms to occur. Depending on the virus, the results could come quickly. The other source would be the Barn's mammalian cell cultures. Amplification of the virus in the cell culture would take longer than in living animals, perhaps several days, but the culture would be purer than in the animal blood and easier to isolate for further study in the future.

When Curt and Mariah left the MCL they reversed the

entry process, removing the suits and hanging them up where they'd found them. Mariah preceded Kennedy into the change room, where she discarded her disposable clothing and gloves in another biohazards receptacle and showered out. Even though she assumed that no particles had breached her suit, she took care to scrub under her fingernails and to blow her nose before leaving the shower area. After getting dressed again, she waited for Kennedy outside the door of the outer change room.

"Thanks for your help," she said, when he emerged through the doorway.

"Nice work. Impressive," he said.

Mariah briefly considered using the compliment as an opportunity to make friendly conversation with Kennedy. She'd wanted to impress him, she realized now, and it was generous of him to say what he'd said. His gruff behavior in Hoffman's office notwithstanding, he'd been nothing but professional, and even nice, today. But Mariah was exhausted. She'd done dozens of necropsies over the years, but today's had been tough. The truth was that she loved dogs, and working on Calvert, who she assumed—irrationally, she knew—was a good dog, had shaken her more than she wanted to admit. Any thought of making small talk with Kennedy was overridden by an overwhelming urge to return to her office, shut her door, and simply close her eyes for five minutes.

"Thanks," she said to Kennedy, angling her body away from him, feeling rude but telling herself it didn't matter. "I'll keep you posted on the results."

Kennedy raised a hand in thanks and good-bye, seemingly unperturbed, and they parted ways.

"Keep your fingers together, dear. You don't want her to nibble you." A young mother watched as her four-year-old daughter pressed against the fence of the Chester County Fair's livestock petting zoo and extended an offering of grain to a young heifer.

The little girl giggled. "She's tickling me, Mommy." The child pulled her hands away from the cow's muzzle.

"They have rough tongues, don't they?" said the mother, smiling. "But they won't hurt you. Let's wash your hands." She looked around for a handwashing station, but didn't see one. She pulled a tissue from her pocketbook and wiped the girl's palms and fingers. She took the child's hand and threaded through the crowd of squealing kids who'd gathered around the enclosure.

"Are you hungry, sweetheart?" she asked. "Let's get something to eat."

CHAPTER SEVEN

When Mariah had gotten back to her office after the necropsy, she hadn't immediately begun working on the results. She'd wanted to get her mind off the dog, so she rested for a few minutes, then worked on her foot-and-mouth disease model and tried to put the necropsy out of her mind for the afternoon.

Now it was late, late enough that her stomach had begun to groan. She'd skipped lunch, the images of the dissected flesh too vivid in her mind for her to work up an appetite, and couldn't really even remember eating breakfast, though she was sure she had. Oatmeal. Cereal. Something light.

Yielding to her hunger, she decided to pop down to the cafeteria for a microwaved cup of soup and a Coke. Minutes later, as she was heading back to her office, head down, deep in thought about the microscope work ahead of her, she rounded a corner and nearly ran into Curt Kennedy, who was standing near her office door. "My God, I'm sorry. Didn't see you," she said, wondering what Kennedy was doing at her office.

Kennedy held up his hands and smiled. "My fault," he said. "I obviously startled you. Just stopped by to see how it's going."

45

"Oh," Mariah said, a little breathlessly. "I'm about to go over to the lab."

"Mind if I join you?" he asked.

Mariah hesitated. She narrowed her eyes at Kennedy. Was he shadowing her because he thought she'd put off the work? Or screw it up? Her mind scrambled for some excuse to turn him away. Not only was she annoyed, but she needed to concentrate and she was afraid he'd be a distraction.

"Just curiosity," he said. "And I figure I'll learn something from you."

"Okay," she said finally, deciding she really had no reason to suspect his motives. "You can help ID the bugs."

In the lab, as Kennedy looked on, Mariah prepared the samples and mounted the first one inside a vacuum column on the scanning electron microscope. She activated the SEM's electron gun, focusing a beam of high energy electrons onto the sample. The result was a three-dimensional image of any particles detected by the electron beam, displayed on a computer monitor. By changing the magnification on the scope, Mariah could focus in on individual particles, revealing an astonishing level of detail.

She first detected several rod-shaped objects averaging about a half micron in diameter, several times bigger than a large virus particle. She focused on one, then swiveled her chair toward Kennedy. "Want to have a look?"

Kennedy bent toward the monitor, his shoulder brushing lightly against Mariah's. "Bacteria," he said. "Looks like the one that causes canine ehrlichiosis."

Mariah stood and pulled a copy of *The Manual of Clinical Microbiology* from a shelf and quickly confirmed *Ehrlichia canis*. She thought back to the necropsy. *That was no ehrlichiosis*, she thought, remembering that Calvert had undergone extensive hemorrhaging. She turned back to the microscope and increased the magnification. A number of much smaller particles came into view, clearly virus particles, spherical in shape, about one hundred nanometers in diameter—more than a thousand times thinner than a human hair—with spiky protuberances all around. Mariah didn't recognize the particles. She stood and invited Kennedy to have another look.

Kennedy spent the better part of a minute at the scope, adjusting the focus, resolution, and magnification. When he finally looked up at Mariah, his expression was puzzled.

"Virus," he said. "Look a little like flu virions. Maybe the dog had canine influenza. But the particles seem a bit big for flu."

"So what else could they be?"

Kennedy shook his head. "They remind me of something I saw a few years ago—in Afghanistan. But it can't be the same bug. Doesn't exist in the Western Hemisphere. This has to be some kind of flu virus. Maybe a new strain. I can ask a colleague at Fort Detrick to have a look. Could I borrow a blood sample?"

"Help yourself, but I hope you can get that ID quick. We need to brief Hoffman tomorrow." Mariah thought again about Hoffman's insistence that they do the necropsy in the MCL. "What was this Afghanistan virus?" she asked.

Kennedy turned back to the monitor and scrutinized the images. "A zoonotic agent, pretty bad. Case fatality rate around 50 percent. Of humans, that is. But no way could it be here."

CHAPTER EIGHT

The next morning Mariah settled into an empty seat at a rectangular table in a small conference room at the Barn. She nodded to Hoffman, who sat at the head of the table. *He really looks military today*, she thought. Ramrod straight, spit-and-polish appearance, even in civilian clothes. She studied his face, looking for a clue as to why he'd called this sudden meeting. No expression. She and Kennedy weren't due to brief him on their findings until this afternoon. She glanced around the table. It was a small group: Hoffman, Kennedy, herself, and three other people she didn't recognize: a gray-haired woman; a blond woman; and a male army officer.

Hoffman leaned forward slightly and cleared his throat. "Thanks for coming together on short notice," he said. "For those who don't know everyone, let me introduce you." He went around the table. The gray-haired woman was Dr. Emily Rausch, the chief of infectious diseases at Pennsylvania Hospital. The army officer was Lieutenant Colonel Wade Davidson, head of the emerging diseases unit at USAMRIID in Fort Detrick. The blond woman was Barbara Wright, director of the Pennsylvania Office of Public Health Preparedness.

Hoffman nodded toward a television monitor in the corner of the room where an image of a balding man in a white lab coat filled the screen. "We have Dr. Richard Blumenthal, the director of the North American Infectious Diseases Division at the Centers for Disease Control, joining us remotely. Rick, can you hear me okay? Good."

Just like Hoffman to be so oddly formal, Mariah thought. He could have left out the long title and just said CDC—especially with this group.

Hoffman turned back to the table. "Dr. Blumenthal's on secure video link from Atlanta. Let's get started. I've double-checked your clearances—what we talk about today stays among us. Bottom line is we have a public health emergency apparently caused by a zoonotic disease. Five days ago a woman from Middle Valley brought a sick dog to a local vet. The dog went into convulsions and died in the exam room. Before it died, it bit the vet." He turned toward the gray-haired lady on his left. "Emily, why don't you take it from here?"

Dr. Rausch leaned forward in her chair. "EMTs from Chester County brought the vet in yesterday," she said. "He was in tough shape—semicomatose, hemorrhaging from the mouth and nose, severe headache, high fever. Died an hour after he arrived."

Mariah's mind raced. This was the vet who had handled the same dog she'd dissected yesterday? And now he was dead? She glanced at Kennedy. Was he thinking the same thing?

Blumenthal cut in from the TV monitor. "So did they take him directly to Penn Hospital?"

Rausch shook her head. "They first tried to admit him at the regional hospital in Kennett Square, but they wouldn't take him. Earlier in the day, the same hospital had admitted the dog's owner—also from Chester County—with similar symptoms. They tried to treat her but couldn't diagnose the illness.

The woman kept getting worse. So they evacuated her to Penn Hospital on a Life Flight helicopter."

"I was afraid of something like that," said Blumenthal. "Now we'll likely have a lot more exposures. How's she doing?" he asked.

"Stable," replied Emily. "We have her in intensive care in a special isolation unit. We've induced a coma, slowed her metabolism. We've also admitted her husband and two young children. Husband's showing symptoms, but so far the kids seem okay."

"Anyone else sick?" asked Blumenthal. "The EMTs, for example?"

"I was coming to that," Rausch said, and Mariah picked up on a hint of annoyance that she sympathized with. Blumenthal was asking obvious questions. She wished he'd let Rausch speak uninterrupted. "So far we've also admitted six medical personnel," Rausch went on. "Three EMTs and a doctor and two nurses from the Kennett Square hospital. Same symptoms. They're in the hospital's isolation wing. Our own attending medical staff are in full protective gear. We're carefully monitoring them."

For several seconds there was silence in the room. Finally Blumenthal said, "So what else are you doing to manage this?"

"The state has responded aggressively," said Barbara Wright from the Pennsylvania Public Health Office. "We've shut down the regional hospital and are in the process of decontaminating the hospital facilities, vet's office, ambulances used to transport victims, and the dog owner's house. We're looking for a common denominator among the illnesses."

Hoffman spoke. "The victims all seem to have had a connection—direct or indirect—to the dog."

"Right, it does look that way," said Rausch. "And so far all the victims are from Chester County."

"Any idea what we're dealing with?" asked Blumenthal. Mariah stopped herself from rolling her eyes, remembering only at the last second that he could see her as well as she could see him. *This guy and his million-dollar questions*, she thought.

"Kandahar hemorrhagic virus syndrome," Hoffman said gravely.

"How could that be?" Blumenthal asked, clearly alarmed. "That's known only from Southwest Asia."

Mariah flashed back to Kennedy's remark in the microscopy lab about the unidentified microbe in Calvert's blood. He'd said it looked like a virus from Afghanistan, but seemed to dismiss the possibility. Had he suspected something then? She watched as Hoffman looked around the table, jaw thrust forward.

"A couple of you aren't familiar with this disease or the background," said Hoffman. "A U.S. soldier on deployment in Afghanistan came down with Kandahar three or four years ago and died a few days after symptoms showed up. Medics got some blood samples before shipping his body back here, so we have it on file."

"So how dangerous is this thing?" asked Wright.

"Pretty nasty," said Hoffman. "Some of you know something about it, but for those who don't, it's tick-borne, first identified on the Afghanistan-Pakistan border in 2011. Most animals, including livestock, are known carriers but don't usually show symptoms."

"What about dogs?" asked Kennedy. Mariah figured he must be thinking about Calvert. It was the first thing she'd thought of after the revelation about Kandahar virus.

"Canines seem to be an exception," said Hoffman. "But the disease is often misdiagnosed as rabies. We know that primates, including humans, are highly susceptible."

Blumenthal broke in. "We sent a team to Afghanistan after the soldier died. As I recall, you were there too, Dr. Kennedy."

Kennedy nodded in affirmation.

"We learned at the time that Kandahar virus isn't airborne,"

Blumenthal explained. "Similar to Ebola, transmission is by close contact with infected humans or animals, through body fluids. And its symptoms resemble Ebola in some ways. Like a flu at first, but often accompanied by a skin rash and changes in behavior. Three to six days after symptoms first show up, the patient starts to hemorrhage—internally and externally. They'll pass dark tarlike stools and bloody urine. Their vomit looks almost like coffee grounds. Many of them bleed out—from the nose, mouth, gums, penis, vagina, virtually any orifice. Even through the pores of the skin."

Mariah winced and looked around the room. Kennedy, Hoffman, and Davidson showed no visible reaction. *They already know all this*, she realized, but Rausch looked tense, and Wright had paled.

"What's the case fatality rate?" asked Rausch.

"About half of confirmed cases end up dying," said Hoffman.

"You're sure you've got an accurate ID from the dog's blood?" Blumenthal asked.

"I did that work," Lieutenant Colonel Davidson said. "Dr. Kennedy provided a sample. Just finished running DNA sequences to confirm it."

"I'd also like to have a look here in Atlanta," said Blumenthal. "Can you overnight a blood sample to us?"

He doesn't trust the Fort Detrick work, Mariah thought.

"No problem," Davidson answered.

"Where are that soldier's blood samples now?" Blumenthal asked Hoffman.

"Here, at the Barn," Hoffman said. "In a secure freezer in Level Four. We also isolated the virus at the time. Stored in the same freezer. The intent was to develop a vaccine. Still is. If we ever get the funding, that is."

"I'm sure I'm not the only one who's thinking that somehow the virus got out," said Blumenthal.

Hoffman rolled a pen between two fingers. "No way," he answered. "Only three people have access to that freezer—a lab scientist, a technician, and me. It takes two keys to open the freezer room. The other two individuals each have only one of the keys. I'm the only person with both. So that freezer doesn't get opened without my being there."

To Mariah, Hoffman's assurances rang hollow, and she had the sense that even he wasn't confident in what he was saying. After all, the infected soldier's corpse had been shipped back to the United States and his blood samples and isolated virus had been stored at the Barn. It seemed like an improbably large coincidence that these cases now were so close to the only location in the country where the virus had been available.

"So can you explain how Kandahar just happens to break out within fifty miles of the only North American source of the virus?" Blumenthal asked, as if reading Mariah's mind.

"Plenty of possibilities," said Hoffman, seemingly unfazed. "An infected tick from a soldier or civilian recently returning from Afghanistan. Possibly on a military dog that operated in theater. Or someone was exposed in the war zone and came back here before symptoms showed up." He paused and appeared to think something over. "Might be a good idea to check regional hospital records for unexplained hemorrhagic diseases over the past couple of years," he said. "And check on everyone who's had contact with the infected patients."

"We can do that," said Wright.

"Okay, here's what I propose," said Hoffman. "We bring in USDA Wildlife Services. They fan out around the dog owner's house and collect as many small mammals as possible—field mice and squirrels, for example. They'll need to be in protective clothing. They sacrifice the animals, remove and identify any ticks, and take blood samples. They also trap free-ranging ticks. They turn over the blood samples and ticks to our scientists at the Barn. We'll do the analyses here in the maximum containment lab."

"What about the human victims?" asked Blumenthal.

"CDC and USAMRIID at Fort Detrick should work together on autopsies of human corpses," Hoffman said.

"CDC can handle this," Blumenthal snapped. "Standard protocol for us. We'll retrieve tissue samples from cadavers and blood from the patients in Penn Hospital's isolation ward, isolate known pathogens or suspect microbes, and amplify them in appropriate media. We'll do the same with the ticks and the dog's blood."

"Let's not get ahead of ourselves, Rick," Hoffman said calmly. "This will be a team effort. I want the scientists here at the Barn to work with the dog's blood. They'll use test animals and expose them to the blood to look for disease transmission. The Fort Detrick scientists will do the same thing with blood samples from infected humans and with pathogens isolated from collected animals and insects."

Hoffman looked around the room. "Any other questions?"

Mariah noted with some embarrassment that she was the only one who hadn't said anything during the meeting. People were probably wondering why she was even there. She was wondering the same thing herself. She racked her brain for something to contribute, but all she could think was: *The vet who treated the dog is dead. He died within five days of being bitten. Five days.*

"Okay, let's get started," said Hoffman. "We'll follow the plan I just laid out. This will be a team effort. I expect full cooperation among team members. Any issues—*any*—I want to know about them immediately. We'll meet here again as soon as we have some substantive results. Out-of-towners can conference in by secure video link. Thanks for your time today."

As they left the conference room, Mariah fell into step beside

Kennedy. "Looks like we'll be spending some more time to-gether in containment," she said. "I'd like to get an early start on the animal work tomorrow. Can you meet me at the MCL at seven thirty?"

"I'll be there," Kennedy said. He looked at Mariah. "Nervous?"

Yes, she thought. "Not really," she answered. "Are you?"

"Damn right I am," replied Kennedy. "Nipah's a pussycat compared to this thing."

That evening in Philadelphia, in a dimly lit booth of a knockoff English pub, Doctor Vector sipped from a pint and studied a small photograph on the table in front of him. He had a good view of the entrance, but in the semidarkness of the cubicle he'd be all but invisible to anyone entering the pub. He could study his contact before being seen. He'd never met this man before. His credentials had seemed impeccable, but Vector wanted a face-to-face meeting to be sure he could trust him to carry out a critical part of the upcoming mission. That would allow Vector to concentrate on preparing his beloved ticks for their crucial assignment.

Vector wore a blue blazer and an open-necked tattersall shirt. The clothes made him feel slightly more at home in the patrician surroundings, but he frequently glanced around the room and twirled a saltshaker as he waited. He scrutinized the photo again. Not a lot of detail, but there was intelligence in the face and the eyes had a dark, hard look about them. A man you wouldn't want to cross. But was he careful, detail-oriented? Reliable? And how would you know for sure, especially at a first meeting?

He saw the pub door open and watched a slight, dark man in a blue Windbreaker and brown slacks walk through the entrance, pause for a millisecond, and take in the room with one swift glance. Vector glanced again at the photo before pocketing it. Definitely his contact. Now the other man was striding toward him. He rose to shake his hand and introduced himself. The man in the Windbreaker abruptly returned the handshake and said his name was Omar, which Vector assumed was an alias.

The two men sat down on opposite sides of the booth.

"Beer?" Vector asked.

Omar shook his head.

"Coffee? Something to eat?"

"Nothing." Omar glanced at his watch. "You brought me something?"

"That's for next time," said Vector. "Today we firm up plans." He looked around the room, leaned forward, and lowered his voice. "The package will be well secured and small enough to hand-carry aboard a plane. You'll deliver it to an overseas establishment where it'll be refined and expanded. That should take a couple of weeks. Then your team will take it to the final destinations."

"What will this package look like?"

"A small container of liquid."

"If it's liquid, it'll have to go into checked baggage."

"Too risky. And we're only talking about a couple of ounces. It'll look like a brand-name bottle of mouthwash—same color and all. One of those small bottles they let you carry onto a plane. Sealed real tight. When you get it, you'll put it in a ziplock bag and add some toothpaste and other stuff."

"You said it would be expanded before final delivery," said Omar.

"Right. We'll need several quarts. We'll produce that at the next location."

"So how do we get all that on a plane?"

"I'll let you know when it's time."

"How many final destinations?"

"Three," Vector said.

"I'll need a dozen people, including an advance team at each location and an American cell," said Omar.

Vector shook his head. "No way. Four men max. More than that and too much risk of detection or compromise."

"You think you know more about how to do this than me?" asked Omar. "You do it my way or we don't have a deal."

Vector stared at Omar, who held his gaze, unblinking. Finally Vector looked away. "Okay," he said. "Your call. But I don't have to tell you that failure is not an option." He reached into his shirt pocket, retrieved a small, folded piece of paper, and handed it to the other man. "Instructions for our next meeting."

Omar unfolded the paper and read it. Then, with a steady hand, he held it above the candle on the table between them, allowed it to catch fire, and waited until it burned down to a tiny corner. He stood, gave a barely perceptible nod, and turned away. Vector watched as he strode quickly toward the exit. For several minutes Vector remained at the table, nursing the dregs of his beer, trying to shake off the nagging feeling that he didn't have as much control over things as he'd once thought.

CHAPTER NINE

When Mariah arrived at the MCL, Kennedy was already there. They suited up and headed to the animal rooms inside the containment area. Mariah had earlier put in a request for twenty laboratory research mice and ten rhesus monkeys. Technicians would have already placed these in cages inside the animal rooms. The monkeys and mice would serve as animal models to evaluate their response to exposure to pathogens that the dog may have carried. Mariah would inject the animals with aliquots of the dog's blood. The responses of the lab animals could give an indication of the potential infectivity of the pathogens to people.

Mariah hated this work. She knew it was an alternative to actually exposing human beings to dangerous bacteria and viruses, but she also knew that the deliberately infected animals might experience debilitating illnesses or excruciating deaths.

They established a routine. Kennedy would retrieve a mouse from its cage and hand it to Mariah. She would then inject several cubic centimeters of the dog's blood with her right hand, while firmly holding the mouse in her left, her fingers clamped across the mouse's neck to minimize the possibility of being bitten. When Mariah finished a mouse, Kennedy was ready with the next one, and they simply traded off. After each mouse was injected, Mariah would use a new syringe and hypodermic needle to avoid cross-contamination. She placed the used needles and syringes into a "sharps" bucket with a protective cover.

By midmorning, Mariah was ready to inject the fifteenth mouse. The needle was poised just above the animal's clavicle. Kennedy had turned to select the next mouse, and as he did so the sleeve of his moon suit brushed against the bucket of used syringes and needles.

The bucket crashed to the floor.

Mariah flinched and her right arm involuntarily jerked downward, stabbing the needle into the back of her left hand. Her thumb had been near the plunger, and now she awkwardly maneuvered it as far away from the plunger's surface as possible without letting go of the syringe altogether, leaving it bobbing in her hand. She'd felt the pain of the needle as it penetrated her skin after passing through the thick outer protective glove and the thinner inner surgical gloves. "I stuck myself!" she yelled, hoping Kennedy could hear her voice above the sound of the air in their suits. *Did I depress the plunger?* her mind screamed. *Did I bump it with my thumb?* Very carefully she pulled the syringe out of her hand and laid it on the work bench.

Kennedy drew a gloved finger across his throat and jerked his thumb toward the exit door. They hurriedly returned the mice to their cages, left everything else as it was, and rushed out of the lab.

Mariah moved quickly. After rinsing in dilute bleach the external surfaces of her moon suit, she shed the suit and headed to a decontamination station. She removed her surgical scrubs, booties, and neoprene gloves. She immediately swabbed the puncture wound with an antiseptic solution. She then stepped into a shower and let the water run over her body from head to toe for a full minute and followed that by washing her entire body with a special cleaning solution. When she was finished, she rinsed off, toweled dry, and cleaned the wound again.

Mariah knew that if the infectious agent had entered her bloodstream, no amount of scrubbing would make any difference. She proceeded to the outer change room, retrieved her clothes from the locker, dressed, and exited into the corridor.

Kennedy was waiting for her, arms across his chest. "Quarantine. ASAP," he said.

The following morning in Middle Valley, the young mother looked at her four-year-old daughter across the breakfast table. "Did you have a nice time at the fair? Wasn't it nice to see all the animals?" she asked.

The little girl nodded and picked at her cereal.

"You haven't eaten anything, sweetheart," said the mother. "Are you okay?"

Her daughter looked up. "I don't feel well," she said.

The mother looked closely. Her face seemed flushed. *Was she coming down with something?* "Can you tell me what hurts?"

"My head. And I have a sore throat." The little girl began to whimper.

The mother placed her hand on her daughter's forehead. Very warm. And her eyes looked bloodshot. "Wait here, sweet pea," she said. "I want to take your temperature."

The mother went into a nearby bathroom, found a thermometer, swabbed it in alcohol, and hurried back to her daughter. The girl was now sitting in a chair, holding her head in her hands. "I know, baby. It's no fun," said the mother. *What time does the clinic open?* she wondered, already mentally rearranging her day's schedule to fit in a visit. She cupped her left hand under her daughter's chin and gently lifted it up. She quickly pulled her hand away. Blood was pouring from her daughter's nose.

The mother ran back to the bathroom and grabbed a box of tissues. When she returned, a pool of blood had formed on the floor and her daughter was sobbing. She pulled out a handful of Kleenex, held it to the girl's nose, and saw the blood seep through. She grabbed a larger bundle of tissue and pressed it against her daughter's face. In just seconds it was soaked with blood. She retrieved a towel from the bathroom. She still couldn't stop the blood flow. *My God*, thought the mother. *She's bleeding to death!* She picked up her cell phone and dialed 911.

CHAPTER TEN

In her small isolation room in the Barn's quarantine wing, Mariah winced when she heard the soft beep on her secure, government-issued smartphone. She pulled the PDA from a pocket of her white hospital gown and punched a key. A text message flashed on the screen: *Call me. Hoffman.*

She stared at the message, stark black letters on a white background, and tried to read more into the three words. She touched the smooth cold plastic, as if the device could transmit the message's meaning through her fingers. Mariah had been waiting for word from her boss. They'd have had time by now to look at the syringe blood under the microscope, and maybe even to get results from the lab mice. But she was afraid to return the call.

Her head began to pound. It felt as if all the blood in her body had pooled up there and was trying to force its way out, all at once. Something wet and vaporous, tasting of stale cider, was bubbling up through her esophagus. Something darker and heavier, like a small dense cannonball, was pushing down on her abdomen. She felt dizzy. The letters on her phone began to blur and fade away as if written in disappearing ink. Was she breaking with Kandahar? Was this the beginning of the end of her life?

Control your imagination, she told herself. She'd felt fine until the phone buzzed, and she wanted to believe that Kennedy was right. As he'd shepherded her into quarantine he'd reminded her that even if any microbes had entered her bloodstream, they were likely to be *Ehrlichia* bacteria, basically harmless to humans. But what if he was wrong? What if she'd been exposed to the deadly virus? Would she ever set eyes again on the golden-green fields and hills and the ink-dark waters of the slow creeks of rural southeastern Pennsylvania, her home? Or would she remain in lonely isolation until she died?

Mariah looked back down at her phone. *Get it together*, she told herself. *You can't put this off any longer.*

She punched in Hoffman's number. "Mariah," he said. "Good to hear from you. How are you feeling?"

"Okay," she said, her heart racing. "Still no symptoms I'm aware of." There was a pause that felt interminable and Mariah wondered if Hoffman wanted her to say more. *You know how I'm feeling! Cut to the chase!*

"My guess is you'll be fine," Hoffman finally said, with maddening nonchalance. "There's no evidence you've been infected. Anyway, the reason I called is we're having another meeting this afternoon. I'd like you to join, by phone. Just an update on what we've learned so far."

"No problem," Mariah said, incredulous and reeling from Hoffman's bizarre lack of emotion. "What time?"

"Four," said Hoffman. "We'll call you and patch you in."

"Thanks for including me," said Mariah. But Hoffman had already rung off.

Doctor Vector sat on the edge of a decaying wooden bench on a forested hill overlooking Pennypack Park Creek in northeast Philadelphia. He ran his hand over a bald area on the top of his head as if brushing back a long-absent lock of hair. He retrieved a clean white handkerchief from his trouser pocket, removed his sunglasses, carefully wiped them, put them back on, and glanced at his watch. Where was Omar? The instructions he'd handed him in the pub were clear. He was already ten minutes late.

A beautiful summer day, birds chirping, flowers in bloom, soft gurgling of the creek over submerged rocks. It meant nothing to Vector. This was the last place he wanted to be right now. Where was that guy?

Suddenly he heard movement on the dirt trail beside the creek, the sound of crunching footsteps. His contact? No, moving too fast. A weekend jogger out for a run. Would the jogger look up and see him, wonder what a man in a suit was doing there, sitting all alone? He should have at least brought a newspaper. But the jogger passed by without a glance in his direction.

He eased back on the bench and casually crossed his legs, trying to look relaxed. Soon there was movement behind him and a low voice. Vector turned and found himself looking into dark, expressionless eyes. Thin build. Jeans and a T-shirt. *Omar*. Vector hadn't even heard him approach.

Omar looked around carefully, ran his hands under the bottom of the bench, and sat down at the far end. "You have the material?" he asked.

Vector withdrew a small wrapped package from an inside coat pocket, and handed it over. "Guard this with your life—literally," he said. "You'll also find a plane ticket to Manila in there. Plus a passport. And a phone number. You leave tomorrow afternoon. Call the number after you arrive in Manila. The guy that answers will tell you your next destination."

When Mariah checked in by phone to the four o'clock meeting, Hoffman announced that every team member had joined the meeting and that CDC's Blumenthal was also on speakerphone. He then told the group that Mariah was in quarantine because of an accidental needle stick. Mariah heard expressions of alarm and concern from around the table, and a barrage of questions, but Hoffman cut them off.

"She's doing fine," he said. "No evidence she was infected, but we want to be on the safe side."

"Yes, thank you—" Mariah said, but Hoffman was barreling on and it seemed as if no one had heard her.

"Thanks for coming together on short notice," said Hoffman. "We've had some disturbing developments. First, it seems that we're dealing with a very hot strain of Kandahar." He quickly summarized results of the lab animals' exposure to the virus, simply saying that more than half the monkeys had died but that the mice were unaffected. He fended off questions, saying that they planned to run more tests.

"I've got a question for our Penn Hospital doctor," boomed Blumenthal's unmistakable, authoritative voice. "How are the patients doing?"

"We're guardedly optimistic with the dog owner," said a voice Mariah remembered as Emily Rausch's. "She's stable and her condition hasn't gotten worse. The woman's kids are doing fine."

"And the others?" asked Blumenthal.

Rausch seemed to hesitate. "The rest of the news isn't good," she said at last. "The woman's husband died, as well as the vet's lab assistant. Plus a doctor at the regional hospital in Buck's Ford. Two of our own nurses and a doctor have come down with symptoms. We've taken in about two dozen new patients in the past couple of days. All the illnesses are consistent with Kandahar. And early this morning we admitted four very sick kids. Same symptoms."

"Damn," said Blumenthal. "I assume the kids are connected with the Middle Valley family?"

"Doesn't look that way," Rausch replied. "They live in the same town but don't go to the same school or otherwise interact with them. But we found out that all four went to the Chester County Fair in Brandywine Heights last week—that's a mile or two north of Middle Valley. Seems they attended a petting zoo there."

Mariah cringed at the news. Kids. And a petting zoo. Of all the places for a deadly virus to set up camp. Not only did this imply that more people had been exposed than would have been if the infected animals had merely been part of someone's private livestock, but it meant that a majority of those at risk would be children.

"Fortunately," said Hoffman, "Brandywine Heights and Middle Valley are pretty rural, so we're not dealing with a substantial human population. The animals are a different story. Large herds of livestock. Horses. Pets. Plus wild animals. The USDA wildlife folks have some preliminary results. The virus is pretty widespread in deer and smaller mammals in the vicinity of Middle Valley. Based on blood samples. And in deer ticks as well."

"Looks to me like we're on the verge of a major epidemic," Blumenthal said. "This shouldn't be just USDA's show."

"I think we need to proceed as we have been, Rick," said Hoffman tentatively.

"Proceed as we have been?" Blumenthal bellowed. "One of the Barn's investigators just stuck herself with a hot agent in the MCL. This kind of work has to proceed slowly and deliberately, and resources are too tight to spread so thin. We should divert more funds to CDC and let us manage the program."

Mariah's breath caught in her throat. In the solitude of her quarantine cell she pressed a hand over her eyes, trying to hold back her rage. The needle stick was a complete accident. If Blumenthal had been in her place, the same thing would have happened when the bucket crashed to the floor—she was sure of that. She opened her mouth to defend herself when she heard someone else speak.

"I was there when Dr. Rossi had the accident," a stern male voice said quietly. Was that Kennedy? Mariah's pulse began to race.

"She was being extremely careful," said Kennedy. "I watched her entire necropsy the day before. I've never seen a more skillful job. The accident the next morning was my fault. I knocked a sharps container off the table as she was injecting a mouse. Obviously it startled her and her hand slipped. So if you're going to blame anyone, blame me. But it sure isn't the first time exposures have occurred when handling infectious agents. CDC itself doesn't have a great track record in that department."

Blumenthal, along with everyone else, seemed to be at a loss for words in the face of Kennedy's anger.

"We have a huge job in front of us if we're going to stop this outbreak before it becomes an epidemic," Kennedy went on. "Every agency involved, every facility, every individual has an important role to play. We have to work together, we have to support each other, but we also have to move fast. All due respect, Rick, but this slow, deliberate stuff from the CDC playbook is bullshit. Lives are at stake. People are dying. Time is death."

Mariah raised an eyebrow. She already knew Curt Kennedy wasn't a man to mince words, but obviously he also didn't care who he ripped into.

The conference room was quiet.

Blumenthal finally broke the silence. "I'm sorry," he said. "That was wrong of me to say what I did. We do need to be working as a team."

"Apology accepted," Hoffman said, sounding uncomfortable. "Here's the bottom line: this agent's obviously hot as hell and it's spreading fast. We'll have to move quickly to contain it. Is there any treatment for Kandahar, Rick?"

"Ribavirin can be effective," said Blumenthal. Mariah thought he sounded contrite, but also noncommittal. She wondered what Kennedy was doing now. Quietly raging? Playing it cool?

"Okay, here's our plan of attack," said Hoffman. "We'll set up a five-mile-radius containment zone around Middle Valley. The area will incorporate Brandywine Heights. Nothing—people, animals—moves in or out until further notice. All pets, domestic animals, and livestock will be rounded up and euthanized. USDA sharpshooters and trappers will cull all mammalian wildlife in the quarantine zone. We'll collect and analyze as many ticks as possible, and continue close surveillance of people to monitor any further spread of the virus. We'll need to try to track down the infected animal in the petting zoo—hopefully there's only one. And we'll commandeer all the ribavirin that's available and begin administering it to symptomatic patients. If we work quickly enough we should be able to keep this from spreading much more."

"I assume we're talking about military enforcement," said Kennedy.

"Right," replied Hoffman. "National Guard. We'll have to get the governor's office involved, and the White House. I'll get a call in to the president's chief of staff. They'll need to call the governor. The sooner we can get the Guard in place the better."

CHAPTER ELEVEN

AUGUST 23

SOUTHEASTERN PENNSYLVANIA

It was a Sunday morning at the Barn and Mariah was finally beginning to shake off the looming specter of a gruesome death. She'd experienced no symptoms since she'd stuck herself—not even a mild headache. She figured that if she'd been infected with Kandahar virus, signs of disease should be evident by now.

She heard a knock on the door and the first thing she saw upon peering through the glass were Curt Kennedy's blue-gray eyes. She opened the door.

"Glad to see you're awake," said Kennedy. "I was in the neighborhood and thought I'd stop by."

Mariah noted with optimism that he wasn't fully suited up but instead was only wearing a simple mask and gown. "Have a seat," she said. She pointed to a black metal folding chair.

"I wanted to be the first person to tell you," he said. "After we got you into quarantine, I checked the syringe you stuck yourself with. The reservoir was full. It doesn't look like you depressed the plunger."

Mariah realized that she'd been holding her breath and slowly exhaled. "I hope you're right," she said, but she knew that Kennedy's reassurance was hardly solid evidence that she hadn't been infected. "You were great in the containment lab," she said. "Not just professionally. You really calmed me down after the needle stick. I appreciate it."

Kennedy nodded professionally, but added an unmistakable arch of his eyebrow. "So did Hoffman tell you anything besides what he said at the meeting?"

"No. He barely told me he thought I'd be okay. He's not the chattiest guy."

"Well, I think you'll be okay too, but I need to be up front with you," Kennedy said. "The news isn't great. After you went into the slammer, I finished the animal injections. Got a technician to help me. I checked on the animals first thing yesterday morning. Really wasn't expecting anything yet. The mice were fine, but almost all the monkeys were already showing symptoms. Off their feed, feverish, runny noses, agitated. I looked in on them again this morning. Most of them were dead. I called Fort Detrick to find out their results from the blood from the human victims. Same story."

Mariah was silent. Kennedy was still looking at her. She thought she saw sadness in his eyes, or perhaps it was weariness. He probably hadn't had much sleep since they left the lab yesterday. "You told me the other day that the Afghanistan Kandahar strain had a fifty percent case fatality rate," she finally said. "Hoffman reported yesterday that 'over half' of the injected test monkeys had died. Now you just said *most* had died. So which is it?"

"The fifty percent rate is accurate for humans in Afghanistan," said Kennedy. "But the rate was much higher for the test monkeys here."

"So this strain is much more virulent?" asked Mariah.

Kennedy nodded. "That's if we extrapolate the monkey results to all primates, including humans. But we still don't have enough data to know for sure."

Mariah looked down at the floor, and was silent. When she looked up again she asked, "Any possibility it can be transmitted through the air?"

"We're checking on that," said Kennedy. "We put the surviving animals in an isolation room with nonexposed ones, separated by varying distances. We'll keep a close watch."

"Hoffman knows all this?"

"I briefed him," said Kennedy. "That was the reason for yesterday's meeting, even if he didn't share all of this info. Look, I know you're worried. But I repeat that there's no evidence you were exposed. My guess is you'll be out of here in a couple of days. If you'd been infected, chances are you'd be showing symptoms by now."

Mariah knew Kennedy was probably right, but she just couldn't shake the notion that her time was limited.

"Listen," he said. "For what it's worth, I've been through something like this myself."

Mariah looked sharply at Kennedy. "You were exposed to Kandahar?"

"No. Ebola," he said. "About twenty years ago, when I was fresh out of grad school. I spent a week in quarantine in a hospital in Africa. I was part of a team that had been searching for the index case for an Ebola outbreak that was burning through the Democratic Republic of Congo. I was being as careful as I could—scrubs, gloves, mask, safety glasses. But the clinic's protective gear was pretty cheap—really inadequate for a hot virus. And they hadn't had any previous experience with Level Four agents.

"It was getting toward the end of the first day of interviews. I came up to the bed of an old man, obviously dying, wasting away. Bleeding from his mouth, nose, even his eyes. When I bent over to check him, he went into a coughing fit. Before I could back away, he reared up and sprayed bloody spittle all over my face. I was wearing the glasses and mask, but the stuff still got on my forehead and I worried about the flimsy mask. I hoped that I hadn't been inhaling when the guy coughed. I flushed my face and eyes with tap water. And I did a little praying."

Mariah waited and watched Kennedy's face. His expression was set, impassive, similar to when she'd first met him in Hoffman's office. But today she had the feeling that he was trying to control his emotions.

"Two days later I came down with a headache and chills," he said. "Temperature of a hundred two. I got a team member to drive me to Kinshasa—we both wore protective gear the whole way. I checked into the hospital there. They put me straight into quarantine. I waited for the hemorrhaging to begin. But I got better, not worse. They discharged me on the eighth day. Turned out to be a mild case of flu. So, bottom line: exposure doesn't necessarily mean infection."

"I'm surprised you don't have nightmares," Mariah said, quietly.

"Who says I don't?" he said.

Mariah and Kennedy sat across from each other in the small isolation room and didn't speak.

"I'd better get back," he said at last. "Hang in there. It won't be long. I know it's got to be boring as hell. I'd be climbing the walls."

Mariah watched him open the door and walk out.

That afternoon Curt Kennedy stood near a makeshift stage at a community playground in Middle Valley, Pennsylvania, as a large crowd gathered. It looked to him as though the entire town had turned out. He estimated the group at about three hundred people.

He saw farmers in coveralls, teenagers with bicycles, mothers pushing strollers, soccer-playing middle schoolers wearing high socks, shorts, and brightly colored T-shirts, young lovers holding hands, stooped grandfathers leaning on canes, and middle-aged men with large paunches that strained against long-sleeved green jerseys bearing the logo of the Philadelphia Eagles and the number and name of a favorite player. To Kennedy, it looked like a cross section of rural America that might have gathered for an annual bull roast sponsored by the volunteer fire department.

But as he looked closely at the faces in the restless crowd, he didn't see eager anticipation. He saw worry and fear. He figured that by now nearly everyone in town would have read the article in the *Inquirer* about the quarantine and animal euthanization plan and that they'd seen or heard about a company of National Guard soldiers that had assembled in the area.

Kennedy heard noise near the stage and watched as four men and a woman mounted the steps and took seats in folding chairs facing the crowd. He saw Emily Rausch and Frank Hoffman, and a man Kennedy recognized as the mayor of Middle Valley, midthirties and the owner of a small insurance company that primarily served the dairy and horse farms of Chester County. Kennedy knew that the man had been elected to the part-time post only six months earlier and that it wasn't usually a busy job.

Another person onstage was a man who was wearing an incongruous dark suit and had Washington written all over him. He held a small sheaf of papers in his hand and Kennedy guessed that they contained notes for a speech. *Mistake*, thought Kennedy. This crowd wouldn't appreciate someone reciting something to them from a script.

Then there was the fourth man, who wore the combat fatigues and black boots of the army. The boots gleamed with a mirrorlike sheen, and Kennedy could see two stars in each of the collars of the officer's starched blouse that signified the rank of major general. *National Guard*, thought Kennedy. With that rank, he had to be the state commander.

The din of the crowd died down. The mayor stepped up to a microphone mounted in the middle of the stage, tapped it a couple of times, cleared his throat, and spoke.

"Thank you all for interrupting your day and coming out this afternoon," he said. "As some of you know, we have a bit of an emergency in the town. We have a few visitors with us who will fill you in on what we're dealing with and answer any questions you might have. Without further ado, let me introduce our first guest, Dr. Frank Hoffman, director of the National Laboratory for Foreign Animal Diseases. Dr. Hoffman?"

"Thank you, Mayor," said Hoffman, stepping up to the mic. Kennedy watched him closely for signs of nervousness, but Hoffman looked poised. "I'll try to keep this brief. I know there will be a lot of questions and we'll do our best to answer them. The National Laboratory for Foreign Animal Diseases—the Barn for short—is a state-of-the-art facility operated by the U.S. Department of Agriculture to protect farm animals from exotic diseases. We do have a situation on our hands. Four days ago we became aware of a new viral disease that's affecting animals in the Middle Valley area. Our scientists are trying to learn everything they can about it. The main threat is to animals, but there's a possibility that the disease could be passed to humans. So we're proceeding with an abundance of caution. We've made the decision to cull all animals within a five-mile radius of Middle Valley."

Kennedy heard a murmur run through the crowd. He knew why Hoffman had used the word *cull*—it was technically accurate—but it smacked of bureaucratic understatement and probably set his listeners on edge.

"Animals will be sacrificed as humanely as possible," said

Hoffman, raising his voice. "And out of the sight of town residents. After they're put down, they'll be safely disposed of."

"Including our pets and farm animals?" shouted a woman from just in front of the stage. "Is this absolutely necessary?"

"I'm sorry, ma'am," Hoffman said. "Unfortunately, domestic animals could be carrying the disease and that presents a risk to public health. It's too risky to spare them. We have no alternative. Owners will be fairly compensated."

More suit-speak, thought Kennedy. These people didn't want "fair" compensation. They wanted Hoffman to be straight with them. As Kennedy watched, the crowd began to get unruly. A burly man had pushed himself forward and was now yelling at the podium. He was wearing oil-stained jeans, muddy work boots, a gray T-shirt with a "Made in Pennsylvania" logo across the front, and a green John Deere ball cap.

"Pardon my French, but this is pure BS!" the man said. "You can't just come in here and kill our animals!"

Hoffman held up his palm and tried to quiet the crowd. He raised his voice above the growing din. "We have no choice, folks. We don't want this disease to spread to the people in this community."

The chorus of voices grew louder. "I thought you said there was only a possibility of risk to humans!" shouted a blonde woman.

"That's true, ma'am. But, as I said, we're proceeding with an abundance of caution."

The "Made in Pennsylvania" man had now worked his way to the very front of the crowd, just below the stage. "Abundance of caution!" he said loudly. "That's what you guys said when you made it mandatory for people to get the bird flu shots a couple of years ago. And what happened? No outbreak, but a bunch of kids sick from the vaccine. And tell me this. What are the troops doing here? And why are they fencing in the town?"

From the gasp in the crowd it was obvious to Kennedy that

this was the first time that many of the townspeople had heard about the fence perimeter.

"We can't allow the free movement of animals into and out of the area," said Hoffman. "We have to contain the disease here."

"What about the people?" someone shouted. "I suppose you're going to imprison us too!"

"Unfortunately, because human beings could be carrying the virus, we don't want to take a chance on their spreading it outside the area," said Hoffman.

Kennedy could see that Hoffman was trying to appear cool and imperturbable, but he also saw him fold his arms and begin shifting his weight from foot to foot.

"So the entire town is being quarantined?" shouted "Made in Pennsylvania." "What are you going to do if we try to leave? Shoot us?"

This was getting out of hand. Kennedy moved quickly to the edge of the stage and got Dr. Rausch's attention. He spoke in a low voice, hoping that he wasn't overheard. "Emily, we've got to tell them the truth."

"We can't tell them everything," she said. "It would start a panic."

"You're already starting a panic," said Kennedy. "People can handle the truth. What they don't like is uncertainty. They can tell when they're being lied to."

"We're not lying to them. Everything Hoffman has said is true."

Another loud question interrupted them. "Who authorized this?"

Now Kennedy saw Hoffman turn and speak quietly to the dark-suited man seated on the stage, who then glanced at the notes in his hand, stood, and moved to the microphone. He spoke in a slow, measured voice.

The man introduced himself to the crowd as a deputy undersecretary of the Department of Homeland Security. "This comes down from the White House itself, ladies and gentlemen," he said. "I want to emphasize that there's no cause for alarm at this point and I want to assure you that DHS is in full control of the situation. We're still in the early stages of learning about this new animal virus. But, as Director Hoffman said, our first, overwhelming priority is to protect people. So far the virus exists only in a small area around this town. If there's even the slightest chance that the virus could spread to humans, we have a responsibility to prevent that. To fail to do so would be criminally negligent."

Kennedy was surprised at the statement by the DHS official that his department was "in full control." Did they suspect a terrorism link? That's what the language implied. Now he heard a new voice, from a young man standing alone, off to the side of the crowd. Kennedy took in his appearance: slim, about six feet tall, with brown hair. Jeans and a striped, short-sleeved, button-down shirt with collar buttons unfastened. Wire-rim glasses. He carried a small notebook in his left hand and held a ballpoint pen in his right hand.

"Tony Parnell of the *Philadelphia Inquirer*," the man said. "Just a couple of questions."

The DHS official turned to Hoffman and spoke in a stage whisper that was audible to Kennedy. "I thought we said no press."

"I'm sorry, sir," said Hoffman, clearly flustered. "I didn't know he'd slipped in. I think it'll be okay. He had the byline on the *Inquirer* article this morning and he followed the press release pretty closely."

"A question for you, General," said Parnell. "How many troops do you have out there and where are they now?"

"Happy to answer that, sir," said the army officer. "For those who don't know me, I'm the commander of the Pennsylvania

National Guard. We have three hundred sixty soldiers in place. They're deployed around the perimeter of the containment zone."

"Do they have orders to shoot if someone tries to break out of the zone?" asked Parnell.

The general paused before answering and the crowd began to grow noisier. "Only as a last resort," he said hurriedly. "If every other deterrent fails. We know that the good people of Middle Valley understand the importance of maintaining this quarantine until we're sure that the disease is under control."

Kennedy strained to hear through the rising murmur in the crowd. Parnell was pressing on, his voice raised.

"One more question," he said. "I've heard that a local family has been isolated in Pennsylvania Hospital for the better part of a week and that the husband has died. Can you tell us straight up, is their illness related to the quarantine here?"

Dr. Rausch started to rise, but Hoffman, sitting next to her, placed a hand on her arm and stood up himself.

"As I said before, we're operating with an abundance of caution," said Hoffman. "We don't anticipate a significant risk to the population. But we can't afford to take a chance. Now, if you'll excuse us, we have to get back to work. Thank you all for your time and understanding."

Kennedy shook his head. *Botched it*, he thought. Sure enough shouts erupted from the audience and several people started to move toward the stage. Kennedy saw the National Guard commander bend his head and say something to his left lapel. Seconds later, from behind a deuce-and-a-half truck that was parked at the edge of the field, a half-dozen soldiers wearing camouflage fatigues emerged. The soldiers, expressionless, lined up between the crowd and the speakers. Kennedy saw that they were packing nine-millimeter Beretta pistols, secured in holsters strapped to their waists.

Kennedy watched Hoffman, Rausch, the general, and the Homeland Security official head to the side of the stage, descend the wooden steps, and stride to a waiting black SUV with U.S. government plates and tinted windows, leaving only the mayor to deal with the angry crowd.

CHAPTER TWELVE

Mariah stared down into her drink, a little surprised at her surroundings. She was sitting at a nice restaurant in downtown Philly and across the table was none other than Curt Kennedy. He'd asked her to dinner, to celebrate her "liberation" from quarantine, he'd said, and she'd agreed and was now wishing she hadn't. They'd been there for fifteen minutes, had run out of pleasantries after ten, and now Mariah couldn't think of a single thing to say. She studied Curt's face, trying to read his expression, hoping her raised wineglass would shield her scrutiny. He was wearing a dark green polo shirt without a logo. She'd agonized about what to wear because she didn't want to dress for a date if this wasn't one, but she didn't want to insult him by dressing too casually in case it *was* one. She'd finally settled on a black skirt, cut just above the knees, and a lacy white blouse with a scoop neck that nicely set off her glossy dark hair, which she'd allowed to fall naturally to her bare shoulders.

Curt leaned forward into the light, smiled slightly, and returned her gaze. He seemed unbothered by the now lengthy silence lingering between them.

Is this actually happening? wondered Mariah. Was she really having a drink with this guy, a professional colleague she hardly knew, a man who struck her as macho and definitely distant? But when Curt had asked her to meet him after several days in quarantine with no one to talk to, bland institutional food, certainly no booze, constant worry that every sniffle, every tiny headache, was the first sign of the end of her life, Mariah would have consented to a date with a serial killer.

No, that wasn't fair. She'd been glad Curt had asked her out. He'd been so professional and kind after her accident in the lab. *So talk to him, Mariah. What are you waiting for?*

"So," she said at last, grasping for any topic she could. "I heard the town meeting was pretty rough."

"That's putting it mildly," Curt said. "You're a diver?" he asked.

Mariah frowned, thrown off by the abrupt change in subject and confused by his question. He nodded at her wrist, and she realized he'd recognized her watch—a Casio, supposedly water-resistant to one hundred meters. "Not yet," she said. "It's been a dream for a while. Just haven't had the time to learn how."

"I could teach you," said Curt. He made a short, sweeping gesture. "After all this is over. The epidemic, that is."

What is this guy's deal? Mariah thought. From what she'd been able to learn, Curt Kennedy was a loner, and a bit of a cipher. No attachments. No personal life that she'd ever heard of. Barely any history whatsoever. And now she'd known him for a week and he'd asked her out and was offering to take her diving? *Is he messing with me?* she wondered, then immediately scolded herself for being so suspicious.

"I heard you were former military," said Mariah, brushing off the diving invitation in a way she hoped he wouldn't notice. "Navy, right?"

"Army at first," said Curt. "Three years in special ops. Then I joined the navy when they offered to put me through medical school. Did some active duty as a navy doctor. I'm still in the reserves."

"So you're a physician too?" said Mariah, not bothering to hide the surprise in her voice.

"Not really," he said. "Not anymore. Haven't practiced medicine for twenty years."

Their food arrived then, and another silence fell between them.

"I'm glad you're okay," Curt said finally, between bites of his burger. "By the way, you did a terrific job on that necropsy."

"Thanks," said Mariah. "But then I go stick myself the next time in the MCL." *Now, why did I go and say that?* she immediately asked herself. It sounded so lame—and self-deprecating.

Curt merely shrugged. "I was the clumsy one," he said. "Hey, let's see if we can get through one course without shoptalk, okay?"

Mariah smiled and nodded in assent. The epidemic, the quarantine, the slaughter of pets, livestock, and wildlife. It was too depressing. If Curt was game for talking about something other than work, she'd do her best to go along with it. And so for the rest of the meal they talked only about themselves and the small portions of their lives that weren't dominated by work. Curt confessed that he was an amateur woodworker, that he made dollhouses—dollhouses!—in his free time, but he wouldn't elaborate, despite Mariah's shocked questions, except to say that his first one had been for his sister. Mariah talked about the book she was reading, *One Hundred Years of Solitude*, and gave Curt the basics of the plot and the bio of Gabriel García Márquez. They both talked lovingly about their dogs, Mariah's West Highland terrier, Dancer, and Curt's black Lab named Rambo, at whose name Mariah rolled her eyes exaggeratedly and laughed. They ordered another round of drinks, and it was during her second glass of wine that she told Curt about her childhood love of horses and about her restless Subaru and those ads—those damn ads!—that had made her buy it, Curt, laughing, knowing the exact ones she was talking about. And later, as Curt was paying the bill, without looking up from scrawling his signature on the slip, he made a passing reference to Mariah's tattoo, which sent a zing of mortification and something else down Mariah's spine. The tattoo—to honor Dancer—was a small terrier, discreet, just above her left bra cup. He must have seen it at some point when she leaned forward. She smiled and said something that she hoped would come off as unflustered. He'd mentioned that he also had a tattoo and said, in a slightly teasing voice, that maybe he'd show it to her someday.

They walked together to Mariah's car. She fished her keys from her purse. Curt stood near her, close enough that she could feel his warmth. As she unlocked her car door she noticed her hands were trembling. She opened the door, turned to thank Curt, and found his face inches away from hers. She stood still for a few awkward seconds and then reached up and gave him a quick hug, brushing his cheek with hers. "Good night, Curt. I had a really nice time."

"Me too. Let's do it again sometime."

Mariah slid into the driver's seat and started the engine. She rolled down the window, smiled at Curt, and wished him good night again.

As Mariah drove back to her apartment, a twelve-year-old girl in the small community of Gradyville, twenty-five miles west of Philadelphia, pressed her nose against her living room's picture window and peered into the darkness.

"Dad, what's that noise?" she asked. "It sounded like a wolf." What she really thought it sounded like was a werewolf, but she refrained from mentioning this to her father. He was an English professor at UPenn and staunchly disapproved of her reading those urban fantasy books, said they were trash, and why couldn't she read stuff that was good for her, like *Jane Eyre*. *Right*. She'd started it, just to get him off her case. *Totally boring*.

There it was again. A howling.

The girl's father laid down an academic journal, rose from his armchair, and walked to the window. Too dark to see anything. Another howl, higher-pitched than before and closer. Had to be a coyote. Normally that wouldn't surprise him. Their house was at the edge of the 2,600-acre Ridley State Park, the closest thing to wilderness that you could get in the greater Philadelphia area. There were coyotes in the park, or at least there had been. Before the outbreak and the animal slaughter.

The man's wife came into the living room. The noise had pulled her away from her computer, where she had been reading about the latest progress on containing the disease epidemic. "What is that?" she asked her husband.

"Probably a dog," he said. "Must have gotten away from the animal control people." He didn't want to say coyote. He didn't want to alarm his daughter any more.

"Go get her, Dad," his daughter said. "Please? Maybe she's hurt."

"That's not a good idea," he said, wondering how his daughter had concluded that the animal was female. "It could be diseased."

"But you can't just leave her out there alone! Couldn't you just put her in the shed? We could put a fence around the door. That way we could get food and water to her. Please, Dad."

"She's right, dear," said the wife. "The dog might be wounded. We can't just leave her out there to die."

The man looked at his daughter. Her lips were trembling. Maybe it was a dog. And it could be hurt. It would be cruel to ignore it, but if it was a coyote, it might be vicious. Probably hungry—since its prey had likely been wiped out—and diseased. If he went out there he'd better have some protection. In case. Boots. Heavy clothing. A weapon. "Okay," he said. "I'll go out the back door. Stay here at the window. When I signal, hit the floodlights."

Before leaving the house, the man detoured down the cellar stairs. He found an old pair of sturdy work boots, canvas coveralls, a thick denim jacket, and leather shooting gloves with the forefingers cut out. He slid a large trunk away from a wall. Behind the trunk was a small door with a padlock. He unlocked the door and retrieved a twelve-guage Remington shotgun and a box of shells. He'd had the gun since he was a teenager. It was a gift from his father, who thought a shared deer-hunting experience would help them bond. That hadn't happened, but he'd kept the gun. He popped two shells into the shotgun chambers, pocketed the rest, dressed in the protective gear, and headed back up the stairs.

Before opening the back door, he listened carefully. He heard another howl, coming from the front of the house. He hoped his wife and daughter would see the animal and perhaps distract it as he approached from the other side. He quietly opened the door and stepped outside.

The night was pitch-black. Not even the sliver of a moon. He remembered it had been clouding up at sunset, but at least it wasn't raining. He crept around the side of the house, stepping carefully to avoid any noises that would give him away. Chances were he'd only find a wounded dog, but any wounded animal could be dangerous.

He reached the far corner of the house, stopped, and peered around. Nothing. He stayed still and listened for several minutes. The howling had stopped. Where was the creature? A slight noise behind him. He turned quickly, in time to see a dark shape hurtling through the air.

The man had no time to raise his gun, let alone fire off a shot. The animal was on him, snarling and growling. The man tried to cover his head with his arms. The animal's momentum drove him backward and he fell heavily, with the beast on top of him. This was one big coyote, the man thought as he sought to defend himself. Had to be over seventy-five pounds. Sharp teeth pierced his denim jacket and penetrated his forearm. He pounded on the animal's head with his other arm. Too late, he realized that he had left his throat exposed.

CHAPTER THIRTEEN

AUGUST 26, MORNING

LANCASTER COUNTY

Dr. Emily Rausch willed herself to relax as the Pennsylvania Hospital ambulance rolled along Route 30, lights flashing, siren wailing.

She'd received a call shortly after arriving at work that morning. An Amish couple had been found dead by their sons in their rural home in Andrews Bridge in Lancaster County. The couple had apparently died a couple of weeks before, or more. The sons had just discovered them and were waiting at the house. Based on the description of the bodies, Emily had activated the hospital's biohazard response team and dispatched another ambulance to pick up the bodies. Her ambulance would bring the sons to the hospital—assuming they consented.

The ambulance slowed, pulled into a long dirt lane, and approached a white frame house with a covered porch and an old-fashioned windmill in the yard. Emily could see several people standing outside the house. *Sure hope the local authorities followed my instructions*, she thought. No one should enter the house until she got there. "Stop here," she told the driver. "We suit up before going any farther."

Dressed in protective gear with full face masks and respirators,

Emily and her four-person team exited the ambulance and stiffly walked toward the waiting group. "Has anyone been inside?" she asked.

"Just the sons," said a uniformed police officer. "They're the ones who called it in. They're waiting over by the shed." The policeman pointed toward a small, rickety building about fifty yards from the house where two middle-aged men were standing with arms folded, staring warily at the emergency responders. "They live over in Lancaster City," the policeman added. "Didn't see much of their parents from what I heard."

Emily turned to one of her teammates. "Get the sons into the ambulance," she told them. "They'll have been exposed." She headed toward the house, followed by the other team members.

Emily Rausch was no stranger to the odor of death, but the stench that greeted her—even through the biohazard suit—was unlike anything she'd ever smelled before. There was none of the normal, vaguely sweet aroma of the deceased that sometimes reminded her of mushrooms growing in dark, damp places. That smell had life in it, even in death—the organic smell of bacteria and other decomposing organisms that thrived on what was left of the former life that nurtured them. But the odor in this house was devoid of life.

The bodies were close together in the bedroom, dressed in nightclothes, skin stretched tight across the facial bones, hands shrunken and curled like claws. The man lay on the floor, his back propped up against the bed. His wife lay in a fetal position on the edge of the mattress, her arm draped over the bed, her hand in contact with her husband's head. A dark stain had spread from her gaping mouth onto the sheets. A darker stain soiled her nightdress below her waist. The front of the man's nightshirt was similarly discolored, and dried blood coated his nostrils and jaw.

Emily quickly examined the bodies and noted extensive

discoloration of the skin and dried blood around every orifice. An autopsy would confirm it, but there was no doubt in her mind. This was Kandahar.

She doled out instructions to her coworkers and exited the house, noting that the second ambulance had arrived. She resisted the urge to pull off her face mask and take in deep drafts of fresh air. That would have to wait. She issued instructions to the ambulance that would serve as a hearse and walked to the ambulance she'd arrived in.

The Amish couple's sons were seated in the back, dressed in protective gear. Emily could see the fear in their faces—and anger. This would take her best diplomatic skills.

"I know how hard this is for you," she said. "I'm so sorry." She let her words sink in and then continued. "I know you're wondering why you're in here, suited up." She looked back and forth between the two men. The fear was still there, but the expressions had softened. "We believe your parents were exposed to a rare virus," she said. "There's been an outbreak in this area. Unfortunately, it's quite contagious. That's the reason for the hazmat suits." She waited for a response. Both men remained quiet. *They know they've been exposed too*, she thought. *They probably figure they're doomed.*

"Chances are you'll both be fine," she told them. "But you should be closely observed for a few days. In case. If you show any symptoms, we can treat you right away. With your permission, we'll take you up to Penn Hospital." Emily watched as one of the men turned toward the other and made eye contact. Were they going to refuse to deal with hospitals? *Please*, Emily pleaded silently. *Please don't make this harder than it already is.* But then the man turned back to her and nodded slightly. Relieved, she reached to open the back door of the ambulance. She needed to call Frank Hoffman. Then she'd give the driver the green light to head immediately to Philadelphia. "I'll be right back," she told the men. The least she could do was sit with them on the ride to the hospital.

As his gaze swept over his surroundings, taking in details that most people never noticed, Omar was virtually certain that only one other person in the world knew that he had just arrived in the Philippines. But he was experienced enough to know that assumptions could be dangerous. Assumptions could get you killed. Vigilance, caution, and preparation, lots of preparation, kept you alive, allowed you to get the job done right.

He had a big job ahead of him, and not much time. He'd need to find a safe house in Manila, a place to lie low until he proceeded to the next destination, a place where he wouldn't need a credit card that could be traced, where questions wouldn't be asked. He had plenty of cash and money could buy almost anything, including silence, especially in an impoverished area like the Philippines. And if money didn't work, there were always other, more persuasive incentives.

He needed a cell phone, one of those temporary, prepaid ones, untraceable, available at almost any chain pharmacy. He'd need another passport, to replace the one he'd flown over on that was in the name of a guy who looked somewhat like him. From what he knew about the Philippines, expert forgeries should be easy to come by. He made it a practice to never use a passport more than once. With today's technologies it didn't take long for the spooks to put two and two together.

He needed local support. He'd have to learn everything he could about the sleeper cell here and vet the most promising candidates. Doctor Vector had tried to insist that the job could be done with a skeleton crew, in fact had only given him a phone number to call. But Vector knew nothing about this kind of work. You needed a team, a team you could trust, to carry out an operation of this magnitude and complexity. He'd have to work quickly to recruit the right people from the local sleeper cell, as he was due at his next destination in three days. But the candidates would all have one thing in common. They'd all be fanatical believers who would willingly give their lives for the cause.

Finally, he'd need a disguise.

He pulled a ball cap down over his eyes and hailed a passing cab, which reminded him that he'd also need his own car. Taxi drivers were observant, and they talked. A car would be easy to come by in the city itself, where, unlike here at the airport, security cameras were few and far between. As he bent to enter the cab's backseat he tightened his grip on his backpack—his only luggage. The pack would never leave him. Never, that is, until he successfully delivered its contents.

Omar directed the cabdriver to drop him off in Manila's Santa Cruz district. They soon arrived at a heavily populated area, crowded with small shops and shantylike houses. Omar told the driver to stop, handed him some pesos, and quickly exited the cab. As the taxi drove off he darted into a narrow alley and entered a small store, where he picked out and paid for new slacks and a T-shirt, another ball cap, and a pair of sunglasses. He ducked into a changing room and emerged seconds later, leaving his old clothes behind. Good enough for now, he told himself. He could be a bit more creative later.

CHAPTER FOURTEEN

At 8:00 a.m. Curt Kennedy approached the entrance to the maximum containment laboratory and saw that Mariah was already there. She smiled and gave him a little wave.

"We've got to stop meeting like this," he said.

"Very funny," said Mariah.

Their task was to retrieve from the secure freezer room a pure isolate of Kandahar virus that had come from the dead soldier's blood and get it to a CDC microbiologist who would try to develop a vaccine for the virus. Hoffman had said they'd intended to do this after the infected soldier's death several years ago but couldn't get the funding then. Now a vaccine was an immediate priority and it seemed that money was no object.

They suited up and entered the secure area. Kennedy consulted a diagram on the wall that showed the layout of the spaces. He pointed toward the main corridor. "Third door on the left. Believe it or not, Hoffman gave me both keys."

"I thought he had to be there whenever the room was opened," said Mariah.

"That's what he told us the other day. But he said he had an out-of-town meeting today, that he'd make an exception for me."

As they approached the freezer room a bulky, moon-suited figure passed by them in the corridor and quickly exited the MCL.

"Wonder who that was," said Mariah. "Not even a wave."

"I swear he came out of the freezer room," Kennedy said, frowning.

"How could that be?" Mariah asked. "There's only one second key and you're carrying it."

He inserted his keys and opened the door. A single chest freezer stood against the far wall. He walked over, punched in some numbers on a pad on the freezer, and opened it. The temperature was set to minus eighty Celsius, the optimum level for long-term storage of virus cultures. But the gauge read minus seventy. Why was it warmer in there than it should have been? Kennedy saw a box with inserts holding a number of small vials, picked out a vial, and read the label: *Kandahar, Afg.* A date was inscribed below. Only about half of the inserts held a vial. There was no sign of an inventory, so there was no way to tell if anything was missing. He looked for a log-in sheet, but didn't see one.

"Let's go," he said to Mariah. She looked startled but didn't question him. They exited the lab and he led the way to the shower rooms.

"Shower out quickly," he said. "I'll meet you outside."

Soon they stood together outside the MCL. "I don't know what's going on," said Kennedy. "I'm pretty sure that the guy who passed us in there had been in the freezer room—and in the freezer. It was warm enough that it seemed like someone had just opened it. And he looked like he was carrying something."

"So what are we going to do?" asked Mariah.

"Try to follow him," said Kennedy. "He can't be far ahead unless he didn't bother to shower out." He started to move, knowing there was no time to waste, but then stopped and turned back to Mariah. His gut was telling him this could be a dangerous situation.

"Look, I'll go ahead," he told her. "I'll give you a ring later."

Mariah shook her head. "I'll go with you," she said firmly.

Kennedy hesitated for just a second. He couldn't take the time to argue and Mariah seemed determined. Maybe he was overreacting. He told himself that he'd minimize the risk to her, pursue the guy carefully, stay far enough back that they wouldn't arouse the man's suspicions. "Okay," he said. "But we'll have to move quickly."

They both heard a noise—the sound of footsteps ahead of them.

Kennedy took off running, with Mariah close behind. They came to a T at the end of the corridor and heard a door banging shut to the left. When they burst through it, they were facing a parking lot. Kennedy heard the sound of an engine and saw a dark sedan pulling away.

"Come on!" he shouted, yanking keys out of his pocket as he broke into a run again. They sprinted to a pickup truck and jumped in. Kennedy fired the ignition and pulled quickly out of the parking space. The sedan was about a hundred yards ahead, moving fast, approaching the exit from the Barn property, where a plainclothes security guard sat inside a small shed. He had a sliver of hope that the guard would detain the speeding sedan, but he doubted that would happen. He'd been arguing for better security at the Barn, but the powers that be hadn't taken him seriously.

The car blew past the gate and turned right onto Route One. Kennedy pressed down on the truck's gas pedal, intending to follow close behind. He cursed under his breath at the sight of the guard, now in the middle of the exit lane, waving *him* over. *So now he decides to do his job.* Kennedy pulled to a stop, rolled down the window, flashed an ID card, and pointed ahead. "I'm after that vehicle. Official government business." Without waiting for an answer, he accelerated and turned onto Route One.

There was no sign of the sedan. Kennedy hoped that it would be delayed by a stoplight. Traffic was light this time of day.

After a few minutes, he saw the car waiting at a red light. He slowed the truck, timing his approach so that he passed through the light a couple of hundred yards behind the sedan after the light turned green. He kept pace for an entire half hour, remaining far enough back so that it wouldn't be apparent that he was following. They drove through Delaware County and into Chester County. Mariah was silent in the passenger seat. He glanced over at her. *She doesn't look scared*, Kennedy thought.

When he turned his eyes back to the road again, the sedan was gone.

Two National Guard soldiers wearing white Tyvek protective suits walked slowly down the length of a long, shallow trench in the middle of a large farm field near Andrews Bridge, Pennsylvania. They wore asbestos gloves and full-face, multipurpose respirators, and carried flamethrowers. Tangled, stiff carcasses of Holstein dairy cows, piled two or three deep, filled the trench. Every few seconds long streams of flame issued from the barrels of the flamethrowers and ignited the corpses. Black, oily smoke plumed from the trench and stained the blue sky with ragged, dark streaks. Farther up the trench, bulldozers pushed more dead cattle into the depression.

A lean, graying man in green coveralls watched the activity from a vantage point upwind of the blaze. The man was the director of emergency management for Lancaster County, and the on-scene commander of the cow-culling operation. A young National Guard lieutenant standing next to him shook his head and spoke.

"Must be thousands of cows in there," said the lieutenant. "And plenty more to go. We'll need to get a move on."

"Approximately twenty-five hundred so far," said the director, with a trace of annoyance. He knew what he was doing, knew how much time the operation would take if it was done right, to his standards. "The trench is a quarter mile long and twenty-five feet wide," he said. "Filled to capacity, it'll hold five thousand animals, about half the dairy-cow population in the vicinity of the farm where the infected cow showed up."

The sounds of gunshots echoed in the background and a steady parade of dump trucks delivered new loads of dead cows to the pit. Backhoes stood ready to scoop earth over the charred bodies when the burning had run its course, and to start another excavation when the first trench was close to full.

The director gazed at the operation and turned back to the lieutenant. "Everything's on schedule," he said. "We'll be done day after tomorrow."

"What's it going to do to the county's farming?" asked the lieutenant.

"Pretty much destroy the livestock business," said the director. "Best-case scenario is that livestock's the only thing it destroys. I could see it collapsing the state's entire economy." Watching the slaughter and incineration made the director feel physically sick, but he knew that the quickest way to kill ten thousand cows in open farmland was to shoot them, and that the safest and most efficient means of carcass disposal was burning.

He'd had a lot of second thoughts about the operation, and a host of questions he didn't share with the lieutenant. What if the containment efforts didn't work? What if the disease spread beyond the quarantine zone, which had now expanded to fifteen miles, and engulfed the entire county, with ten times as many cows? How many National Guardsmen would it take to shoot a hundred thousand cows? How long would it take to dig five miles of trenches to accommodate the carcasses? How many dump trucks? Backhoes? Flamethrowers? Would the burning carcasses contaminate the groundwater and the air? And what about the psychological effects on soldiers who, hour after numbing hour, would have to fire point-blank into the brains of helpless farm animals?

He'd read about a 2002 homeland security exercise involving a hypothetical foot-and-mouth disease outbreak on five American farms. In ten days the virus had spread to thirty-five states. The exercise predicted that National Guardsmen would have to kill millions of farm animals, including pigs and cows, to stop the disease from spreading farther, that the soldiers would run out of bullets, that a ditch at least twenty-five miles long would be required to bury all the carcasses, and that all this would be in plain sight of the public. It predicted riots in the streets.

He forced the negative thoughts out of his mind and concentrated on the work of the soldiers. With luck, they'd be done by sunset, but for most of the Guardsmen it would be the longest day of their young lives. He would do his part to ensure that the soldiers had frequent breaks, plenty to eat and drink, and a chance to relax and chat about something other than the mass slaughter of farm animals.

Mariah unconsciously tightened her seat belt. They'd lost sight of the sedan and now Curt was speeding down the narrow rural road. She sat rigidly, jaw clenched, her eyes focused ahead.

"You okay?" Curt asked.

She turned quickly and looked at him. "Fine," she said, embarrassed by the obvious catch in her voice. "Just trying to figure out where that guy went."

Curt nodded then suddenly leaned forward. "Got him," he said, pointing.

Mariah saw the sedan some distance ahead and then felt the truck decelerate. They maintained a distance of several hundred yards behind the other vehicle.

Soon the sedan turned right. Curt followed, onto Union-ville Road, then Doe Run, bordered by fields and horse farms. Minutes later, the sedan turned left onto a narrow, paved road, then right into a cornfield, raising a cloud of dust above the head-high stalks.

As Curt and Mariah reached the turnoff he eased the truck into the entrance of the dirt road and stopped.

"Aren't you going to follow him?" asked Mariah.

"Too risky. No easy way out if he sees us. Wait here." Curt got out of the truck and jogged down the lane. He was back in five minutes. "The road's about half a mile long," he said. "House at the end. Looks kind of abandoned. I didn't go all the way in."

"Now what?"

"We wait." Curt started the truck, backed out onto the main road, and drove about a quarter of a mile beyond the dirt lane. He turned the vehicle around, facing the lane, and parked the truck off the road, partly hidden by tall corn.

"So what's going on?" asked Mariah as Curt turned off the engine. "And who exactly was that?"

"My guess is someone made a duplicate set of keys to the freezer room," Curt said. "If they had access to the originals, it wouldn't be that hard. Pretty standard lock and key arrange-ment. Surprising. Thought Hoffman would have been more careful."

"But how would they have gotten both of Hoffman's keys?"

"If he was trusting enough to give them to me, he's probably done it for others."

"Pretty stupid if you ask me," said Mariah. "So what do we do?"

"For now we watch," said Curt. "I hope you're okay with that. Pretty boring, I know."

"I'm fine. We need to figure out what's going on."

"I don't believe in coincidences," said Curt. "Kandahar shows up not that far from the Barn and the only North American source is in a freezer in the Barn. And someone—whoever we were chasing—was in there just before us today." He turned his head and looked toward the cornfield.

For several minutes neither of them said anything as they kept their eyes on the entrance to the dirt lane across the road. Mariah clasped her hands together in her lap, feeling keyed up but willing herself to stay calm. Even two feet away from Curt, she sensed energy radiating from him. She glanced over. He was staring toward the lane, his lips pressed together, eyes narrowed, attentive to the surveillance. She focused on his profile, the strong chin, crooked nose, small, ragged scar on his right cheek. She felt like touching it. Now he was turning toward her. She quickly looked away.

"You were looking at me," he said. "Did I cut myself shaving or something?"

"No, nothing like that," she said. "I was just wondering about that scar."

Curt smiled. "Oh, that. Definitely not a shaving cut. Got it when I was younger. Wrong place at the wrong time. I guess it's kind of ugly."

"No, not at all. Hardly noticeable."

"You're being kind." Curt was silent for a minute and then looked over at Mariah. "The other night in the lounge," he said. "I mentioned making dollhouses."

Mariah nodded, hoping he'd go on but not wanting to push it.

"I told you I made the first one for my little sister," he said. "Lucy. I was twelve. She was seven. She'd been diagnosed with leukemia. She was in chemo. Really brave. Never complained, even when she lost all her hair. It got so she'd be comforting me instead of the other way around. I made the dollhouse to cheer her up."

"Did she recover?" Mariah asked quietly.

Curt shook his head and began to watch the lane again.

Mariah cleared her throat. "I'm sorry," she said. "I lost both of my parents when I was young." She felt like she owed him this.

"What happened?" Curt asked, looking at her with concern.

"My father was a cop in Philly. He was killed on the job. Drug bust gone bad. My mother was killed a couple of years later, in a car crash. I was nine. My grandparents raised me." She saw Curt open his mouth, but then, ahead, she noticed dirt rising again above the cornstalks. She pointed.

Seconds later, the dark sedan appeared, turned left onto the main road, and sped off.

"Government plate," said Curt.

"Should we follow?"

Curt shook his head, started the truck, and pulled out into the road. He parked by the dirt lane, opened the glove compartment, and withdrew a spool of white thread. Mariah watched as he walked down the dirt lane and did something with the thread that she couldn't make out.

"What was that all about?" she asked when he returned.

"Tied it off to cornstalks on each side of the lane," he said, buckling his seat belt. "Strong enough that the wind won't break it, but if a vehicle comes through it'll snap." He glanced at his watch. "We'll come back first thing in the morning. If the thread's intact, we'll check out the house."

"Shouldn't we run this by Hoffman?"

"No need. Besides, he's out of the office today. If we see anything unusual, we can always fill him in."

Mariah didn't like it. Too cloak-and-dagger, not her thing. And maybe dangerous. She wanted to object. But she was letting her imagination get the better of her. If no one returned here before tomorrow morning, it should be safe enough. Plus there was definitely something suspicious about that person they'd seen in the MCL. And, she admitted to herself, she felt safe with Curt.

CHAPTER FIFTEEN

Mariah was behind the wheel of her Outback with Curt beside her. They were heading back to the cornfield. From the corner of her eye she could see that Curt was looking at her.

"So what do you think of Hoffman?" he asked. It was the first thing beyond pleasantries he'd said since she'd picked him up twenty minutes earlier.

"He's okay, I guess," Mariah said. "Why?" She was careful to keep her eyes on the road ahead. She'd offered to drive so that Curt could pay closer attention to the surroundings.

"Just wondering," said Curt.

Mariah thought about the question. She respected her boss, but he made her a bit uncomfortable. She didn't think she should share that with Curt, and she couldn't really put her finger on what bothered her, hadn't really thought about it that much. "He obviously knows his stuff . . ." she said, letting her voice trail off.

"But?" said Curt.

Mariah glanced over at Curt, then turned back to the road. "He can be a bit over-the-top with that America first shtick," she said.

"That's no act," said Curt. "Do you know what happened?"

"I heard his wife was killed by terrorists in London in 2005. She was on a double-decker bus that got bombed."

"Right," Curt said. "On the upper level. The explosion threw her about fifty feet into an iron fence."

Mariah shuddered, picturing the scene and then trying not to. "That's awful," she said. "Was she killed instantly?"

"She lived for several days. Hoffman got there as soon as he could. The doctors thought they could keep her alive. But they told him she'd never be the same—not just physically. Permanent brain damage. And she was suffering, even drugged up. Hoffman told me he could see it in her eyes. So he gave the doctors permission to let her go."

"I can't even imagine," she said, rewinding through her interactions with Hoffman over the years, trying to see him in a different light. "But he seems to have been able to move on."

"I guess so," said Curt. "But it took a while. His wife was his whole life outside of work. No kids, no siblings, and his parents died when he was in his twenties. He'd always talk about her. Brought her by the lab a few times. She seemed sweet, devoted to him." Curt sipped from a cup of takeout coffee. "He went into a deep depression after she died. He was working at Fort Detrick at the time. Took a leave of absence. There was a rumor that he was hospitalized for a while in a psychiatric ward, but I don't know if that's true. When he came back to the lab a year or so later, he seemed okay. And he worked his ass off. Understandable. Probably good therapy. He was always a strong leader and his people respected him. So when the Barn directorship opened up, he was a logical choice."

"Mmm," said Mariah. She wasn't sure where Curt was going with this. Was he sticking up for Hoffman? Scolding her for misreading him? Had Hoffman *asked* him to say something? *Stop it*, she told herself. She was being paranoid. Curt had no reason to care about how she felt about her boss. Nonetheless, she resolved to be more open-minded about Hoffman, about people she didn't know well in general.

"Here we are," said Curt, pointing off to the right. "Just pull into the lane entrance."

Mariah braked the car, turned onto the dirt road, and stopped. She waited while Curt got out and walked up the lane. He returned seconds later.

"Thread's intact," he said. "Drive slowly and try to keep the dust down."

At the end of the lane they saw an old white farmhouse surrounded by cornfields. The house needed paint and there were no cars in the driveway. A faded sign in the front yard read Beware of Dog. But no dogs rushed up to greet them. Curtains were drawn across the windows.

"Doesn't look like anyone's living here," said Mariah, easing the car to a stop near the house. Curt was only half listening. He appeared to be scanning the outside of the house. "What are you looking for?" she asked.

"Video cameras, hidden alarms," said Curt. He got out of the car and walked toward the house. Mariah followed him.

They tried to peer through the drawn curtains into the darkened interior of the house. Where the curtains hadn't quite closed they could see most of a living room and adjoining study. Fireplace along one wall, an old couch, a couple of armchairs with worn cushions. They walked to the side of the house and looked into the kitchen. The kitchen windows had no curtains. A dirty bowl and cup lay in the sink and a covered pot sat on top of the stove. A yellowing copy of the *Philadelphia Inquirer* lay on the counter.

"Let's check the garage," said Curt. As they approached it he stopped and pointed toward the far end of the building where a tall, stainless-steel pipe projected several feet above the roof line of the garage. "Looks like an exhaust vent," he said. He walked back around to the front of the garage. Mariah followed and watched him as he tried to raise a large overhead door. It wouldn't budge. He tried an adjacent small door but it was locked.

Curt moved around to the left side of the garage and looked at a window, midway up. He retrieved an old pallet from a pile of debris and propped it against the side of the garage under the window.

"Almost as good as a ladder," he said, positioning his feet at the top of the pallet and stretching toward the window. He pushed up on the frame. "Locked and the shade's drawn, but there's a gap at the bottom," he said. "Whoa, what's this?"

"What do you see?" asked Mariah.

"I'm not sure," said Curt. "My tool bag's on the floor of the front seat. Mind bringing it over?"

Mariah brought him the bag and watched as he removed a small, high-intensity LED flashlight, held it against the bottom of the window, and turned it on.

"Some kind of lab," Curt said. "I can see a lab bench, stainless steel by the look of it. Drop-in sink, gas jets. And there's a refrigerator and upright freezer next to the bench."

Mariah waited while Curt played the flashlight beam along the interior of the garage. "What the hell?" he said. "There's a large biosafety cabinet in there. That explains the exhaust vent outside. And that's not all. A growth chamber of some kind. And animal cages."

He stepped off the pallet and reached back into the tool bag. He removed a small tool and a pair of gloves and safety glasses, which he slid on. He climbed back onto the pallet, secured a suction cup on the tool against the bottom of the window, and began to turn the tool's rotating arm.

"What are you doing?" asked Mariah.

"Cutting a hole in the glass." Slowly and carefully Curt rotated the arm. "This thing's got six tungsten-carbon cutting blades. Super sharp, which is a good thing. Window's pretty thick."

Mariah watched with a mixture of surprise and apprehension. "What was your previous profession again?" she asked. "Cat burglar?"

Curt chuckled but didn't answer. After several minutes, he stopped and peered at the window. He shook his head in disbelief. "Only about halfway through," he said.

Then they both heard the noise of an approaching vehicle.

Tony Parnell of the *Inquirer* stood at the edge of a crowd of several hundred people at Stony Creek Park in Brandywine Heights, Pennsylvania, just outside the newly expanded quarantine zone. The day was clear and hot. Off to the southwest, across the Chester-Lancaster county line, Parnell could see a thin plume of black smoke curling from a hayfield and drifting toward the park, borne along by a fresh breeze. Even at that distance, he could practically taste the smoke—acrid, oily, and redolent with the scent of burning flesh—and it was all he could do to keep from gagging. He noted a four-foot-high, woven-wire fence running along the edge of the park and stretching to the northwest and southeast as far as the eye could see. The fence appeared to be topped with a row of electric wire. National Guard soldiers, spaced evenly apart, stood between the fence and the crowd. The expressionless soldiers held rifles, in some cases clutching them so tightly that their knuckles showed white. Their helmets seemed too big for their heads. They occasionally licked their lips and their eyes darted from crowd member to crowd member.

Parnell studied the crowd. Some carried signs reading Don't Kill our Pets! and Free the Animals. Other signs, evidently displayed by religious zealots, decried the abandonment of God and proclaimed the imminent end of days. But to Parnell, most of the demonstrators seemed to be average citizens reacting viscerally to what amounted to a military-enforced government takeover of a small rural town. He didn't blame them. If it happened in Middle Valley, he thought, it could happen anywhere.

Parnell also knew that his fellow journalists hadn't helped matters. While he felt that his front-page article about the Middle Valley town meeting had been factual, detailed, and, he hoped, objective, other reports had been sensational, even lurid, building with teasers like "Deadly Epidemic Strikes Rural Pennsylvania Town" and climaxing in breathless accounts of historic global scourges like the black death. Several quoted retired infectious disease experts who provided graphic accounts of deaths from flu pandemics and gruesome hemorrhagic diseases like Ebola and, in some cases, drew sobering links between environmental degradation, global climate change, and the inexorable spread of worldwide plagues.

Even the *Inquirer* had helped fan the flames. He thought back to the paper's provocative editorial following the Middle Valley town meeting: *The officials' airy assurances and dismissive responses to the queries of concerned residents raised more questions than they answered. For instance, if the scientists are confident that the disease is not dangerous to humans, why is the town being quarantined? Why are so many animals—including pets, livestock, and wildlife—being sacrificed? Would the armed soldiers encircling the town shoot a fleeing resident who disobeys an order to halt? Is the disease far more serious than the experts are admitting? Is Middle Valley expendable?*

Parnell turned his attention to the other side of the fence, where a smaller group had gathered, many with dogs on leashes or other pets cradled in their arms. The assemblage included a rider on horseback.

The crowd in the park had started to chant, repeating the

same refrain, over and over: "Free the animals! Stop the slaughter!" A tall, lanky young man with curly, longish brown hair and wearing a bright green T-shirt with an Animal Rights League logo, led the chant, bellowing through a bullhorn. Other green T-shirts speckled the crowd. There were several TV cameras and reporters with microphones. To Parnell, it was obvious that this was not a spontaneous demonstration. Its seeds had been planted back at Middle Valley.

Parnell didn't fault the authorities for the actions they'd taken. The disease had to be contained, and from what he'd learned about its virulence, enacting a quarantine and sacrificing exposed animals was the only feasible response. But the communications had been a disaster—clumsy, misleading, even arrogant.

He watched as the young man in the green T-shirt approached a National Guard soldier and screamed at him through the bullhorn, "Let them out!" The young soldier stiffened, but his face remained impassive and he stared straight ahead. His fingers tightened around his gun. The crown began to yell louder. Parnell edged back. This could get ugly. He could see that the soldier was trying to remain professional, not making eye contact, the training kicking in. But his lips were pressed tightly together and Parnell detected a slight tremor in his face. The protester would have seen that too, would have sensed the fear. If this was a veteran demonstrator, Parnell thought, he should know enough to back off. A young, inexperienced Guardsman could be unpredictable.

A shout erupted from the other side of the fence. The horse and rider had approached the border. The helmeted rider appeared to be a female. The horse pawed and stamped at the ground. The rider was bending low, head alongside the horse's neck, whispering in the animal's ear. The young man turned away from the soldier, toward the horse and rider, and raised his hand to the horsewoman in what appeared to Parnell to be a sign of recognition, a greeting.

Now he was bellowing into the megaphone again, directing a new chant at the crowd on both sides. One word, repeated over and over. *"Go! Go! Go! Go!"* The man was crazy, thought Parnell. Should he intervene? No, that was the Guards' job. He was just a reporter. But now the crowd began to pick up the chant.

Parnell watched the horse and rider, hoping they wouldn't respond, knowing they probably would. The rider turned the horse, walked it back about fifty feet from the fence, and turned it again. The crowd's attention was now totally focused on horse and rider. The chants grew louder. Parnell looked around the crowd. Where was the Guard commander? *There.* A lieutenant, looked like he could still be in college. *Come on*, Parnell thought. *Take charge.*

The rider was still leaning forward, her cheek against her horse's shoulder, her hand caressing its forehead. The young Guard commander was staring hard at the demonstrator leading the chant. *Please*, mouthed Parnell. *Get control.*

Finally, the officer moved up to the fence, turned, and faced the chanting crowd. Standing straight, with his hands clasped behind his back, he began to speak. *Come on, talk louder*, thought Parnell. The throng continued to chant. *"Go! Go! Go!"* The Guardsman raised his voice, trying to project over the cries. Parnell was close enough that he could hear the officer. He was trying to *reason* with the demonstrators. *You're going to have to be a lot more forceful than that*, the reporter thought. He turned and looked over the fence at the horse and rider, who were directly facing the fence. The woman continued to bend low over her horse's neck and whisper into its ear.

Then, with a sick feeling of helplessness, Parnell watched the crowd on both sides of the fence clear an opening, like a runway, leaving only the National Guard soldiers standing their ground. He quickly backed away, keeping his eyes on the horse and rider. He reached the far edge of the crowd, positioned himself on a slight elevation where he had a clear view, and waited, hoping against hope.

It happened quickly. Parnell saw the woman apply pressure to her horse's sides with the heels of her riding boots. The horse moved forward in a steady canter, the rider erect in the saddle. The crowd was now cheering. Steps away from the fence, the horse dipped its neck and lowered its front legs, effecting a braking action that brought the rear legs farther under its body. As the rider leaned forward, the horse, in a fluid motion, now shortened its neck, shrugged its shoulders, and shifted its weight back, momentarily compressing the hind legs before they quickly flexed upward in a sudden, graceful surge of power.

As his reporter's eye fixed these details in his mind, Parnell watched the horse arc over the barrier, clearing it by at least a foot.

For what seemed like an eternity to Parnell, but which he later determined could not have been more than a second or two, the crowd fell silent. All motion, except that of horse and rider, seemed to stop.

Then everything seemed to move at once. A National Guard soldier in the pathway of the leaping horse stepped forward. He raised his rifle. With horse and rider still in the air, the soldier fired off a quick volley. The rider flew off the horse, hit the ground, rolled several times, and came to a stop, where she lay motionless. The horse, blood gushing from the right side of its neck, continued to gallop, scattering the crowd, before its forelegs buckled and it pitched headfirst to the ground.

For a moment no one reacted. Then, led by Green T-shirt, the crowd surged toward the soldier who'd fired the shot, screaming profanities. The scenes and sounds registered in Parnell's mind like jerky frames in an early talkie movie. Demonstrators enveloping the soldier. Thudding sounds and muffled screams. Other Guardsmen moving in, rifles at the ready. The Guard commander bellowing into a bullhorn. The sharp report of another gunshot. A demonstrator going down. Another demonstrator holding a rifle wrestled away from a Guardsman. The Guard commander now speaking into a two-way radio. Reporters and TV crews rushing to their cars and mobile vans. The piercing wails of approaching sirens.

Parnell shook his head and scribbled furiously in his notebook. *Now everything has changed*, he thought.

CHAPTER SIXTEEN

Mariah turned quickly toward the entrance lane and saw a cloud of dust rising above the cornstalks and funneling rapidly in their direction. At the rate it was moving it would be on them in less than a minute.

"Get the car!" Curt yelled. As Mariah raced to her Subaru he retrieved the cutting instrument, stepped off the pallet, tossed it into a nearby patch of high weeds, and gathered up the rest of his tools.

Mariah pulled alongside Curt and slowed enough to allow him to open the door and jump in. She glanced in the rearview mirror. No sign of the vehicle yet, but the dust cloud had almost reached the clearing.

Curt pointed toward the cornfield. "That way," he said. "Stay to the edge."

She followed a rutted tractor lane at the boundary of the field. It had been dry lately and an early-morning rain had already evaporated from exposed surfaces, but she hoped it was still damp enough in the shade of the corn to keep some of the dust down. The corn wasn't quite high enough to hide the car.

They were a hundred yards into the lane when she saw a

white, late-model van in her side-view mirror. She opened her mouth to tell Curt.

"I see it," he said, his eyes on the side-view mirror. "Can you go any faster?"

Mariah pressed down on the accelerator. The car started to skid on the firm soil, kicking up clods of dirt. Had they been spotted?

"Van stopped in front of the house," Curt said, twisting around to look behind him. "Two guys. They got out. Walking around the house now."

Mariah let out the breath she realized she'd been holding. If the men in the van had seen them driving off, they would have followed. But she knew that it would only be a short time before they checked the garage. They'd see the displaced pallet and the matted grass below the window. They might even discover the scoring in the windowpane. They'd certainly find the tire tracks in the field. They'd put two and two together.

She drove as fast as she could over the rough terrain. They soon reached a hedgerow at the end of the field. Curt pointed toward a gap in the hedge that provided access to farm tractors. A paved road lay just beyond. Mariah shot through the gap and jerked the wheel. The car fishtailed on the dirt and slid onto the asphalt surface. The tires gripped the road.

Soon they were heading south on Homeville Road. Mariah was breathing so hard that she could barely hear the tires humming along the asphalt. Her pounding heart felt like it was trying to force its way out of her chest. Curt's voice came from a long way away.

"Nice driving," he said. "You looked like a pro back there."

"Yeah, right," she said, grateful for his efforts to calm her down but unable to get into a joking mood. "Think we shook them?"

"Maybe," said Curt.

But then Mariah glanced at the rearview mirror and pressed her lips together to hold back a violent expletive. "I think they're behind us," she said.

Curt turned around. "Floor it. We should be able to outrun them."

Mariah depressed the accelerator as far as it would go. A light rain had resumed and was beginning to speckle the dusty windshield. Her chest tightened as if a giant had her in a bear hug. It seemed to be pushing blood into her head. She started to get dizzy. She pressed a button to crack her window, and air rushed in, buffeting her upper body and clearing her head. She raised the window back up but left a gap of several inches at the top. The speedometer read ninety-five.

She glanced again in the rearview mirror. The van was keeping up. Was it closing? Her gaze darted over to Curt. His eyes were fixed on his side-view mirror.

"They must have a supercharger in that thing," he said. "Can you get any more speed?"

"Only on downgrades. What are we going to do?"

"Just keep driving as fast as you can. Maybe we'll find a side road after a curve and slip in there before they see us again."

The rural two-lane road had plenty of curves as it twisted through the countryside, but Mariah couldn't see any turnoffs. The road was now starting to slicken with rain. Narrow gravel shoulders separated the pavement from deep drainage ditches. Mariah struggled to control the car on the wet, winding surface. The van was still closing. There was nothing she could do about it; she couldn't go any faster. The gap narrowed. The bastards must be doing well over a hundred, she thought. Curt was quiet. She figured he didn't want to distract her. Or maybe he was pondering a strategy. The van was right behind them now.

They moved onto a long, straight section of road. A burgundy Volvo wagon approached from the other direction, the first car

Mariah had seen since they had entered Homeville Road. Maybe she could get their attention. She flashed her lights several times in succession. The oncoming car slowed down. It passed her. Mariah could see a couple in the front seat and a small face pressed to the back window. The driver gave a friendly wave, oblivious, probably thinking she was simply warning them of a cop ahead. Then the car was gone. Mariah despaired. Couldn't they see that she was being chased by the van?

The van was now riding the rear bumper of the Subaru. Was their plan just to crash into her? Mariah had kept the accelerator to the floor, but the van was much faster. She saw it swing into the oncoming lane, and it pulled alongside her. The front passenger window rolled down. Mariah could make out two men in the front seat wearing dark wool caps pulled low over their foreheads. The passenger extended his right arm out of the open window.

Mariah screamed and ducked just as a bright flash erupted from the van window. She heard glass shattering and felt sharp fragments falling on her face. She smelled acrid smoke. Her hands had come off the steering wheel and she saw Curt reaching for it. She heard the Subaru's tires biting into dirt, then felt a weightless sensation. *Airborne*, she thought uselessly. Then, simply: the end, nothing, black.

Doctor Vector slammed down the phone. "Goddamn idiots," he snarled under his breath. He should never have gotten involved with a sleeper cell. That had been Omar's idea: use well-trained, America-hating fanatics for on-the-ground operations here and overseas and tell them only what they needed to know. They'd die for the cause, Omar had said, and even if they knew too much, they weren't likely to reveal it—especially since the United States now considered waterboarding a form of torture. But Vector knew that these terrorists could be brutal and about as subtle as attack dogs. And sure enough, they'd chased down and killed the man and the woman who'd discovered the garage lab when all that was called for was a good cover story for plausible deniability. But now it would be all over the press.

But the mission would not be compromised. Vector was sure of that. All of the elements of the main plot remained in place and were clicking along nicely. He would find a way to deal with this latest setback.

CHAPTER SEVENTEEN

AUGUST 29

PHILADELPHIA

Mariah was back in quarantine. She had to be, she decided as she struggled to open her eyes against the pounding in her head. The walls all around her were stark white. There was a TV monitor on a ceiling bracket beyond the foot of the sterile, steel bed. But slowly she realized she wasn't alone. She had company. A face swam into focus, above her and just to her left. Curt's face. Curt. Had he become infected too?

"Hey, Mariah," he said softly. "Glad to see you awake. You've been out for a while."

Mariah tried to sit up. Something was tugging at her arm. Curt was standing beside her with what she now recognized as a worried look.

"Careful," he said. "You're on an IV."

"In a hospital?" asked Mariah, taking in her surroundings.

"You don't remember anything?"

Mariah pressed a hand over her eyes and didn't answer. What was there to remember?

"After the guys in the van fired at us—you recall that?"

Now pieces floated back to her. "Okay," she said. "Homeville Road. The Volvo. The van pulled beside us. A gun . . ."

"Yes," Curt said gently. "After they fired at us, we went off the road, hit a tree, and caught fire. The guys in the van must have thought we were gone. They drove off. I got their plate number. We got a lucky break. The driver of that Volvo that passed us going in the other direction saw the accident in his rearview, turned around, and came back. Had a fire extinguisher, by some grace of God. He doused the flames and pulled us out. Brave guy."

Mariah looked closely at Curt. "Were you hurt?" she asked.

"Just a couple of cuts and a bang on the head. I'm fine. You should be okay too. You had a mild concussion, but should be back to normal pretty quickly. But for now you just need some rest." Curt smiled down at her. "I'll be back a little later to see how you're doing."

Later that morning at the Barn, Curt Kennedy settled into a chair in Frank Hoffman's office and studied his boss's face: thin lips pressed into a narrow line, deeply furrowed brow, dark circles under the eyes. *The man hasn't slept*, thought Kennedy. *And he's pissed. Not that I blame him.*

"How's Mariah doing?" asked Hoffman.

"Concussion, but she'll be okay," said Kennedy. He found that he had clasped his hands together as he spoke. Thinking of Mariah lying unconscious in the hospital bed, before she came around, made his jaw clench. "Overnight in the hospital. They'll be springing her sometime this afternoon."

"What the hell did you think you were doing?" Hoffman asked, his eyes locked on to Kennedy's.

"Somebody was coming out of the freezer room when we got there yesterday," said Kennedy. "They were obviously in a hurry. I thought we ought to follow them. Good thing we did. They were driving a government sedan."

"You're suggesting this is an inside job?" Hoffman's arms

were resting on his desk and Kennedy could see that his fists were alternately clenching and relaxing. He wouldn't bring up his concerns about Hoffman's key control.

"Not necessarily," he said cautiously. "But it's a reasonable assumption. Look, Frank, I'm sorry I went out there behind your back. I figured I'd better act quickly. And you were out of town."

Hoffman slammed his fist on the desk. "Sorry? Goddammit, Kennedy, who do you think you are! You had no right. I should fire you both. Maybe have you arrested."

As Kennedy stared back at Hoffman, he saw his boss starting to relax, his shoulders no longer hunched up to his neck, the veins in his neck starting to look less prominent. "They did try to kill us," Kennedy said, "so obviously someone had something important to hide."

"So what happened at the farmhouse?" asked Hoffman gruffly. "Give me all the details."

Kennedy related the previous day's events. He voiced his conviction that someone was working with dangerous pathogens—maybe Kandahar—in a home laboratory.

"Did you get inside the garage?"

"No. The van showed up as I was looking through the window."

"Did you get a good look at the occupants of the van?"

"No. All I could see was two people in the front. Both males. Obviously they must have been watching the place. Probably CCTV, well disguised. Those goons showed up pretty fast. I did get a plate number." Kennedy jotted it down and passed it to Hoffman.

Hoffman glanced at the paper and set it on his desk. He was silent for the better part of a minute. When he spoke again his voice was lower and more controlled. "Here's the deal. I'm worried about your safety. I want you two to head right out to the West Pacific—Saipan. You can get moving on the Nipah work."

"That's crazy, Frank," said Kennedy. "You need our expertise to help stop the spread of this virus back here. And what if this was an act of terrorism? Don't you want all hands on deck?"

"I don't disagree," said Hoffman. "But whoever was chasing you will find out that you lived. They may already know. Your lives will be in danger. Better that we discreetly get you out of the country for a while. And we'll do our best to keep this out of the press."

So he's worried about publicity, thought Kennedy. "You think they won't track us down in Saipan?" he asked.

"Not right away."

"You can't send us out of the country," said Kennedy again. "You need us here."

"My mind's made up. I'm booking you on the first available flight."

"But Mariah's just getting out of the hospital. She's had a concussion. She needs to recover."

"Fine," said Hoffman. "I'll delay it a couple of days. But you guys will have to lay low until then."

When Kennedy tried to object, Hoffman waved him off. "Check back with me this afternoon," he said. "I'll give you details then." He motioned toward the door.

CHAPTER EIGHTEEN

The president of the United States sat behind his uncluttered desk in the Oval Office and looked directly into the TV camera. He spoke in a clear, level voice. "My fellow Americans. As most of you know, many of our citizens in the northeastern United States are dealing with a major crisis."

The president described the epidemic in Pennsylvania. He was straightforward about the nature of the disease, the human casualties, the risk of further spread, and "the critical importance of a secure quarantine zone." He apologized for the culling of wildlife and domestic animals but emphasized that it was necessary to protect the human population. He assured the nation that "all available resources" were being devoted to the crisis and that there was "outstanding cooperation among federal, state, and local authorities." He expressed his gratitude to the first responders, including law enforcement, medical, and veterinary personnel, and to the National Guard, all of whom were "working around the clock" to contain the disease so that it did not spread beyond southeastern Pennsylvania.

The president paused and leaned forward, his eyes still fixed on the camera. "This is not an easy time for any of us, especially for those brave citizens in the affected area," he said. "The nation will weather this crisis, as we always have, and we will be stronger for it. But we all must do our part. Above all, we must obey the law. On Friday, a terrible incident took place near Philadelphia. An unruly crowd of demonstrators challenged the National Guard and tried to break through the quarantine barrier. Tragically a soldier and a demonstrator were killed. This only happened because a few selfish individuals decided to take the law into their own hands. Those people are now in custody. We cannot and will not allow anarchy. The quarantine zone is essential to assure public safety and stop the spread of the virus. I am committed to doing everything I can to guarantee the security of our nation, and we will not rest until this disease is eradicated." He paused. "Thank you all. Good night and God bless America."

The president waited until the television crew gathered their equipment and left the room and then turned to his chief of staff. "What do you think, Al?" he asked. "How did it go?"

Alphonso Cruickshank was uniquely qualified to answer the president. Trained as a lawyer, he had ascended to a partnership in a large Boston law firm, but ninety-hour workweeks played havoc with his family life. So he resigned from the firm and took an in-house legal position at the *Washington Post*, where he eventually became general counsel. The position had given him an unusual ability to understand the workings of the press and the legal maneuvering necessary to navigate the stormy political waters of the nation's capital. Even so, Cruickshank carefully considered his answer before responding to the president. "Quite well, sir," he said. "I think the American people will believe you're leveling with them. But the Guard did show their inexperience. Let's just hope the press supports you. You know how they can be."

"There's not much I can do about that," said the president.

"I think there is. It's all about the information flow. If they think that's drying up or somehow being manipulated, they'll be ruthless."

"You're suggesting more briefings."

"That's right," said Cruickshank. "I think you should meet with the White House Press Corps every other day. At least until we turn this thing around."

The president winced. "I'd rather spend time in a lions' cage. But I know you're right."

Mariah poured two glasses of white wine and handed one to Curt. They sat across from each other at her small dining room table. Curt had offered to take her out to dinner to celebrate her release from the hospital, but she'd insisted on his coming over to her apartment, mostly because she really didn't feel like going out in public.

Curt raised his glass and clinked hers. "To life outside work," he said.

"Is there really such a thing?" Mariah asked wistfully, and then chided herself for saying something so wonkish. Her dog was sniffing at Curt's pant leg. "Dancer, leave him alone," she said.

"She just smells my mutt," Curt said, smiling down at the dog. "Seems to be pretty interested. Maybe we should get *them* together."

Mariah wasn't sure if that was Curt attempting to flirt or just making a joke.

"The forensics people thoroughly searched that garage," Curt said, turning back to Mariah, serious now. "Completely cleared out—no sign of any equipment. Even the vent pipe was gone."

"Any sign of virus?" Mariah asked.

"Hoffman said someone wiped everything down with bleach. The odor was still pretty strong. No trace of the pathogen."

"Fingerprints? Other evidence?"

"They're still looking," Curt said. "Hoffman says the van license plate was stolen, so that wasn't any help, and that supposedly government car we followed? No record that any had been signed out from the agency car pool."

"So if I have this straight . . ." said Mariah slowly, focusing on her plate. "Then, excuse me, but what the hell?"

Curt shook his head and shrugged. "They turned it all over to Homeland Security."

Mariah cocked her head, raised her eyebrows.

"Now we leave for Saipan on September first. And until then Hoffman wants us away from the lab," said Curt. " 'For our safety' are his words."

"September first—that's the day after tomorrow!" said Mariah. When Curt didn't answer, she asked, "And it's supposed to be safer in the Marianas?"

"In theory, it would take longer for the bad guys to track us down."

Mariah put her fork down and was silent for several seconds. She stared straight ahead, lips pressed together, her arms tightly crossed. Finally she refocused on Curt, her eyes locked on his. "You're not just a scientist, are you?"

"What do you mean?"

"That whole business at the farmhouse. You obviously knew what you were doing. You've done that kind of thing before. You're some kind of spy, right?"

Curt looked at her steadily. Then he said, "I'm with an outfit called the Bio Investigative Service. We work closely with USDA."

Bio Investigative Service? Mariah had never heard of it. Was it a cover for something? "So you don't actually work for USDA?" she asked.

"No, I do," said Curt. "USDA is my employer of record."

"But your real employer is this 'Bio' organization," said Mariah. When Curt didn't reply, she said, "Does anyone else at the Barn know?"

"A couple."

"Hoffman?"

"No."

"But you're still taking orders from him."

"Right," said Curt.

It was obvious to Mariah that Curt wasn't going to say anything more, so she asked him, "Has Hoffman pulled us off the Kandahar team?"

"He's not saying that. Remember, we were supposed to go to Saipan anyway."

"But they need us here now for this disease outbreak," said Mariah, struggling to keep her voice from rising. "That's far more important."

"I told him that, but he insisted." Curt was speaking calmly, in a way that made Mariah feel like she was being managed. "We'll be back on the team once they find the guys who tried to kill us," he said.

"Can't you get your 'investigative service' people to overrule Hoffman?"

"In the first place, they'd probably agree with him that we're in danger," said Curt. "Second, they'd only intervene in extreme circumstances."

"Well, Christ!" she said, her anger finally getting the better of her. "These are extreme circumstances, Curt. I can't believe you went along with this. No way I'm going to Saipan. Not with everything that's happening around here. We're needed more than ever. I assume you've been listening to the news."

"You mean the incident in the park," said Curt. "With the horse and rider."

"Incident! Full-scale riots are breaking out. The disease is spreading. Hospitals are overwhelmed. They're having trouble bringing basic supplies—like food—into the area. If we don't get this thing under control quickly, we're looking at a major catastrophe. Homeland Security should understand that. They'd want us here to help out. Who knows the science better than us?"

"We can't refuse a direct order," said Curt. "Maybe it even came from higher up. Like the White House."

"I doubt that," said Mariah. She picked up her glass and swallowed the last of her wine. She was feeling slightly reckless. "I think it's Hoffman's bright idea. He's covering his ass. He doesn't want us killed on his watch."

Later that evening, after Mariah had made it clear she was done talking about Saipan, their dinner had continued to go south, their small talk becoming terser and more awkward until finally Kennedy left for home. Once back at his apartment, he dialed a number from a secure phone. Bill Cothran answered on the third ring.

"Nice to hear from you," said Cothran. "How was your trip back from Hawaii?"

"Uneventful," said Kennedy. "Which is good when you're flying."

"I heard a bit about your latest adventure," Cothran said. "I'm up to speed on the disease outbreak. And the agency's involved now. You guys both okay? It's Mariah, right?"

"We're fine," Kennedy said. "Yes, it's Mariah. Mariah Rossi. But look, Hoffman's sending us to Saipan. He's concerned about our safety. But Mariah thinks it's bogus, doesn't want to go, thinks we'll be more useful here, and the thing is, she's right. We're critical members of the research team."

"So why call me?" asked Cothran.

"Figured you could do some checking around. Maybe dig

up some information that will help me make a better case to Hoffman. It'll have to be pretty quick. We're scheduled to fly out day after tomorrow."

"You know this isn't in my job description."

"Get serious, Bill," Kennedy said. "Even you can't define your job description."

Cothran chuckled. "Okay. I'll need some details. Anything that might be relevant. Even if it doesn't seem important. Go ahead. I'm listening."

For ten minutes, Kennedy spoke without interruption, and when he finally finished Cothran said, "Longest I've ever heard you talk, Kennedy. Let me see what I can find out. Plan to be there in an hour or so. I'll call you back."

While Kennedy was wrapping up his conversation with Cothran, three shadowy figures in black sweatshirts and tight nylon stocking caps crouched in drizzly darkness near a wire fence in rural Chester County. They silently watched an approaching National Guard soldier. They waited until he had passed their hiding place and begun to move away on his patrol down the fence line.

The trio's leader quickly reviewed some numbers in his head. Patrolling Guardsmen were spaced a thousand feet apart. Walking speed of three miles per hour, 250 feet per minute. The trio was hiding midway along the soldier's route. It would take two minutes for the soldier to reach the farthest extremity of his patrol, two more minutes to get back to them. That gave maybe two minutes for the three men to act, once the Guardsman got far enough away.

The trio leader began to count off seconds in his head. When he was satisfied that the soldier was out of sight and earshot, he signaled to the other two. They emerged from bushes and crept toward the fence. One pulled a pair of wire snips from his pants pocket and began to cut.

Seconds later, they were inside the fence. They moved quietly toward an old barn a hundred yards away, barely visible in the gloom. They knew that a small flock of sheep was sequestered inside the barn and that, if they didn't act, it would be the last night on earth for these animals. In the morning they'd be rounded up, packed into slat-sided cattle trucks, transported to a distant field, and executed.

The insurgents, who preferred to think of themselves as guerrilla warriors, stopped halfway to the barn, crouched again, listened, and carefully looked around. The leader pointed toward the barn, where a solitary figure was standing just outside the door. "Another Guardsman," he whispered. He was annoyed and more than slightly surprised. "I'll take care of him." He waited until he was sure that the sentry was facing away from him, then stealthily approached, slipped up behind him, and slit his throat. He gestured to the others to move up.

The guerrillas made their way to the front door of the barn, but found it padlocked. The man with the wire snips shined a pencil flashlight on the lock. "No problem," he said. He retrieved a screwdriver from his pocket and began to back off the screws on the hasp.

A loud klaxon noise blasted into the night.

The trio leader cursed. Old barns like this never had alarm systems. "Hustle!" he yelled at the man with the screwdriver. Seconds later, the hasp was off the door. The three slid the door open and rushed inside. They heard bleating noises and soon found the sheep, clustered in a pen at the far end of the barn. They ran to the pen, opened the gate, and tried to shoo the animals out. The sheep wouldn't budge.

The leader, who'd worked on a farm when he was younger, entered the pen and located a large ewe. He pushed on the animal until it began to move toward the gate. The rest of the sheep followed in a shapeless mass, as if tethered to the ewe, reaching the opening more or less at the same time, creating a bottleneck that was broken only by the combined efforts of the three animal rights activists. The sheep finally cleared the gate and began to scatter, bleating in confusion and fear. Running back and forth behind the sheep, the three men tried to herd them, to move them toward the gap in the wire fence. After a brief struggle they had the animals under control.

Then sirens pierced the night air.

The sheep dispersed again, moving in all directions, leaving the insurgents exposed in the open. Illuminated by flashing blue lights, a half-dozen armed National Guard soldiers wearing helmets and bulletproof vests stormed through the fence opening, weapons at arm's length. One of the soldiers shouted into a bullhorn, "On the ground, facedown. Now!"

The guerrilla leader reached into his belt, pulled out a .45-caliber pistol, and began firing, triggering a fusillade of bullets in return. By the time the shooting ended, the three insurgents lay motionless on the ground. One soldier was sitting, clutching his bleeding arm. The sheep had congregated in a tight cluster against the fence.

Close to midnight, Kennedy answered his ringing phone.

"That guy you saw in the lab?" said Cothran without preamble. "The one you followed to the farmhouse. We have no clue who that might be. Of course, you didn't give us much of a description."

"Not too easy to do," said Kennedy. "The guy was wearing a moon suit."

"Right," said Cothran. "But we do have some information about that van that followed you from the farmhouse. Picked it up on surveillance video at Philadelphia airport two days ago. Three guys inside. One was dropped off at the terminal."

"ID?" asked Kennedy.

"Van windows were tinted so we couldn't make out the occupants. The one who was dropped off looks Middle Eastern or maybe Asian. Image doesn't match anything on our databases. Video tracked him into the terminal. Ticketed to L.A., where he connected to Taipei."

"Let me guess," said Kennedy. "Passport and ticket were in a fake name."

"The name is real enough," said Cothran. "*Was*, I should say. The real guy died about a week ago."

"So our mystery man is in Taipei now?"

"No, Philippines," said Cothran. "He bought another ticket to Manila. Video shows him leaving the airport there. In a cab. No sign of him after that. We have assets searching the city."

"It's important that some of your 'assets' have microbiology expertise," Kennedy said.

"You think he's carrying virus?" asked Cothran. "Was any missing from the freezer room?"

"Impossible to tell," said Kennedy. "Couldn't find an inventory. But I think we have to assume this guy smuggled some out of the country."

"I don't disagree," said Cothran. "But as for microbiology expertise, it's too late to find anyone else with your knowledge, and you and Mariah have been involved from the beginning."

Kennedy's thoughts stopped short, confused. "Mariah?"

"Yeah, the plan is she'll work with you. She's got more lab training than anyone else we're going to be able to pull up on this kind of notice. You're just going to have to keep her from getting killed. Nothing too hard."

Kennedy spit out a laugh. He saw the logic in the plan, but he preferred to work alone and Mariah didn't have any experience in this kind of shit. "Don't you think it's a little dangerous for her?" he asked.

"A bit late to ask that now, after what you two have already been through," said Cothran. "Anyway, we'll have an overwatch at all times."

"So someone will run this by Hoffman?"

There was a long silence on the other end of the phone. Kennedy thought Cothran might have hung up. "We're not going through Hoffman," said Cothran finally. "Too risky. From what you told me and what we've learned, this looks like an inside job."

"So you don't trust Hoffman?"

"He doesn't need to know," Cothran said.

Kennedy took a breath, tamped down his questions, thanked his old friend, and the men bid each other good night.

She'd lived in Kennett Square, Pennsylvania, her whole life, all eighty-five years in the same old stone house just north of town, set back from a little lane off Unionville Road, with a picket fence bearing heirloom climbing roses running along the edge of the yard and a worn brick walkway to the front door bordered by perennial plantings that hadn't been tended for a while. She knew practically everyone in the area, had taught many of the town's residents at the local middle school, had served on the planning board and as a volunteer docent at the Brandywine River Museum, and until recently, read stories twice a week to preschoolers at the local library.

Now she was all alone. She'd lived by herself for more than ten years, since her husband had died, here, in this house. Their kids had moved out of state soon after graduating from college. But she'd stayed active and enjoyed entertaining a steady flow of visitors who'd drop by, often unannounced, to share tea, her famed ginger cookies, the latest town gossip, and memories.

But the visitors had stopped, and she was prohibited from even leaving her home. Since August 22, the town and surrounding area had been quarantined. Now, since her illness had come on, she'd become a prisoner in her own house.

For the first few days of her isolation, the phone calls had helped. But they'd become strained, even with her children, and then they'd finally ceased. It was as if they'd written her off. They probably figured she was already dead. She wasn't there yet. But she'd lost the will to make a call herself.

She understood why she'd been abandoned, and she forgave her friends and neighbors. Almost two weeks earlier, she'd come down with a bad cold. A visitor had come by, had seen her hacking and feverish, and refused to enter the house. She'd seen no one since, except for the town health officer, through the window, when he'd posted a sign on her front gate. The flu, or whatever it was, since seemed to have abated. But she was so weak.

She leaned back in an overstuffed armchair and adjusted a blanket on her lap with bent, arthritic fingers. How long since she'd last eaten? Three days? Four? Kind neighbors had been delivering daily food parcels. They'd been bringing them over after dark, probably to avoid a direct encounter with her. She was grateful for their kindness, but now she no longer had the energy to go out to get the parcels and they were piling up inside the gate.

She knew better than to expect help from outside the area. She'd seen the TV reports. Thousands of people sick. Health facilities overwhelmed. National Guard food trucks attacked. She faced the reality: she was on her own.

She tried to recall how long it took to starve to death. Two weeks or more, she'd read somewhere, depending on the person's condition. She hoped that at her age, it would be quicker, much quicker. If she had a gun, she told herself, she'd end it now.

CHAPTER NINETEEN

SEPTEMBER 1

LOS ANGELES

Mariah opened her eyes and shifted in the uncomfortable faux-leather seat in the United Airlines departure lounge at LAX. The flight to Honolulu was leaving in less than an hour. No way was she going to be able to doze off in the crowded, noisy lounge. She picked up a magazine she'd brought with her and idly thumbed through a few pages. Two weeks ago the last thing she'd wanted to do, or even imagined as a possibility, was to head overseas for an assignment. Now she was resigned to it, and deep down, though she wouldn't admit it to anyone and maybe not even to herself, she was even looking forward to it, mostly because she'd be with Curt.

Curt had explained that they weren't going to Saipan, despite what Hoffman apparently still believed, but were headed to Hawaii, where someone would meet them with details about where they'd go next, and that the assignment could be risky but they'd have good security. Beyond that, he hadn't told her much except to say that it had to do with the guys in the van. One of them may have taken some Kandahar virus. Mariah wondered who was making these new arrangements and why Hoffman was in the dark, but Curt hadn't answered and she assumed it had something to do with his intelligence connections, so she didn't pursue it.

The last couple of days had been a whirlwind, but Curt had helped her with everything. A battery of immunizations, a list of stuff to purchase and pack, not much but some things she'd never have thought of, and even arranging for his own dog sitter to look after Dancer while they were gone. She'd asked how long they'd be away, but he was noncommittal, which led her to believe that they wouldn't return until the mission, which was equally vague, was accomplished.

Kennedy had been standing over by the terminal window. Now he walked back to Mariah and sat down next to her. "Don't want to freak you out," he said in a low voice. "But I think someone's tailing us. Don't turn around. Slender guy, five ten or so, fortyish, short black hair, wearing dark slacks and a striped shirt. He's standing over in front of the Burger King."

Mariah hadn't noticed anyone suspicious. "Probably the security you mentioned, right?" she said.

"The detail here ended at the TSA screening line. Why don't you get up and stretch your legs a bit? You can walk by him. I'll watch his reaction. But don't let on that you're aware of him."

Mariah stood and strolled slowly away from the gate area. She passed by the man whom Curt had described. She glanced at him quickly, trying to avoid eye contact. He was reading a newspaper. Did his eyes stray above the page, briefly locking on to hers?

She bought a packet of mints from a nearby shop and returned to her seat in the departure lounge. "Well?" she asked.

"He watched you when you walked by. Just for a second. But long enough for me to know his interest wasn't just casual."

"Did he follow me?"

"He's too professional for that," said Curt.

"You think he's on our plane?"

"I know he is," said Curt. "I first noticed him on the way to security. Got a glimpse of his boarding pass."

"We need to get him out of the picture," said Mariah.

"Agreed. Any ideas?"

"Yeah. Let's let TSA earn their pay," said Mariah. "Want to take care of it, or shall I?"

With a slight smile, Curt retrieved his cell phone and walked back to the terminal window, out of earshot.

Minutes later, two TSA agents strode into the waiting area and approached the man. The agents spoke quietly to him and started to take his arm. Mariah could hear the man objecting. One of the agents spoke louder: "Now!" The agents led the man away. Minutes later, the United Airlines gate agent announced boarding for first-class passengers.

As Mariah and Curt tried to relax on the long flight from Los Angeles to Honolulu, Tony Parnell sat in front of a monitor at his cluttered desk in the *Inquirer*'s brightly lit newsroom. His work area consisted of an L-shaped cubicle with a computer, telephone, two-drawer file cabinet, wastebasket, and perhaps fifteen square feet of surface area that was smothered by unruly piles of papers and books. A privacy screen separated his desk from his neighbor's on the other side, but, at eighteen inches, the barrier's only real function was to prevent Parnell's mess from cascading into the other reporter's territory.

For nearly an hour, Parnell scrolled through the latest tweets, blogs, and more formal reports, including the most recent White House press release, about the Kandahar outbreak. Then, shaking his head, he pushed his chair away from the desk, picked up his cup, and, realizing his coffee had gone cold, set it back down. He sighed, loud enough for the female reporter on the other side to look up with a puzzled expression.

HANK PARKER

Parnell was having trouble grasping how quickly the outbreak had exploded into a major regional epidemic. Given the
speed at which this disease was spreading, he figured it was
only a matter of days before it reached Philadelphia itself. He
thought of his family at home in the city. *Time for a personal
contingency plan.*

Later that morning the president of the United States sat at
his designated spot at the center of an oval conference table
in the White House Cabinet Room, where he'd convened an
emergency meeting. A hazy gray light from the cloud-covered
sky outside filtered through high, thick windows behind him.

From his seat at the table, Alphonso Cruickshank had a good
view of the man who had hired him. Cruickshank knew the
strain the president was under, but still his boss had entered
the Cabinet Room today engaged in lighthearted banter with the
vice president and wearing his characteristic wry smile that
somehow signified both authority and equanimity.

Now the president leaned forward in his high-backed brown
leather chair and looked around the table. His gaze took in each
cabinet member in succession before he settled on the homeland security secretary. "Any update on last night's rioting in
Wilmington?" he asked.

A great fit for the position, thought Cruickshank, looking at
the DHS secretary. He'd directed California's Emergency Management Agency before taking the cabinet position. Cruickshank
reflected that the president had a knack for recruiting leaders
who were not only highly competent but also balanced loyalty
to their boss with a willingness to speak frankly.

The secretary cleared his throat. "We shifted some more
Guard resources there," he said. "Things are under control now,
but we had some significant casualties. About a dozen soldiers

and even more civilians killed. Scores wounded. We're trying to get firm numbers."

"Even worse than I'd thought," said the president.

"We're working with the governors to deploy all available National Guard troops in the northeastern U.S. to the quarantine zone," said the secretary.

"Can we bring in active-duty troops?" asked the president.

"The Posse Comitatus Act would prevent that," said the secretary of defense. "We can't use active-duty military inside U.S. borders."

The president looked down the table at his attorney general. "What about an exception for a critical domestic law enforcement situation, Fred?"

"I think we *could* legally justify an exception to the act to quell domestic violence. But it would probably be challenged in the courts. We'd lose time."

"Excuse me, Mr. President," said the DHS secretary. "We're also facing a severe shortage of health workers. We've got a substantial military medical infrastructure. I believe we could use active-duty medical personnel in a health emergency. We're not talking about using lethal force here."

"Good idea," said the president. "Make it happen." For the next several minutes, he listened to updates from each of the cabinet members. Following protocol, they reported in order of the presidential line of succession. Most of the news was distressing: looting and severe shortages of food and medical supplies in quarantined areas; overseas trading partners refusing U.S. agricultural exports; Canada and Mexico closing their borders to American citizens; and in the near future the prospect of a stock market collapse and a run on banks.

Finally, the president turned to the secretary of health and human services. "What's the latest on the medical side, Annette?" he asked.

Cruickshank studied the face of Dr. Annette Torres as she formulated her response. She was exceptionally well qualified for the position, having headed the infectious diseases department at the Cleveland Clinic and then serving as the hospital's CEO for four years before coming to Washington.

"The situation's not good, Mr. President," said Torres. "The outbreak's spreading and we've got cases now all through Chester, Lancaster, and Delaware counties in Pennsylvania. Nearly a thousand victims hospitalized. Over three quarters of infected patients have died. Fifty new cases a day."

The president shook his head. "How are the hospitals handling this?" he asked.

"Penn Hospital's maxed out," said the secretary. "We've worked with state authorities to establish new quarantine wings in two regional hospitals, but it looks like we'll need a lot more beds. We're drawing up plans now to transport patients to facilities outside the region."

"Can that be done safely?"

"Yes, sir," said Dr. Torres. "We'll be using mobile isolation facilities—basically mini-medical-quarantine units on wheels." She glanced down at notes in front of her and then looked up at the president. "We do have a proposal for better containment," she said. "We clear out an area outside the quarantine perimeter. That would give us a depopulated buffer zone."

"A no-man's-land," replied the president. He was silent for a moment. Then he said, "How much farther out, and how many people are we talking about?"

"Another ten miles, to just outside the Philadelphia city limits. An additional quarter million people or so."

The president whistled softly. "And what would we do with all those evacuees?" he asked.

"Unfortunately, they'd have to be in quarantine for a week or so," said Torres. "To be sure they haven't somehow been infected."

"And where are we going to house a quarter of a million citizens?"

The secretary hesitated before answering. "I've talked this over with Defense and Transportation. A remote area out west. Nevada or Utah. One of the military bases. We'd transport them by train. A continuous shuttle."

"My God."

"What choice do we have, Mr. President? It would only be a temporary detention. Until we control the disease spread. After that, they'd be free to go."

The president nodded. "Any chance this thing could be airborne?" he asked.

Cruickshank leaned forward, his eyes on Torres, saw her hesitate before she told the president that it was "unlikely" that Kandahar could be transmitted through the air. *So she's not ruling it out*, thought Cruickshank. He clenched his jaw. If this thing could be carried by the wind . . .

As Cruickshank was considering the dire ramifications of an airborne disease, the conference room door opened. The chief of staff looked over and saw a Secret Service man standing in the entrance, looking intently at him. Cruickshank rose, walked to the door, and stepped outside, closing the door behind him.

"I have an urgent message for the president, sir," the agent said. "Looks like we have another outbreak."

"Another Pennsylvania location?" asked Cruickshank.

"No, sir," the agent said. "Omaha."

CHAPTER TWENTY

Mariah and Curt followed Bill Cothran to an office on the second floor of a nondescript beige building on the outskirts of Honolulu. Cothran gestured toward chairs around a small conference table.

As they sat down, Mariah tried to figure out who Cothran was. Before they'd left the airport, Curt had told her he was "with security," but hadn't offered anything more. It was obvious, now, even through the haze of Mariah's jet lag, that Curt already knew Cothran, that in fact there was a friendship there that seemed to go back a ways. She looked around the office, saw a couple of framed diplomas, a shelf of technical books and unlabeled binders, no photos. A sign over the front door of the building had said Pacific Enterprises, which she thought was kind of a dead giveaway of a CIA front. And she'd been impressed with a flat panel by the door that seemed to respond to facial recognition. At least it opened when Curt had looked directly into it.

For the next ten minutes, Cothran briefed Curt and her on the latest events in southeastern Pennsylvania.

"Entirely predictable," said Curt.

"Agreed," said Cothran. "I'm just not sure what else could have been done to contain this earlier. Especially since it took so long to learn about the second outbreak in Lancaster County."

"There'll be plenty of lessons learned from this," said Curt. "Beginning with prepositioned emergency supplies in every metropolitan-area county in the country. A better communications plan from the outset. And a crash program for developing and stockpiling vaccines for every disease that's a significant risk."

"In fairness, we had no reason to anticipate a Kandahar outbreak in the States," said Cothran. "It wasn't common even in Afghanistan."

"But it's an internationally reportable disease requiring BSL-4 handling, a designated select agent, and a potential terrorism threat. Plus, our soldiers were exposed to it in Afghanistan. For me, that's enough to justify an aggressive U.S. prevention and response effort."

"I can't argue with that," said Cothran.

"You said they're making progress on a Kandahar vaccine," said Curt. "Are the virus stocks well secured?"

"Fort Detrick and CDC are doing most of the work," said Cothran. "DHS has arranged for twenty-four/seven security at all the locations where the virus is stored—CDC, Fort Detrick, and the Barn. They need to do a thorough inventory at the Barn. The records were pretty sloppy, so no way to know for sure if any had been taken before. And of course someone could have grown more to replace what they removed."

"But we've got to assume that the guy we saw took some," said Mariah.

"Afraid so," said Cothran. "In fact, we're worried that some of it might have been brought into the Philippines." He filled Mariah in on the video images at the Philadelphia airport, Taipei, and Manila. "And there's no record of this guy in any of our databases," he said.

"Why would he bring the virus to the Philippines?" asked Mariah.

"Maybe he's planning to sell it to one of the rebel groups down in Sulu or Mindanao," said Cothran. "Like Abu Sayyaf. They have connections to al-Qaeda and, we think, even ISIS. Bottom line is we need to find this guy. We're doing our best to track him down. And if he's got the virus with him, that's where you guys come in. You'll know how to handle it. By the way, you'll have a cover—I think you'll like it, Mariah. You're a scuba diver, right?"

Had Curt told him that? "Not yet. It's something I've always wanted to do."

"Well, you should know how to play the role. Your flight leaves tomorrow morning. Direct from Honolulu. Someone will meet you in Manila." Cothran reached behind him, pulled an envelope off his desk, and handed it to Mariah. "Your tickets. And new passports. No visa needed. Your stay shouldn't exceed thirty days."

"I thought your work was in security," she said with a wink. "It seems like a bit more than that."

"Oh, no, not at all," Cothran said, leaning back and waving her off in a way that seemed forced. "I make a half-decent bureaucrat, that's all. However," he said, sliding a thin sheaf of papers across the desk toward her, "I'm authorized to inform you that you've been granted an upgraded clearance. Read through this, ask any questions you'd like, and sign in the designated place."

Mariah hid her surprise and skimmed several paragraphs that were mostly focused on the dire consequences of revealing classified information. She wondered again what she was getting into. She had so many questions to ask Curt—but she suspected he probably wouldn't answer them. *Well, what the hell,* she thought. She scrawled her signature, handed the papers back to Cothran, and opened the envelope he'd given her a minute before. Two plane tickets and passports, both in the name of Anderson. She looked up at Cothran, questioning.

Cothran smiled. "You're newlyweds."

Doctor Vector drew a cup of water from a lab sink and swallowed two Tylenol. He'd come down with a bad cough and a headache, was feeling unaccountably tired, and he had this persistent itching, especially under his armpit. He'd been putting in long hours for months now and it was beginning to wear on him. Worse, he'd somehow allowed ticks to escape from the garage lab, despite all of his painstaking precautions. What had he done wrong?

He forced the second-guessing out of his mind. The past could not be undone. He had to focus on the future. His work would soon be finished and then there would be plenty of time for rest. It was coming down to the wire. Now it was time for another feeding, to fatten up his charges, to prepare them to go into battle as healthy and well fed as possible. A wry, apt expression popped into his head: *An army marches on its stomach.*

And it *was* a war, he reminded himself.

He looked around his new lab, deep inside an abandoned warehouse in South Philly. Roomy enough, but kind of cobbled together compared with his old lab by the farmhouse. Still, he couldn't complain. With the help of those idiot goons, he'd quickly cleared out the old lab and resurrected a new one here. Too quickly, in his opinion. But he'd had to move fast or see the destruction of his research.

He placed the empty water glass in the sink, but as soon as the glass thunked against the sink's steel basin, Doctor Vector felt the itch under his arm yet again and froze. His heart began bucking wildly in his chest. A thin film of sweat broke across his brow. The lab around him dropped away as his mind connected the dots of the past few days. Headache. Coughing. And this itch—this infernal itch. He tore off his lab coat, pulled his T-shirt over his head, and twisted the skin of his armpit closer to his face.

Idiot! he screamed silently at himself. Another mistake, made in haste. In his rush to clear out the garage lab, he'd let down his guard, had failed to rigorously follow the careful protocols he swore by. And now here was a tiny tick, embedded in his skin, swollen with his blood.

How had it happened? he asked himself, knowing already that it didn't really matter. Had he neglected to count every tick during the transfer, including those that were in the process of feeding? Had he failed to securely cap a container? Had he somehow missed a newly hatched larva or just-molted nymph? But he knew it made no difference how old the tick was. At any age it would be a teeming reservoir of Kandahar virus, which was now undoubtedly in his system, coursing through his blood-stream, making its way into his liver, his kidneys, his heart, his brain. The worst symptoms would show up soon. The cough and headache he had now were nothing compared to losing his mind and bleeding out. Did this also mean sure failure of the mission? How much more time did he have? At least a couple of days, he was sure of that. Enough time to finish the job?

He forced himself to concentrate. He willed the cold, rational, calculating scientist's part of his brain to take over. *One thing at a time,* he told himself. First he'd do what he could to treat himself: medication, then tick removal and disposal, antiseptic, full body check. After that, back to work. He opened a medicine cabinet and took out a bottle of ribavirin.

Tony Parnell leaned back from his computer and sighed. The best story of his career and he wished it wasn't happening. A disease that killed most of its victims was now threatening the city of Philadelphia, his home turf, a place that already seemed half-dead with dusk-to-dawn curfews and National Guard troops roaming the streets. But he had a deadline and a word-count limit and he'd already compiled so much information that he didn't know how he could meet either. And now there was the latest shocking news. With the assistance of the *Inquirer*'s managing editor, who had close ties to the FBI, Parnell had been carefully cultivating high-level sources in law enforcement, all "anonymous" of course. Yesterday one of these sources had told him about another apparent Kandahar outbreak, in Omaha, Nebraska.

Parnell opened the bottom drawer of his file cabinet, fished out a road atlas, and did some rough calculations. Omaha was more than a thousand miles from Philadelphia. So a viral disease that supposedly wasn't airborne had suddenly jumped halfway across the continent? Had someone from the Philadelphia area flown out there, unknowingly infected? Was this thing airborne after all and had it somehow been transported across half the continent by the winds? Or had it been deliberately introduced?

A deliberate release into the Midwest would be bad enough. But whoever did it probably wouldn't stop there. And if Kandahar was airborne the consequences could be much worse, especially if it got into the wrong hands. His source had revealed that the intel types were now suspecting that the viral strain had been bioengineered for greater lethality. That suggested a terrorist connection.

And what might terrorists do with an airborne disease? Parnell envisioned scenarios where they'd use a crop-duster airplane or modified car exhaust system to distribute the hot agent, or get it into the air-handling systems of public buildings or mass transit facilities. They could even incorporate it into a small bomb and detonate it in a crowded area. And because the virus was so infectious, a modification that would allow it to be transmitted through the air from the sneezes or coughs of infected persons would mean that the disease would be passed along as rapidly as a flu virus. But this bug was much deadlier than even the most lethal strains of flu.

There was no way he could work all of this into the article, and most of it was purely speculative. But he owed it to the public to at least inform them about this apparent second outbreak in Omaha. He pulled a business card from his wallet and reached for his phone.

Doctor Vector knew that everything he'd done to deal with the tick bite, even administering ribavirin, would ultimately do no good. Advanced symptoms of Kandahar virus were already apparent. He'd effectively been dealt a death sentence. It was just a matter of time.

But time was what he desperately needed. Ten days to be exact. He hoped the ribavirin would delay the advance of the disease long enough to buy him the time. He told himself to be positive, to focus. He mentally reviewed a list of tasks and checked them off in his mind. The first job was to thoroughly clean out the lab, leaving no sign of the work that had taken place there. He'd start with the animals.

He unlocked a door on the far side of the lab and entered the animal room. He wheeled a large cart over to the cages of mice, loaded the cages onto the cart, and pushed the cart out the door, through the main lab, and into the hallway. He entered another room three doors down. An incinerator stood in the far corner.

He walked over, ignited the fire, pulled on a pair of thick gloves, and pulled the first mouse out of a cage, taking care to close the cage door afterward. Holding the mouse in one hand, he opened a small access door on the incinerator door with the other.

There was no time to first euthanize the mice. Not that it mattered to Vector. He held no particular affection for these animals. The ticks, of course, were a different story, even though one had been responsible for his impending death. But that was not the tick's fault. He had only himself to blame. He proceeded to dispose of the remaining rodents with his characteristic attention to detail.

Vector then returned to the main lab and approached the insect growth chamber. He'd need about a thousand gravid ticks for the mission. The ticks would fit into a special small container, one that he'd already designed and fabricated. It looked like a large pillbox and was sitting on a nearby lab table. He scrutinized the labels on the racks inside the growth chamber, removed a few vials, and secured them inside the special box. There were still thousands of ticks left over. He'd have to dispose of them. *His pets*. He pushed the emotion out of his mind. This was no time for sentimentality. Then he had a thought. A backup plan. *A Plan B*.

He retrieved a portable cooler from a storage closet. This was the container that he'd used to transport the ticks from his original lab at the farmhouse. It took him only a few minutes to transfer the ticks from the growth chamber into the cooler and securely seal the cooler lid with duct tape. They should be comfortable enough in their new, temporary home. There was some air inside the cooler, but even so ticks could go a long time without air. He'd fed them earlier in the day. That meal should hold them for a while. They'd live at least as long as he would without another feeding. And by the time he was dead, his Plan B soldiers—he thought of them as his special ops forces—would be deployed to feed to their hearts' content.

Between fits of coughing, Vector carried the cooler to the

warehouse exit and wrestled it into the back of a nondescript, windowless cargo van that was parked in the lot of the warehouse laboratory. After locking the van and placing the key under the right front bumper, he paused for breath, pulled out his cell phone, and sent an encrypted message to the leader of the local sleeper cell that Omar had set up.

He slowly made his way back to the lab. Once he was inside, the coughing began again, at first as a kind of wheeze, then erupting into uncontrollable hacking that left him gasping for breath. He spat blood into a handful of Kleenex, staggered to the bathroom, and flushed the tissues down the toilet. He took a few seconds to catch his breath and then returned to the lab.

He poured some Clorox onto a cleaning cloth and began to wipe down surfaces. He wasn't concerned with preventing the spread of disease. Rather he was trying to do everything possible to disguise the purpose of the laboratory. At this stage there was nothing he could do about the equipment, but if he was thorough about the cleanup, no one would be able to link the lab to the Kandahar virus. At least not at first. He knew the authorities would eventually figure out the purpose of this lab. But by that time it would be too late.

Several hours later, his work was done. Vector wearily straightened his shoulders and looked around. He'd miss this place but it was time to leave. He turned off the lights and left the room. He'd do all he could to get a good night's sleep. He had a long flight in the morning.

Very early the next morning, a three-car passenger train passed under a bridge, approached a sharp curve just south of Elkton, Maryland, and began to slow down. The train held several dozen residents of southeastern Pennsylvania who lived in the mandatory ten-mile-radius evacuation area outside the virus quarantine zone. At 2:00 a.m., less than thirty minutes away, the train would pull into Aberdeen, Maryland. There the passengers would be discreetly transferred to a U.S. Army train that would transport them to their final destination: Dugway Proving Ground in Utah.

The engineer rubbed his eyes and stared at the tracks ahead. This was his first run to Aberdeen since he'd gotten the call from TSA the day before. If it went well, there would be many more runs in the days ahead, most carrying a lot more passengers. This was supposed to be a trial run. They'd told him that there could be protests and that the passengers might even resist, but the boarding had been completed without incident. Probably because of the heavy presence of National Guard troops at the Wilmington station, he thought. But he knew that the residents of the evacuation zone were furious about their forced deportation and they had many sympathizers in the surrounding region, people who feared that the depopulated area might soon include them.

The engineer was startled from his thoughts when his eyes caught on something ahead, beside the tracks: several dark figures barely illuminated by a half-moon periodically hidden by scudding clouds. *Probably homeless people*, he thought. Maybe living under that bridge he'd just passed. Vagrants seemed to have made the tracks their home along the northeast corridor. It was well known throughout his industry that there just weren't the resources to guard the train lines, or even to keep the fences intact.

The engineer kept his eyes closely on the figures. There had been several recent incidents of rocks being thrown at trains in this area. The engine's windows were reinforced and a projectile, even a bullet, probably wouldn't penetrate them. But a large rock could do real damage and would be a major distraction. He slowed the train further, down to thirty miles per hour, and blew a short high-pitched blast on the train whistle. He saw one of the figures, a hefty-looking man, separate himself from the rest of the group, stand right by the tracks, and begin waving his arms.

With a flash of realization, the engineer understood that these people were not vagrants, or a pack of kids up to no good. These people intended to stop the train. They'd probably try to disembark the passengers. *Well, good luck with that*, he thought. No way was he stopping. He accelerated slightly and blew past the waving man by the tracks.

But then, several hundred yards ahead, where the track started to curve, he saw a large, motionless dark shape on a crossroad, pointed toward the track, well back from the rails. *A truck.* As the engineer watched, it began to move, slowly, toward the rails. Were they planning to park the truck on the track, assuming he'd stop the train? Were they idiots? Did they know nothing about momentum, mass times velocity? Even at thirty miles per hour, there was no way he could avoid plowing into the vehicle at this distance. He had only one chance. Speed up and hope to get by it before it reached the tracks. The advantage lay in his favor. He was already moving and the truck had been idling and would take several seconds to get up to speed. He pushed the throttle forward and leaned on the whistle lever. The train accelerated quickly and began hurtling down the tracks. It soon reached a velocity approaching eighty miles per hour.

He made it, clearing the truck by scant feet, moving past it into the darkness, the train's wheels screeching on the steel tracks, the whistle blasting shrilly into the night.

Too late he remembered the curve.

The engineer quickly hit the air brakes, then immediately engaged the emergency brake. The deceleration was almost immediate, and drastic, the train slowing to half its speed in a matter of seconds. But with the sudden slowing and the sharp leftward curve came instability. The train lurched and began to tilt to the right as another law of physics, inertia, kicked in, naturally trying to move the train straight ahead despite the curvature of the track.

Halfway into the curve, the train tumbled off the rails, plowing up a deep furrow of earth as it plunged into an abandoned field littered with refuse. When the train finally stopped, the engine and passenger cars lay on their sides. The sounds of screaming penetrated the night.

CHAPTER TWENTY-ONE

Mariah glanced around the airy, spacious lobby of the Manila Hotel, noting the high ceilings with lazily turning overhead fans and comfortable old rattan furniture. "Kind of old-world," she said to Curt.

"Right. A lot of history," he said. "MacArthur stayed here during the war. A little dated now but the security's good. And it does have a romantic appeal."

Mariah looked at him. Was that a teasing smirk on his face? *Lots of luck, fella*, she said to herself. Then she remembered that they were supposed to be newlyweds.

A young man rose from a chair in the lobby and approached Mariah and Curt as if he'd been expecting them. So this was the guy Cothran had said was going to meet them in Manila? He seemed really young and struck Mariah as nervous and maybe even a little angry. She did like that he had gray-blue eyes, like Curt's, but they seemed out of place with the man's dark hair. She figured the anomaly must be a feature more common than she'd imagined, like birthmarks, just something she'd never really picked up on before. There were a lot of things about other people that she hadn't been noticing, she admitted to herself.

She'd been so focused on her work, so wrapped up in her own little world, a world that was now getting larger.

Curt grinned, extended his hand to the young man, and turned toward Mariah.

"Meet Angus Friedman," he said. "Angus, Mariah Rossi." For a couple of minutes, they made small talk, how their flights went, that sort of thing, as Mariah tried to size up Angus. What she had first thought might be anger now looked more like disappointment. Maybe he was expecting a more modern hotel. It was pretty clear that he already knew Curt. And what about the Cothran connection? Was Angus CIA too? Sure didn't look like it. But then she didn't have any basis for that judgment, except from the movies.

"Angus, we're going to check in and freshen up a bit," Curt was saying. "Want to join us for dinner later? Say seven thirty?"

Mariah could see a struggle on Angus's face between acting professional and showing his disappointment. He definitely seemed to want to say something of meaning to Curt, but instead just replied, "Yes, sir. See you then. Thank you."

Curt seemed oblivious to Angus's strange tone. He went up close to him and asked, "Do you have some information for us?"

Angus nodded. "Our fugitive flew to Jolo yesterday. That's in the province of Sulu."

"I know where it is," said Curt. "Do we know why he's there?"

"Not yet, but he was accompanied by an Abu Sayyaf guerrilla—you know, the local Islamic terrorist group."

Mariah was close enough that she could hear. She now figured that Angus must work for Curt's organization, which she now suspected was a branch of the CIA. What was it again—the Bio Investigative Service? He obviously knew what was going on. Was he going to join them on the search for the fugitive?

"We do have a first name," said Angus. "Omar. That's it. Even that's probably an alias. We've got an agent embedded with Abu Sayyaf. Our guy thinks Omar may be Pakistani. He still hasn't shown up on any databases."

"So what are we doing to catch this Omar?" asked Curt.

"We're booked on a flight to Jolo early tomorrow morning." Angus reached into his pocket, pulled out an envelope, and handed it to Curt. "Here are your tickets. Seven thirty departure."

"I'll arrange for a cab," Curt said. "Let's meet in the lobby at five thirty a.m. We'll plan to make it an early evening tonight."

Later that evening, after a frustrating dinner with Curt and Mariah at a restaurant near the hotel, Angus returned to his hotel room. There was no way he was going to be able to sleep. Why did that woman have to come? Why couldn't he get a single moment alone with Curt, to tell him what he'd failed to tell him back in Honolulu because there hadn't been time? Why couldn't Cothran have just told Curt instead? Why did it have to be up to him? He was feeling so many things—angry, anxious, and even a little jealous that the woman seemed to be Curt's girlfriend. He needed a walk. He knew it could be dangerous to go out at night in this area. But he had to clear his mind before the next day's operation.

He gathered up his wallet and passport and left the room. The waterside walk down Roxas Boulevard was pleasant and had a calming effect. After a while he stopped and sat on a bench overlooking Manila Bay and tried to sort through a jumble of thoughts, some in conflict with others. Foremost in his mind was that, after all these years, he now had a father again. He'd known about Kennedy for months, ever since Cothran had revealed his identity during the agency's background investigation. At first he'd been overcome with emotion.

But now Angus was struggling with the reality of coming face-to-face with his long-lost father.

Of course he was thrilled to finally be reunited with Curt, a man whom he'd instantly liked and admired. But Angus had grown up without a dad, had, over time, adjusted to the loneliness and rootlessness that had come with that, had developed a core of independence and self-sufficiency that he sensed could be threatened by the insertion of a father figure into his life. Especially a father figure as dominant as Curt.

And what about Curt? Angus wasn't at all sure what his reaction would be to the sudden intrusion of a son that he'd probably long assumed he'd never see again. Would he be viewed as a complication in the man's busy, shadowy life, even an encumbrance? If Angus told him the truth, would Kennedy be able to accept it?

And then there was the question of Mariah. It was obvious to Angus that she and Curt had a close relationship, maybe even a romantic one. What would Angus's appearance on the scene do to that relationship? And how would Mariah respond?

Finally, there was the mission. If the three of them were to successfully complete it, they'd need utmost focus on the job at hand. The emergence of complicated family issues could distract them from their all-important task. Maybe he should wait until they'd accomplished the mission before telling Curt the truth. But how could he concentrate effectively with this secret buried within him, crying for release like an animal trapped in a cage?

Finally, Angus made a decision. He'd go back to the hotel and wake up Curt and just tell him. Just get it out. It was the only way he'd be able to think clearly in the morning. And, in the end, he'd have to be thinking clearly if this operation was going to be successful.

As he began to walk back a car passed slowly on his side of the road and eased to a stop just ahead of him. The passenger door swung open and a man stepped out and turned to face Angus. In the man's hand was something dark and heavy-looking. As Angus's mind finally registered that the man was looking at him, the man raised the dark object, and that was the last thing the young man saw.

CHAPTER TWENTY-TWO

Kennedy followed the hotel security guard to the elevator and down the hall to Angus's room. Angus hadn't met them in the lobby at the arranged time, and he hadn't answered his phone.

The room was empty except for an open suitcase lying on the bed, which obviously hadn't been slept in. Kennedy checked the bathroom. The space smelled of aftershave. A damp towel was draped over the tub. Dirty clothes hung on the back of the bathroom door.

Kennedy walked back into the bedroom and quickly searched it. Nothing was amiss and there was no evidence of any struggle. Nothing unusual at all, not even a note. There was no sign of a wallet.

Kennedy thanked the guard and returned to his own room. To maintain the honeymoon ruse, he and Mariah had shared a room, but that was all they'd shared. Even if he'd been tempted— and Kennedy admitted to himself that he definitely would have been tempted under other circumstances—it was obvious that Mariah was keeping him at arm's length. He could hear her in the shower. He grabbed his phone, punched in a number, and Cothran answered, "Pacific Enterprises."

"Batman here," Kennedy said.

"What's up?"

"Our new player seems to have disappeared."

Long pause on the other end. "Did you meet him?"

"Yes, last night," said Kennedy. "But no sign of him this morning."

"I'll contact the team managers and track him down. It shouldn't take us long. I'll call you right back."

"I'll wait here."

Minutes later his phone rang. "We can't reach him either," said Cothran. "Can you proceed on your own?"

"Yes, no problem."

"We'll be in touch. Watch for a text. Safe travels."

Angus groaned and tried to stand on tiptoes to alleviate the aching pain in his shoulders. His arms were suspended over his head and stretched backward, his wrists bound together by a nylon line that hung over a metal pipe beneath the ceiling of a large dingy room that smelled like rotten fish. He was naked from the waist up. His face was caked with blood and one eye was swollen shut. With his good eye, he tried to make out his surroundings, thinking it would be important to note and remember every possible detail. Looked like an old storage building. Overhead door at one end. Concrete floor with dark stains and muddy tracks. Flickering fluorescent lights with half the bulbs burned out. Rows of empty shelving on the far wall. An old army-green forklift with a flat tire.

He thought back to the previous evening. Car pulling over on Roxas Boulevard. Guy getting out, holding an object that looked like a blackjack. Waking up sometime later in a dingy hotel room, couple of guys standing over him asking questions. Contents of his wallet strewn on a table. They'd said they knew he was a software engineer, that he must be rich. They'd wanted him to give them the names and phone numbers of family members who could provide a million-dollar ransom. He'd refused to talk. They'd hit him again and he'd blacked out for the second time. When he'd awakened he'd found himself in this warehouse, with two hooded men standing guard over him. From the sound of their voices Angus knew these weren't the same guys who'd captured him.

He heard a door open. Short, thick guy wearing a black hood with eye slits, carrying something in his right hand.

"Ready to talk yet?" the man asked.

"Fuck you," Angus slurred.

Searing pain across his lower back. What had they hit him with this time? Angus turned his head. He could see that the man was holding a whip. There was something on the end of the tail, looked like a cluster of fishhooks. The man raised his arm again and swung. Angus moaned through gritted teeth.

"We know you're CIA," the man said patiently, in an accent that Angus couldn't place. "Just tell us what you're doing here and we'll let you go."

Angus knew that even if he talked, they'd probably kill him. How did they know who he was? Had they picked up on him at the airport? Did they know about Curt and Mariah? Doubtful. They'd have put two and two together by now if they knew he was working with the two Americans. The questions weren't leading in that direction.

More likely something in his wallet had given him away. *Think.* Was there anything incriminating in the wallet? Credit cards, driver's license, even his passport were all under the name Andrew Hyatt. Business cards identified him as a representative of a U.S. software company. The wallet held other business cards with names of local computer companies. Then Angus remembered. On a small piece of folded paper, tucked deep inside his wallet, was a special phone number that Cothran had given him. He'd ignored Cothran's warning to not write it down, to just memorize it. He was afraid he'd forget the number and figured that the number by itself, without an association, wouldn't be incriminating. Stupid rookie mistake. He now realized that any professional worth his salt would track down the number, figure out that it wasn't just an innocuous U.S. embassy line. And it seemed that the guys who'd originally captured him for ransom had figured it out and traded him to these new guys for a nice profit.

Fine, they suspected he was a spy. But they wouldn't get any information from him.

Angus watched as the hooded man walked to a table in the corner of the room. The man picked something up and came back toward him. Angus squinted to make it out. As soon as he realized the object was a syringe, fear swept over him. He had little hope now that he'd be able to hold anything back. He was sure he'd even tell them the one secret he'd been trying to let Curt in on.

Later that morning, Mariah sat rigidly in a South East Asian Airlines thirty-passenger turboprop commuter plane and clenched her teeth as they flew through low clouds toward Jolo airport in the province of Sulu. She had a window seat but wished she didn't. The pilot had announced that the flight could be rough. The outer fringes of a fast-moving typhoon were brushing the area. Mariah could feel wind buffeting the plane.

She looked over to Curt. He sat stiffly, his jaw clenched, staring straight ahead. *Doubt he has a fear of flying,* Mariah thought. Was he thinking about Angus? Curt had told her that instead of joining them on the flight, Angus would meet them later in Jolo, but he hadn't explained the change in plans.

The plane gave a sharp jolt. Mariah cinched her seat belt tighter and gripped the arms of her seat. Curt had turned toward her, an amused expression on his face.

"So what happened to the dollhouse you made for Lucy?" she asked, not realizing until later, when she thought back on the moment, that she'd asked the question defensively. She'd felt nervous because of the plane, and because of Curt seeing her nervous, and she'd brought up the sensitive topic of his sister as a way of putting him back on his heels.

Curt looked down. "I guess my parents gave it away," he said.

"But you kept making them?"

"No, I switched to more masculine things. Toy boats, wooden guns, that sort of thing. And a tree house. My father helped me with that one. It wasn't until I got out of graduate school that I started building dollhouses again. Still do it. Helps me stay connected to Lucy."

"What do you do with the dollhouses now?"

"Give them away. I go up to Penn Hospital quite a bit to visit the kids in the cancer ward. Every time I finish a dollhouse, I take it with me and leave it for one of the little girls."

Mariah started to respond, then caught herself. She wanted to compliment him, but didn't know how he'd take it. She doubted that he'd ever talked with anyone about this aspect of his life, and she was glad he was opening up to her, but she didn't want to embarrass him by probing too much. So she finally said, in a tone that she hoped conveyed admiration at his generosity, "So that's why you wanted to go to medical school?"

Curt raised his head and turned toward her. "Basically, yes. The navy gave me a really good opportunity. But after a few years of treating patients—soldiers and sailors with everything from STDs to PTSD, I pretty much burned out. And got fed up with bureaucracy. But I got interested in animal diseases because so many of them can be transmitted to humans. Left active duty and went back to school, this time on my own dime except for what the GI Bill covered. Earned a PhD in microbiology." He chuckled. "So look what happens. I end up working for the federal government. Back to the bureaucracy."

The plane banked low and approached the runway with wobbling wings, touched down, bounced a bit, and then taxied to the end of the runway as the passengers broke into a smattering of applause.

As she exited the aircraft with her duffel bag, Mariah felt a little ridiculous. She was wearing a straw hat, a floral sundress, and sandals. Curt was decked out in a Hawaiian shirt, shorts, and wraparound sunglasses. They were trying their best to look like a young couple on a diving holiday. They'd booked a flight for the following day to Puerto Princesa in the Palawan Islands and had reserved a four-day dive package through Evergreen Dive Adventures—a flight and a vacation they had no intention of taking, Mariah thought ruefully to herself. They'd even chatted about their diving plans while they'd waited in the terminal for the flight to Jolo, and had gotten into an animated conversation with another passenger about the province of Palawan. Mariah wished that the dive resort was their real destination.

Angus rubbed his raw wrists and rotated his aching shoulders. He was alone in the storage shed for the first time since they'd brought him here. And for the first time he wasn't half hanging by his arms from an overhead beam, steeling himself against the next physical assault, trying to summon up every ounce of his resistance to keep from spilling his guts.

But, in the end, he'd talked.

He thought back to his training, to a stooped, gray-haired man with a road map's worth of lines on his face and deep-set eyes that resembled tarnished copper coins on old parchment.

Everyone has a breaking point, the veteran had told him. The object was to hold out as long as you could and reveal as little as possible.

Angus had held out as long as he could. For more than a day he'd withstood the beatings and the sleep deprivation. Then they'd brought out the syringe. He'd figured it contained some kind of truth serum. Angus had learned enough about these psychoactive drugs to know that their efficacy was questionable. But he also knew that recent advances in neurobiology increased the likelihood that more effective pharmaceuticals were under development—if they weren't already out there. If they injected him, he might not have any control over what he said. He couldn't take that chance.

So he'd given his captors some information, enough to lead them to believe he was telling the truth. He admitted that he was with the agency, revealed Curt and Mariah's names, and confirmed that he was working with them. But he'd told them it was about an international drug cartel and that his colleagues had already left for Thailand, in pursuit of the ringleader. He figured the story would at least buy him some time, maybe allow him to escape somehow and warn his colleagues.

But they'd been back within hours. They'd called him a liar and claimed they had ready access to a worldwide information network, that Curt and Mariah had never left the Philippines, and that they now had the two Americans in custody. If he didn't talk, they said, didn't tell them everything, they would kill his colleagues. Angus had no way of knowing if they were bluffing about holding Curt and Mariah, but he had no reason to doubt it and every reason to believe that they would carry out their threat. And that was something he would do everything in his power to prevent. He could never live with himself if his actions led to his father's death.

But Angus also figured that even if he talked, these thugs

would probably kill Curt and Mariah. He decided to take the chance that they were bluffing about the capture. He refused to talk more.

So they'd injected him.

Hours later, when he'd emerged from a fog, his captors told him what he'd disclosed. His CIA experience, his history with Cothran, Curt, and Mariah, their reasons for being in the Philippines, and the one thing that he'd hoped against hope that he'd never reveal: that Curt was his father. And now he had to live with what he'd done.

Very early the next morning, Mariah and Curt exited their hotel into a driving rain, loaded their bags into the back of a dark green Land Cruiser, and climbed in, Curt in the front and Mariah in the back. The driver introduced himself as Lieutenant Ray Alvarez, from the U.S. Navy, as he slowly pulled away from the curb and flicked the wipers up to a high speed. Mariah shivered in the Cruiser's AC.

They soon left the city behind. Mariah strained to see where they were going, but all that was visible was what the headlights illuminated: the road immediately ahead and a fringe of dark bushes along the sides. At first Alvarez and Curt talked to each other in a kind of shorthand that made Mariah wonder if this was another guy Curt already knew, but soon she decided that this was simply the way military people communicated. She gathered that Alvarez and his team comprised a United States–Philippines task force that worked in counterterrorism throughout the region. "Essentially," she heard him to say to Curt, "we focus on Abu Sayyaf."

"We have recent intel," Alvarez said, "that Omar was sighted with an Abu Sayyaf element near Mount Dajo. That's about five miles from here, in the middle of the national park. Plan is to capture the guy. He could be carrying this virus, but we're not even sure what to be looking for, let alone how to handle it safely. He might even threaten to release it somehow. That's where you come in."

"Expecting any action?" asked Curt.

"Most likely not. We'll have the element of surprise. But you never know for sure. We do know about your own special ops background, Dr. Kennedy, but it's probably best that your partner remain behind. She'll be safe at our base camp."

"No way," Mariah said quickly, surprising even herself. "Curt and I are a team. Besides, you said you aren't expecting opposition." *Actually, I'm pissed that you'd even consider leaving me out of this*, she thought to herself. She was *part* of this mission, and she was damned if she'd be left out of this important phase of it. "We stay together," Curt said. Mariah cheered inwardly.

"Fine," said Alvarez. "Your call."

The paved road gave way to a dirt track. The early-morning blackness grew darker. Branches began to brush against the side of the Land Cruiser. Mariah imagined that the jungle was closing in all around them. She saw dark shadows loom up and then disappear in the headlights. Some of the shadows looked animate. She could no longer distinguish between the road and the dense surrounding rain forest.

When the forest finally receded, Mariah realized that they'd arrived at a clearing. The rain was still steady. She and Curt donned camouflage-colored ponchos, climbed out of the Land Cruiser, and followed Alvarez around to the back.

Mariah watched as Alvarez reached into the back of the vehicle and pulled out a hip holster attached to a web belt. He opened the holster, took out a pistol with a black rubber grip, released the magazine, and handed the empty gun to Curt, grip first. "I assume you've used a Beretta," he said.

Curt nodded and gave the gun a thorough visual inspection,

then took the loose magazine from Alvarez and removed all the rounds. Inserting the empty magazine into the pistol, he carried out a complete function check with the gun pointed toward the sky. He replaced the cartridges in the magazine, reinserted the magazine, and secured the safety. He reached for the web belt, secured it around his waist, and holstered the gun. He saw Mariah watching him, an eyebrow arched.

"I was a soldier," he said. "Remember?"

By now, Mariah could see that at least a hundred men had assembled in the clearing and lined up in military formations. She heard unit leaders giving instructions to their troops in English and in an unfamiliar language that she assumed was Tagalog. The troops then started to move out, on foot. She and Curt followed.

"Mariah," Curt said quietly as they started down the road. "Stay right behind me, okay? Don't let me out of your sight."

Mariah nodded and followed behind him silently. She focused on his back and plodded along, trying to make as little noise as possible. She marveled at how quietly a hundred men could move through the night. Her eyes began to adjust to the darkness and she found that, even in the rain and gloom, she could see the soldiers closest to her and Curt.

After a while—Mariah was finding it hard to judge time and she didn't want to illuminate her watch face—they left the road and headed deeper into the jungle. The dense vegetation blocked much of the rain. They appeared to be following a narrow trail. The ground was wet, muddy, and crisscrossed with fallen tree trunks and limbs. Mariah slipped several times. The air was so thick with humidity that she found it hard to breathe. Cicadas buzzed incessantly from the dripping trees. Smaller insects, mostly mosquitoes by the sound of them, jabbed at her face and tried to crawl into her mouth, nose, and eyes. They seemed oblivious to the DEET she had slathered on earlier in the Land Cruiser. She was certain that many of them carried the pathogens for malaria, dengue, perhaps even yellow fever, and who knew what else.

The air smelled of rotting vegetation. She heard guttural squawks, low cooing noises, and loud, crowlike *kra*s. She figured birds would be sleeping. It couldn't be later than 4 a.m. Could some of the noises be monkeys? She'd read that long-tailed macaques were abundant in this part of the Philippines. Were there any dangerous predators in the Philippines jungle? She thought about venomous snakes and then shook her head to try to make the thought disappear.

She was breathing hard with exertion. The rain had finally let up, but the heavy air somehow seemed no less wet.

Curt stopped without warning and Mariah almost ran into him. He turned and held a finger up to his lips. Mariah hardly dared to breathe. She imagined that the thumping of her heart was echoing off the dense jungle foliage.

She heard a loud cracking noise that sounded too sharp and clipped to be a breaking branch. Then the sound of a string of exploding firecrackers. Curt pushed her roughly to the ground, dove down beside her, and whispered hoarsely, "Ambush! Stay low! Don't move!" She remained motionless, listening to snapping noises whipping above her and softer, chunking noises as the bullets hit something solid.

Something fell with a thud on the ground near her. She heard a low moan. A soldier? *He must have been hit!* thought Mariah. She resisted an overwhelming urge to rise up and run, instead flattening herself as low as possible to the ground, willing herself to slow her wildly beating heart and to wall out the snapping noises overhead. She pressed her moist hands against the ground to keep them from trembling, and swallowed down the acid bile rising in her throat. She heard the moaning again. *I've got to help the guy*, she thought.

Suppressing her fear, she quietly crawled toward the sound. In the pitch-black she relied on her ears to guide her. She bumped against something, reached out, and touched a man's head. Her hand felt wet and sticky. She heard a man trying to speak. Was he saying "please"? Then he was silent. She found the man's wrist, felt for a pulse, then let go.

She heard more gunshots, closer, and forced herself to remain still. She hoped that it was return fire from the task force and not the insurgents. Then the sounds began to recede. A sign that the ambushers were on the run? Trying to help the wounded soldier had momentarily given her something else to focus on, but now the fear came flooding back. *God, let this be over soon*, she said to herself. *Or at least let it get light again.*

Mariah lay as motionless as possible for a long time. She assumed Curt was nearby but didn't dare call out to him. It grew quiet. Even the jungle noises had stopped. As she waited in the silence, dark shapes in front of her began to look animate. She couldn't stand it. She had to know what was out there. She reached into a pocket, pulled out a small flashlight, and switched it on. She could see that she was in a clearing surrounded by dense jungle foliage. She heard the sound of approaching voices. She switched off the light and stayed still, hoping she couldn't be seen. She could hear men conversing in an unfamiliar language. The voices grew closer.

Then she felt rough hands on her shoulders.

CHAPTER TWENTY-THREE

SEPTEMBER 4 (SEPTEMBER 5, PHILIPPINES TIME)
JOLO, PHILIPPINES

Mariah struggled against a rope that tightly bound her wrists. Her back was to a large tree, her arms tied together on the opposite side of the trunk. A man she didn't recognize stood in front of her, his hand raised to eye level, a knife gripped in his fingers, its curved blade streaked with rust. Two other men stood nearby, rifles aimed at her.

The man with the knife slipped the blade under the top button of Mariah's long-sleeved shirt and gave a little tug, severing the button. One by one he repeated the process until her shirt was open at the chest. He then worked the blade under the front of her bra, sliced it, and pulled the severed halves away with a gentleness that made Mariah feel she was about to vomit.

As the man stepped back, appraising her, Mariah struggled to restrain her rage, to control an urge to spit in the man's face and scream at him. But she knew that would be a mistake, that it would only provoke him more. So she focused on details of what she was seeing, letting her scientific training kick in. *Middle-aged*, she noted. *Bearded face, matted hair, uneven teeth stained reddish.* Probably from betel nut, a kind of seed, she'd read, that people chewed in this part of the world. The man wore flip-flops, baggy trousers, and a ragged T-shirt with a Chicago Bears logo. He was licking his lips now, lifting his hands and leaning toward her.

Okay, she thought to herself, *but I'm not going down without a fight*. Her arms were still tied behind her, but he hadn't gagged her. She'd bite him, tear a piece off his face if she had to. She tensed herself as his face closed on hers, his tongue still flicking across his lips.

A volley of shots rang out. Mariah instinctively squeezed her eyes shut but then forced them back open to see the man pitch backward, fall to the ground, twitch, and lie still. Mariah heard more gunfire and saw the other two men who'd been standing silently off to the side go down. One lay motionless and the other clutched his bleeding right shin and moaned.

She heard a familiar voice behind her.

"It's okay, Mariah," said Curt, approaching her and averting his eyes at the same time. "I'm here. Are you okay?"

Mariah simultaneously felt relief and something else. Embarrassment. And *shame*, she told herself, knowing immediately how illogical that feeling was. "I'm fine," she said. "Just get me untied."

Now that he'd made the decision, Tony Parnell felt a sense of relief. His source had reported that the Omaha scare was a false alarm even though the city's residents had panicked. The suspected Kandahar outbreak had turned out to be some kind of pneumonic plague. Nasty bug in its own right, even caused hemorrhaging, and the single Nebraska infection had apparently been passed along by a dog to its owner. But it was nothing like Kandahar and no further cases had cropped up.

Still, Parnell was sure there'd be plenty of other Kandahar reports in the days ahead. The country was terrified and even a minor, innocuous bug could be perceived as a suspected case.

Diagnostic labs would be working day and night. Local authorities would be imposing their own quarantine zones. Common cold and flu victims would be presumed Kandahar cases and would be isolated from the rest of society.

Fearing exposure to the deadly virus, citizens were trying to flee the country, but other nations were refusing to land U.S. flights, and Canada and Mexico had closed their borders. *The feds need to take charge*, Parnell thought. The social order was breaking down. Soon it would be every man for himself.

Which is what led Parnell to make his own decision. He would immediately move his family out of Philadelphia. His wife's sister had a place in rural Pennsylvania, up near the New York border. Plenty of room, few neighbors. His wife and young son would be safe there. At least for the time being.

That afternoon, back at the soldiers' camp, Mariah wanted nothing more than to take a long nap and wake up with no memory of what she'd just been through. She shuddered as her mind continued to flash with images of filthy, matted hair, rusty knifepoints, stained teeth, and the calm, leering approach of that human animal. She had no doubt about what those guys intended to do to her. Thank God Curt had arrived when he had. But now he seemed to be keeping his distance.

Despite her exhaustion, she forced herself to keep moving, offering to help with the other men from Alvarez's team who'd been wounded in the ambush. She didn't mention to anyone that her training was in veterinary medicine, no one asked, and she simply moved from soldier to soldier, cleaning and stitching up the wounds that appeared in front of her. Caring for the others helped take her mind off what she'd been through, but she knew the respite was only temporary. When she'd done what she could for the last of the men who'd been waiting in the camp's makeshift infirmary, she glanced at her watch assuming it would be late in the afternoon, and was shocked to see it was just after 1:00 p.m. She felt as though she hadn't slept for a week. She stood there, looking out at the surrounding rain forest, trying to decide whether to offer more help or simply succumb to her fatigue and curl up on a cot somewhere, to sleep a long dreamless sleep.

Then Curt arrived. From the puzzled look on his face, Mariah knew he'd probably seen her staring off into space. He asked how she was doing and then told her that the man they'd shot and captured had revealed the location of the guerrilla camp and that he and a team of soldiers were heading there now. Mariah noticed that Curt was wearing a new ball cap with the task force logo emblazoned on it. *They've probably made him an honorary member*, she thought to herself. *They haven't offered that to me.*

Mariah tried to push the cynicism and exhaustion out of her mind. The thought of being alone, of not having anything to do while Curt was gone, terrified her. And so, as Curt turned to leave the tent, she said, abruptly, "I'll come, too."

Angus figured it had been about twelve hours since he'd coughed up the information. So far only one person had come back into the building, just long enough to leave him a bottle of water and a cup of cold rice. They'd left him untied. At first he didn't understand why, but when he'd tested the only apparent way out of the windowless storage shed, a heavy metal door that was obviously padlocked on the outside, he grudgingly accepted that he was trapped.

Or was he?

Now Angus began a methodical search of the building, not sure what he was looking for, just *something*, anything, that could help him escape. The shed was ruggedly built, smooth concrete walls and floor, looked like it might have been constructed back in the 1950s. The ceilings were high, a couple of vents up near the roof line, but no ladders, no way to scale the walls even if he could pry out the vents, which at any rate seemed too small for him to fit through. Tools? One old screwdriver and a small wrench on a low shelf. He pocketed both of these. A short section of two-by-four leaning against a wall. Maybe he could bang it against the door, alert people outside. But would he alert the wrong people, his captors, who he was pretty sure wouldn't be too far away?

He stood in the center of the shed and began a slow, 360-degree turn, taking in every detail, concentrating, thinking.

The forklift.

It looked like it hadn't run for decades, but that part didn't bother Angus much. He had some mechanical skills and knew quite a bit about cars. Except this wasn't a car, wasn't remotely like anything he'd ever driven before. Still it would have an engine, a clutch, accelerator, brakes. How hard could it be?

He walked over and inspected it. All the pieces seemed to be there, even a key in the ignition. It had a flat tire, but that was no big deal. He wouldn't be driving it far. He hoisted himself up into the worn seat and turned the key.

No sound, not even a clicking noise.

Dead battery. Angus hopped down, checked the cables. They weren't connected. Made sense. They'd have uncoupled them so that the charge wouldn't draw down as fast in storage. He scraped some corrosion off the terminals with a piece of scrap wood, hooked up and tightened the cables with the wrench in his pocket, and tried the starter again.

The engine turned over, coughed, wouldn't fire. *Check the gas.* Sure enough, empty. He sniffed the tank. Diesel. There had to be some gas, somewhere.

He found a rusting petrol can tucked behind the forklift seat, uncapped and smelled it, and poured a couple of gallons into the tank. On the third try, the motor sputtered, backfired, and caught. Loud, badly out-of-tune engine sounds reverberated off the walls. If his captors were anywhere near, they'd come running. And if they weren't nearby they'd surely have lookouts watching the building. He'd have to move quickly. He revved the engine and pointed the forklift toward the front door.

The machine didn't go very fast and Angus was scared guards would discover him before he reached the wall. But in what felt like hours, but was only a few seconds, the forklift reached the loading dock door and tore it off its hinges. Because of how slowly the lift was moving, Angus was able to jump off before the machine propelled off the dock to the pavement below.

The loud crash finally brought the guards.

As Angus struggled to his feet after his leap off the forklift, he saw two men moving toward him at a dead run. *"Itigil kung nasaan ka!* Stop where you are!"* shouted the first man in Tagalog.

Angus quickly dropped back to the ground and rolled toward the forklift just as he heard the loud retort of a gunshot. The forklift now screened him from the men. That would give him an advantage. Even though they would know he wasn't armed, they'd have to approach cautiously. Most likely they'd split up and come around the lift from opposite sides. He had maybe thirty seconds to consider his options. The most sensible course of action was to simply surrender. That should assure his survival, at least for the time being. But they'd lock him up again, even more securely than before. And he'd have no way of saving Curt and Mariah.

He decided to fight.

He remembered the screwdriver in his pocket. A weapon, after all. His agency training had taught him how to kill with flimsier objects than a screwdriver, especially if he had the element of surprise. But two armed men at the same time? Then he saw the petrol can lying on the ground next to the forklift.

He reached for the can, unscrewed the top, and sprang to his feet. In less than a second he took in the scene. Guard one rounding the forklift on the left, perhaps ten feet away, arm extended, gripping a pistol. Guard two on the other side, slightly farther away, apparently unarmed. Without hesitating Angus propelled himself toward the first man and hurled the open gas can toward the man's head. Even as he registered the quick sequence of events that followed—the can hitting the man square in the face, diesel fuel splashing into his eyes, a scream, a gunshot that apparently went wild—Angus was already tackling the man, locking his left arm around the man's neck, retrieving the screwdriver with his right hand, driving it into the man's right eye, feeling the man go limp. Angus grabbed the man's gun and turned just as the second man leaped at him, clutching a knife.

Angus fired, fired again, and quickly rolled out of the way. The second man fell and lay still, blood beginning to ooze from his open mouth. Angus shakily stood up, pocketed the gun and the knife, and surveyed his surroundings. He appeared to be in an alley lined with low buildings that looked like more warehouses. He heard the sounds of traffic at the far end of the alley, where he figured a main road must cross. There were no nearer noises, but the gunshot would have carried some distance. It was time to get out of there. Before leaving, he searched the pockets of the two dead men, found some cash, and pocketed it.

Forcing himself to walk at a normal, unhurried pace, to avoid attention, he moved down the alley to the main road, flagged down a jeepney, and climbed aboard. First stop: U.S. embassy.

As they followed the soldiers along the narrow jungle path to the guerrilla camp, Curt could feel Mariah distancing herself from him, and he thought he knew why. He'd found her half-naked, tied to a tree, on the verge of being raped. She had to be a bundle of raw nerves, of conflicting emotions—lingering terror, gratitude that he'd rescued her, shame to have been found so helpless, so vulnerable, so exposed. It would take time for her to recover psychologically, and Curt resolved to be as gentle and supportive as possible.

He also assumed that Mariah was reacting to the violent gun battle and, especially, to seeing him shoot and kill two men right in front of her. Sooner or later, he figured she'd ask the question, the one about the first person he'd ever killed. Mariah had a way of probing into him. And if he answered, there'd be more questions, questions he could never answer, not even to her.

As they traipsed through the jungle he thought back to the first time he'd taken the life of another human being. Mogadishu, Somalia, late 1992. His first mission as an Army Ranger. The United States was supplying food to the starving, war-torn city. He was in command of a platoon whose task was to protect the airlift from blocking efforts by warlords and gangs. On a sun-seared October day he was accompanying a rifle squad on a patrol, and without warning a small, thin Somali wearing a dark T-shirt and ball cap emerged from a doorway, his rifle raised and pointed at the lead member of the squad. Curt fired off a quick burst and dropped the Somali before the ambusher could get off a shot. He warily approached the body, feeling no emotion at first, not even satisfaction, just a dull sense of having performed as expected. Then he saw what he'd done.

His first kill was just a kid. Curt knew it was hard to tell age in this part of the world. Most people looked older than they were. Even teenagers might have passed for late twenties. But the boy who lay in a crumpled heap at Curt's feet, arms flung out to the sides as if in supplication, could not have been more than thirteen. Curt had aimed at his victim's chest—this was the first time he'd fired his weapon at another person and he couldn't bring himself to go for a head shot—so the boy's face was unmarred and strangely peaceful. His eyes were open and his mouth had formed a small circle as if his last word was "Oh."

The other Rangers had searched and secured the area and then gathered around Curt. No one had spoken at first. Curt hadn't been anticipating anything like congratulations, or even an acknowledgment of what he'd done. After all, it was expected—and he was an officer. But the other men would have checked the body, would have seen that the KIA was just a boy. Finally, the squad leader, a corporal a couple of years older than Curt, had turned to him with a look that was both sympathetic and apprehensive and asked if the squad should move out.

Curt had nodded assent and told the corporal that he first needed to take a leak. He'd ducked behind a building, bent over, and puked. By the time he'd rejoined the squad a minute later, he'd pushed the incident out of his mind. And there it had stayed, buried, except sometimes in the vulnerable, early predawn hours.

"Everyone hold up." Alvarez had stopped in the trail and was pointing ahead. Grateful for the interruption to his thoughts, Curt scrutinized the dense foliage and made out a large thatch-roofed hut that nearly blended into the jungle. The building looked deserted but smoke still curled from dying cook fires, giving off the smell of burned rice.

Alvarez motioned for silence. He sent two soldiers to scout it out.

The soldiers reported that the building seemed to be abandoned. Alvarez signaled to Mariah and Curt to follow him.

Doctor Vector passed through customs and immigration at the Ninoy Aquino International Airport in Manila, and walked slowly through a mass of noisy people greeting arriving passengers, doing his best to suppress a hacking cough that had grown much worse on the flight from the States. He carried a small bag with a couple of changes of clothing and a toiletry kit, and an oversized briefcase with a panel separating an upper section with a foam pad and some innocuous paperwork from a lower level that contained disguised, sophisticated weapons that would never set off any metal detectors or arouse the suspicions of inspectors.

Vector had swallowed two more ribavirin pills in the plane's restroom before the aircraft had begun its pre-arrival descent. He had enough of the antiviral pills to last another week, just enough time to complete the mission. He knew, because he'd waited too long to start the course of ribavirin, not knowing until it was too late that he'd been exposed to Kandahar, that the medication could do little more than delay the inevitable. But that would be enough. All he needed was to buy some time. To summon all that remained of his fast-dwindling reserves of energy. And to do all he could to hide his symptoms from others.

But disguising his illness was becoming more and more difficult. The coughing was bad enough. Now he was frequently spitting up blood and his eyes were bloodshot. A rash had broken out on his upper body. He was so weak that he had to stop frequently to catch his breath.

He joined the taxi line outside the airport, and willed himself to be patient as he waited his turn. When he finally reached the head of the line and approached the waiting cab, a well-dressed European-looking man dashed in front of him and began to open the cab door. Vector screamed at him and roughly pushed him aside. The man stumbled, caught his balance, and swiveled toward Vector, his fist raised. A nearby Filipino policeman rushed over and positioned himself between the two men.

Now I've done it, thought Vector. Uncontrolled anger and

aggressiveness could be telltale symptoms of Kandahar. He should have prepared himself for such a reaction, done all he could to suppress it. He forced himself to be polite to the cop.

After admonishing both of them, the policeman affirmed that the cab was Vector's and that the other man should join the end of the line. Vector breathed a sigh of relief, entered the taxi, and gave an address to the driver.

When they entered the hut, Mariah saw that the interior was dry and comfortable, with walls and a floor of tightly spaced bamboo splits. A large, dark hardwood table with a dozen chairs occupied the center of the main room. There was a two-way radio and other electronics equipment in the corner. She watched as Alvarez pried the lids off several wooden boxes.

"Ammunition, grenades, claymores," he announced. He turned to Mariah. "Let's have a look around. Keep your eyes open for anything of possible interest."

Mariah wasn't sure what to look for. She didn't see any documents and she doubted the insurgents would have left any incriminating information behind. She stood by the doorway and scanned the room, looking for anything that seemed the slightest bit unusual.

She immediately spotted something out of place—a reed mat with brightly colored geometric designs lying on the floor near the communications equipment. She couldn't imagine the Abu Sayyaf guerrillas being concerned with aesthetics in their jungle hideout, and the mat didn't appear to be in the right position for a prayer rug. She walked over to it and slid it to one side with her foot.

The bamboo flooring beneath had been cut in a large square. She called to Alvarez and Curt.

"Good eyes," said Alvarez, taking in what she'd found. He

pulled a long, straight-edge knife from a leather sheath hanging from his waist. He slipped the tip of the blade under a cut section of the bamboo and pried upward until he could fit his fingers under the flooring. As he began to lift, metal subflooring came into view.

"Better stop there, Lieutenant," said Curt. "Who knows what's under that thing. Might want to move your men back. Mariah, you too." After the soldiers and Mariah had moved outside the hut, Alvarez carefully removed the bamboo section, exposing a hinged, square steel plate secured by two heavy-duty screws. He backed off the screws and swung the plate up, revealing a set of stairs descending from the opening. He turned to Curt, with a questioning look on his face.

Curt shook his head and joined Mariah outside the hut. He told her what they'd discovered under the flooring and asked her to help him search the surroundings. They soon found a large vent pipe, partially obscured by vegetation. "Looks like we're dealing with an underground lab," said Curt. He walked back to the hut, followed by Mariah.

Curt opened the duffel bag they'd brought from the States and he and Mariah rigged up a makeshift containment chamber by erecting a polyethylene enclosure directly above the steel plate. They entered the enclosure and sealed it tightly to the floor with duct tape.

Within the cramped enclosure they put on portable biohazard suits packed in the bag. Each suit was equipped with a full hood and battery-operated respirator, which was basically a fan that pulled air through a HEPA filter into the hood, assuring that the air was purified for breathing. Fully charged, the batteries should last at least four hours, but Curt knew that it had been several days since they were last charged and that the tropical heat and even moderate exertion could reduce their run time. They'd have to work quickly.

He retrieved a small sack from the duffel bag. The sack contained a set of tools, more polyethylene sheeting, a package of swabs, test tubes, ziplock bags, and two sets of disposable surgical scrubs. If they became exposed to any pathogens down below, they'd have to leave their biohazard suits behind, decontaminate as well as possible, and change into the scrubs.

He directed his flashlight into the opening. The steps led down to a large metal door. Curt began to descend the steps, aiming his flashlight ahead, followed closely by Mariah, who closed the hatch behind them.

Not until he arrived at the entrance of the U.S. embassy in Manila did Angus begin to breathe more easily. The cab ride from the warehouse area had taken nearly thirty minutes in heavy traffic and narrow, congested streets, a half hour that had seemed more like half a day. Angus had carefully watched the surroundings the whole trip, frequently turning to look behind him, but hadn't seen anything that looked even remotely threatening. Still, his stomach had been in knots the whole trip.

One more immediate challenge remained: to convince the Marine guard at the embassy gate to let him through, or at least to call inside, even though he had no passport, no identification whatsoever. Angus had one thing in his favor. He remembered the phone number that Cothran had given him back in Honolulu, and chided himself. He should have had more confidence in his memory from the beginning. Then he might have avoided all this.

Mariah followed Curt down the stairs below the floor of the hut and waited as Curt cracked open the metal door at the bottom, revealing thick rubber gasketing around the edges of the entrance. They stood back and listened. After several seconds of silence, Curt opened the door completely and shined the light inside. He motioned to Mariah to follow him. They moved together along the wall of a long corridor and soon came to another closed steel door. Curt tugged it open and flipped on a light switch just inside.

Mariah's breath caught. She was looking at a state-of-the-art biological laboratory. Here, beneath a ramshackle hut in the heart of a jungle, were stainless-steel lab benches, shelving with glassware and supplies, sinks, fume hoods, and storage cabinets with hazardous chemical labels.

She and Curt began to explore. Two large doors on one side of the room opened into a walk-in freezer and cold room. Another door led into an equipment room. Mariah was astonished at the collection of high-end scientific instruments: a flow cytometer/sorter; a high-pressure liquid chromatograph with mass spectrometer; a PCR thermocycler; a fluorometer and spectrophotometer; and image analysis/stereology inverted microscopes and a confocal microscope. A desktop computer, monitor, and printer sat on a table along one wall. A locked steel cabinet stood next to the table. Curt pried the cabinet door open with a screwdriver and revealed a portable safe with a combination lock. He removed the safe and told Mariah they'd take it with them and find a way to open it when they were back at base camp.

They found more doors leading out of the main lab. One opened into a microscopy space and another into a tissue-culture and histological preparation room. Inside one heavy steel door they discovered two generators, a large air-conditioning unit, and air-handling equipment. They opened yet another door at the far end of the main lab. Inside was a changing room with lockers. Just beyond they could see showers. *This place gives the Barn a run for its money*, Mariah thought. Curt removed the plastic bags containing the disposable surgical scrubs and placed them in an empty locker. On the other side of the showers they found another room with biohazard suits suspended from hangers along the wall. Mariah could see a door just beyond and assumed it was the entrance to a MCL. Was it hot inside, teeming with dangerous pathogens?

She looked at Curt but couldn't make out the expression on his face. Her breathing had shallowed out into short gasps, and she willed herself to calm down. She watched Curt walk over to the far door and pull hard on its lever to overcome the negative air pressure sucking the door in the other direction. She followed, shutting the door tightly behind her.

The first thing Mariah noticed in the lab was a complex apparatus consisting of a plastic cylinder and tubing inside a stainless-steel frame. The apparatus sat on a table. She leaned closer to read a label—*FiberCell Systems, Inc.*

"Do—" She'd forgotten how loudly she had to speak to be heard through the mask of her biohazard suit. She started again, louder: "Do you know what this thing is?"

"Looks like a bioreactor," Curt said. "They manufacture vaccines—or high-density concentrations of viruses. I've seen one at Fort Detrick, but never would have expected something this elaborate out here in the jungle."

Mariah leaned closer. "The cylinder is half-full," she said. "Some kind of liquid." She retrieved swabs from her bag, wiped the apparatus in several places, and sealed the swabs inside test tubes.

As she finished her task she saw Curt investigating a biosafety cabinet in a corner of the room.

There was a machine of some kind inside the cabinet. She didn't recognize it but thought it looked a little like a small grinding mill. She saw Curt bring his hand up to his face mask. Was he double-checking the seal?

Curt carefully approached the cabinet and took several swab samples from the surface of the machine and surrounding area.

There was one more door inside the MCL that they hadn't yet gone through. Curt opened the door and Mariah followed him inside. She could hear a loud roaring that sounded like the air-handling units back at the Barn. She also heard piercing cries similar to those she'd heard in the jungle early this morning. Then, even with the biosafety suit on, she was overcome by the powerful odor of ammonia and animal feces.

The room was dark. Curt flicked on a flashlight, quickly found a light switch, and illuminated the space.

Mariah gasped. The room was lined with cages. Inside the cages, emaciated macaque monkeys paced back and forth. One large, healthier monkey glared at them and began hurling itself against the bars of its cage. Soon all the monkeys, or at least those that were still alive, were screaming. Monkey corpses lay on the bottom of several cages. Mariah looked closer and saw blood oozing from the mouths and noses of some of the macaques. She looked into their eyes. Blood was seeping from the corneas. The eyes seemed to plead. Mariah immediately thought of Reston Ebolavirus. There had been a deadly outbreak in 1989 in Reston, Virginia, among macaque monkeys imported from the Philippines for research purposes. Exposed humans weren't sickened. But the Reston monkeys hadn't shown external bleeding like the ones in this room. That damage was mainly internal. Mariah shook her head and fought back tears. She wanted to help these animals, but she knew it was too late for them.

She had to fight her natural response to get the hell out of this place. She was no agent. This was way beyond her day-to-day job. But she did know about lab work and could calm herself by trying to respond logically to what the surroundings called for. She and Curt took swab samples from a number of locations around the animal room amid the monkeys' frantic shrieks. Mariah was careful not to get too close to the especially agitated monkey. She knew that long-tailed macaques had sharp teeth and a nasty habit of biting handlers.

They finished taking samples and headed toward the door. Curt stopped just before the exit. As Mariah waited, she saw him bend over to examine something on the floor. It looked to her like a spray gun of some kind. He examined it closely and took swab samples from around the nozzle. Finally, he straightened up and turned toward the exit.

The large macaque monkey crashed against its cage door, forcing it open. With its teeth bared, it covered the distance to Curt in less than two seconds and leaped at him.

Mariah reacted instinctively. As Curt pivoted away from the attack, she picked up the spray gun and threw it at the monkey, striking it on the shoulder. Stunned, the macaque momentarily paused. Mariah heaved open the door. She and Curt dashed through, slamming the door shut just as the monkey gathered itself for another attack.

Then they heard the sound of gunshots.

A line of six two-and-a-half-ton military cargo trucks lumbered along in the darkness on westbound Route Three and entered the city limits of West Chester, Pennsylvania. The trucks were filled with food and medical supplies for the besieged residents of the city who'd been cut off from the rest of the world for nearly a week.

The National Guard soldiers manning the trucks had been well briefed. They knew they'd be facing a potentially hostile populace and that the residents of West Chester were on the verge of panic, having already depleted the area's food reserves and believing that they were facing starvation. The soldiers also knew that several inhabitants had died from a lack of critical medications. The soldiers were armed, but had been warned that if confronted, they were to use their weapons only as a last resort.

The trucks stopped in front of the West Chester City Hall. A National Guard major stepped from the lead truck and looked around. Not a soul in sight. A good sign, thought the major, though he wondered where the mayor was. The governor's office had contacted the city leader earlier to inform him that the resupply would take place at 2 a.m., when the townspeople would be asleep. The mayor was asked to meet the trucks and direct them to a secure warehouse where the supplies could be stored and distributed from. He'd been strongly advised not to share this information with any other West Chester resident.

The major returned to the truck. Had the rendezvous point been changed? He needed to contact his superiors to see if he'd missed any information. He started to open the truck door to make a radio call and heard a noise behind him.

The major turned to see a large crowd of men emerging from around the corner of the city hall building, advancing quickly toward the trucks. The men were armed with clubs and tire irons. A few carried shotguns. As the crowd grew closer the major could hear angry murmuring and he saw menace in the faces of the men. He faced a decision: confront the group, find out what they wanted, and try to calm them down, or alert the soldiers and prepare for a possible attack. He chose the former option, in part because he wasn't sure there was time to notify his troops, who were sequestered with the supplies in the canvas-covered cargo beds of the trucks, and in part because he wanted to keep things from escalating.

The major walked toward the crowd, his bearing erect, affecting what he hoped was a confident demeanor. He stopped a few feet away from the apparent leader of the group, a large, bearded bear of a man wearing an old sweatshirt with the sleeves cut off, and started to ask him what they wanted. Ignoring the major, the man signaled to the people behind him, who stepped around him and advanced toward the trucks.

The major turned and shouted toward the soldiers in the vehicles, but he doubted they could hear him. He saw the driver of the lead truck open the door, his pistol drawn, but the crowd was already there. He heard the blast of a shotgun and saw the driver fall.

Alerted by the noise, the rest of the Guard soldiers erupted from the backs of the cargo trucks, but the confrontation was over quickly. The mob was prepared for the soldiers' resistance.

By the time the crowd had stripped the trucks of their supplies and loaded the goods into waiting pickups, five soldiers lay motionless on the ground. The remaining Guardsmen, disarmed by the crowd, stood by helplessly, many bleeding from wounds or clutching broken limbs. The major, holding a handkerchief to a laceration on his head, watched as the attackers piled into the pickup trucks and drove away.

At the sound of the gunfire in the lab, Curt switched off the hallway light and whispered to Mariah to remain quiet. Hardly breathing, she stood in the darkness, pressed against a wall, wondering what she'd do if they were discovered, listening to the rogue macaque throw itself repeatedly at the door of the room she and Curt had just fled. They had no weapons, not even the tools they'd used earlier.

Minutes later Mariah heard a door open and heavy footsteps approaching. She reached out for Curt and grasped air instead. Where was he? She saw the bright beam of a flashlight playing across the room and heard movement, close, and a murmur of voices. The light switched off. Mariah held her breath, forced herself to remain motionless. Then a bright light glared into her face, and a man was shouting: "Got her! I got her right here!"

Mariah kicked the man with all her might. The flashlight flew out of his hand, smashed against the wall, and went dead. She inched away in the darkness and heard the sounds of thudding and muffled groans. Finally, a voice she recognized as Curt's called out.

"Mariah," he said. "Where are you?"

"Where are *you*?" she cried as a delayed surge of fear rose up her throat and threatened to choke her.

The overhead lights switched on, and Mariah shielded her eyes with a shaking hand. As Curt moved toward her she looked over his shoulder where two men lay motionless on the floor. She wasn't sure they were still alive. She wasn't sure she wanted them to be.

Omar willed himself to control his emotions, to snuff out the incandescent anger that was smoldering inside him. When his men had called to tell him that the young CIA employee, Angus Friedman, had gotten away, his first, irrational impulse had been to go directly to them, to execute them on the spot, with his own hands. But he knew that wouldn't do any good. He needed them and it was too late to line up replacements. Besides, he acknowledged, he was ultimately responsible for the escape. He should not have underestimated Friedman, should never underestimate any field operative who worked for American intelligence.

Now he needed a plan. Doctor Vector was due in the Philippines today. His flight had probably already landed, and he'd be arriving in Jolo by evening. Even though the guy was an egotistical idiot, he was controlling the mission. At least Vector believed he was. The mission had to succeed. At all costs. If

Vector found out that Friedman had escaped, he'd be furious. And, Omar had come to learn, when Vector got angry, he'd lose perspective and judgment, be capable of making irrational decisions. The mission would be jeopardized. Omar knew he'd eventually have to disclose Friedman's escape. Was there a way to do this that wouldn't set off Vector, that could actually be used to the advantage of the mission?

Omar took a deep breath, straightened his spine, bent his knees, and rhythmically contracted and relaxed his diaphragm. As he squatted, he extended his arms and rotated through a series of slow, precise, coordinated movements. Omar was a devout Muslim but had long since realized that there was much to learn from other cultures, including the ancient Buddhist practice of moving meditation known as tai chi.

By the time he'd finished his routine, Omar had decided on the path forward.

CHAPTER TWENTY-FOUR

Mariah and Curt entered a small, windowless conference room air-conditioned to the point of frigidity. A group of five or six was assembled around a table, and Mariah was surprised to see Bill Cothran among them. The portable safe from the underground lab sat in the center of the table.

Cothran stood and shook hands with Curt and Mariah. "Glad to see you're both okay. Understand you've had a rough time—especially you, Mariah."

"No problem, I'm fine," she said. But she didn't feel fine, and she hoped it didn't show. She felt exhausted and twitchy. She sat down and clasped her hands together on her lap, afraid they would tremble if she placed them on the table. She noticed that Lieutenant Alvarez was at the table too, and that his arm was in a sling. She knew there'd been a massive gunfight aboveground while she and Curt had been exploring the underground lab. Men, Curt told her, had been killed, and Alvarez had taken a bullet to the shoulder. She assumed other holes were about to be filled in. She wondered what was in the safe. She could feel Curt watching her out of the corner of his eye and suppressed a shiver.

"I've got great news," said Cothran. "I just got a call from the embassy in Manila. Friedman showed up there. He'd been captured by people likely connected to this whole thing. They weren't gentle with him, but he managed to escape and we're briefing him now. Physically he'll be fine, but they got to him."

Mariah noticed that Cothran was primarily directing his report to Curt and Curt was nodding. "The important thing is he's safe," said Cothran. "We'll deal with the exposure as it comes."

After pausing for a moment, his eyes on Curt, Cothran continued: "He's on his way down here," he said. "I'll let him give you the details. We've got plenty to cover already this morning." He remained standing and introduced the rest of the group: a U.S. Navy commander from the Joint Special Operations Task Force; his Filipino counterpart, an army colonel; and a clean-shaven civilian man from the U.S. embassy in Manila. CIA, Mariah guessed.

The colonel gave a concise report on the discovery of the Abu Sayyaf facility and the gun battles. He estimated that the ambush force had been composed of fifty to seventy-five insurgents. Between the two firefights the guerrillas had sustained twenty-one KIA and seventeen captured. The task force had suffered only four casualties, not counting wounded. *Four men died*, thought Mariah. *That's what you need to say, Colonel. Four men woke up this morning not knowing it would be their last day on earth.* She wrapped her arms across her chest and tried to keep warm.

Cothran nodded toward Alvarez. "As you can see, the good lieutenant was wounded in the second battle," he said. "Fortunately, it's superficial. He'll live to fight another day."

"Where are the guerrillas now?" asked Mariah.

"Pretty much melted into the jungle," said Alvarez. "Our troops are conducting a thorough search of the camp and surroundings. We did capture one guy. He's in a secure location here at the camp and he's being questioned right now." He nodded toward Curt. "Dr. Kennedy's helping us."

Mariah kept looking at the safe on the table and wondered how they were supposed to pretend it wasn't there. Cothran interrupted her thoughts. He was asking her to brief the group about the underground laboratory. She made an effort to control her voice, which she thought sounded high-pitched and shaky. "They were operating a state-of-the-art bio lab down there," she said. "It included an MCL—Level Four by the look of it. And the latest equipment—even a bioreactor that looked like it was being used to manufacture virus. Plus an animal room." Mariah paused, remembering the monkey attack, then forced herself to continue. "They were experimenting with macaque monkeys," she said. "Most were sick and dead—a hemorrhagic disease. We're guessing they were deliberately exposed to Kandahar virus."

The embassy man shifted in his chair and drew back a bit from the edge of the table. "I'm surprised you weren't exposed yourselves," he said warily.

"We wore protective gear," said Mariah. "We took a number of swab samples. They're being analyzed in Manila."

"We discovered a fine-particle grinder," Curt added. "And a spray gun. Sure looks like they were trying to aerosolize the virus."

"Shit," said Cothran with a grimace, and Mariah realized that he must have been hearing some of this for the first time. She'd stopped trying to sort through the hierarchy of these shadowy, hypercompetent men. "An aerosolized virus. That's all we need," said Cothran. "Anything else? Go ahead, Curt, make my day."

"We did find that safe," Curt replied, pointing to the center of the table. "Might be worth checking out the contents. And while we're at it, I suggest bringing in a trained microbiology team to thoroughly investigate the lab—and look for the virus."

"I agree," said Cothran. He turned to the man from the U.S. embassy. "The University of the Philippines has some expertise and they have that new Level Four lab," he said. "That's where we sent the swab samples. It'll be quicker to bring a couple of their scientists down from Manila than to fly a team over from the States. Should be able to get them here by this evening if we make it highest priority. They'll need to be cleared, of course."

There was a knock on the door and a navy enlisted man entered. The navy commander motioned him to the table and turned to the rest of the group. "A machinist's mate," he said. "He has some special skills."

The enlisted man placed his ear next to the safe's combination lock and lightly grasped the dial. He slowly turned it forward and backward several times. In less than a minute, the safe clicked open.

The commander reached inside and pulled out a packet of documents. He glanced at them and passed them on to Alvarez. "Tagalog. Can you translate?"

Alvarez leafed through the sheaf of documents and held up the top sheet of paper. "Looks like a who's who of the lab workers. Mostly Pakistani and Indonesian names, a number with advanced degrees in microbiology or medicine." He pulled several more documents from the file. "These are architectural renderings of the laboratory and its various rooms. There should be blueprints somewhere. And there are technical drawings and specifications for scientific equipment. Wonder why they would just leave all that info lying around."

"Hardly lying around," said the navy commander. "It was in a secure underground lab, locked in a safe. And they probably had contingency plans to burn the stuff if the wrong people showed up. We obviously surprised them. But they did have time to remove the hard drive on the computer in the lab. Smashed it. We're trying to recover data, but it doesn't look hopeful."

Curt made a quick sketch of the particle grinder he'd found in the lab and handed it to Alvarez. "Any manuals for this in there?"

Alvarez glanced at the drawing. He looked through the documents again. "Not that I can see." He turned to the naval officer. "Anything else in there, sir?" he asked.

"Just this," the commander said. He reached inside and pulled out a fat, letter-sized manila envelope sealed with a metal clasp. He opened the envelope, pulled out several sheets of paper stapled together, and scanned them quickly. "Can't read it," he said. "Some foreign language." He handed the documents to the civilian.

"Urdu," said the man. "And there's a number in the first paragraph: 11/9."

"Sounds like a date," said Curt. "If it is, it would be September eleventh—9/11. Most of the world uses the reverse order of month and day."

For several seconds no one said anything, which Mariah figured was because they were all considering the obvious implications of the date.

"There's more in the envelope," said the commander as he grasped it and turned it upside down. Several stacks of paper currency tumbled onto the table. Cothran reached across, picked them up, and leafed through them. He looked over at the others with a puzzled expression on his face. "Euros," he said. "And pound sterling."

Shortly after 9:00 a.m., several dozen men and women marched down Chicago's South LaSalle Street, heading for the historic, Art Deco Field Building in the Loop District. Their destination was the Bank of America retail space on the west side of the Field Building's ground floor. Many of the marchers were masked and dressed in black. Several carried heavy objects—metal pipes, crowbars, and aluminum baseball bats. They reached the front of the building and stopped. As expected, the bank's doors were locked, and not just because it was a Saturday. Since the nationwide run on the banks earlier in the week, the federal government had closed all financial institutions until further notice. Most citizens had accepted this, knowing that without such a strong measure, the entire banking system—and the national economy—could collapse.

But the Chicago marchers had a different view. About half of the group descending on the bank consisted of depositors determined to retrieve their personal savings. They'd been persuaded that the government was going to confiscate all private bank holdings, a belief fed by the remaining marchers, the ones dressed in black, anarchists and petty hoodlums who sought to capitalize on a disaffected populace, who came to sow disorder or, simply, to loot.

A large hooded man pushed his way to the front door, raised a crowbar over his head, and smashed it against the glass. The glass was designed to be shatterproof, but after several heavy blows, a spiderweb of cracks spread across its surface. Other masked marchers moved in, wielding their own weapons.

Minutes later, the glass was shattered, allowing the door to be opened from the inside. The crowd surged in, oblivious to the sirens wailing in the distance.

That evening in Jolo, Mariah walked beside Curt as they headed back to their quarters. The sweet fragrance of tropical flowers permeated the still, soft night and the subdued light of a quarter moon seeped through the forest canopy. She felt secure next to Curt—and at peace.

Curt had his arm around her waist, his hand resting on her

hip. Mariah walked slowly and leaned lightly against him, feeling his warmth through her thin blouse. "Alvarez was right about that fermented coconut drink," she said.

"The *tuba*, you mean."

"Right. It does sneak up on you."

"The scotch probably didn't help."

Mariah pressed against Curt, her shoulder against his arm. Maybe it was the drink and feeling the effects of the past couple of days. The adrenaline wearing off, with only the fear left. She was crying now. Curt tightened his grip around her waist and wiped away the tears on her face. Soon they approached a cluster of small, thatch-roofed huts and ascended a set of steps to one of the cottages. Mariah fished in her pocket and handed a key to Curt.

Curt opened the front door, flicked on a light switch, and looked around. "Not bad," he said. "All the comforts of home."

"Not bad at all." Mariah gazed at the hut's interior and took in the bamboo walls with prints of bright, tropical scenes, comfortable rattan furniture, a colorful reed floor mat, and an inviting queen-sized bed.

Curt handed the key back to her. "I'll be next door if you need anything." He turned to leave.

"Curt?" She saw him hesitate. She wasn't ready to say good night to him, not yet. "I'm really not sleepy," she said, holding his gaze. To her relief, he eased past her and stepped into her cabin as if they'd come to some kind of agreement.

"Sorry I can't offer you anything to drink." Mariah kicked off her sandals, walked over to an upholstered wicker couch, and sat down with her long legs curled under her on the cushion. "I like Bill Cothran," she said, trying to hide her nerves. "You can tell his real passion is epidemiology. Why do you suppose he went to a desk job?"

Curt sat down next to her, close, but not as close as Mariah found she was hoping for. "Money, I'd guess," he said. "He spent so much time in the field that it affected his marriage. Hefty alimony and child support payments after the divorce. His kids are grown now, but it's been so long since he practiced science that it would be too hard for him to get back into it."

"Is that why you never got married?" asked Mariah, feeling bold. "Too much time in the field?"

"Partly, maybe," Curt said, watching her. "Basically, never met the right person. What about you?"

"Same here," she said. "Never met the right guy."

She realized that Curt had moved closer to her, not touching, but near enough that she could feel a kind of radiant energy through her thin, paisley honeymooner's blouse, decorated with palm trees and flowers. She looked at his hands, and her mind involuntarily flashed to the hands of the man who'd held the knife up to her face in the jungle. Without really meaning to, she edged away from him, ever so slightly.

Curt was looking closely at her. "I know it's been rough for you," he said. "I wouldn't even blame you if you were a little afraid of me. After what I did to those guys in the jungle. And the underground lab."

Mariah hesitated before answering. "No, it's okay," she said. "Sometimes we have to do things like that." She was trying to be matter-of-fact, but she knew her voice sounded strained.

"Under the right circumstances," Curt said evenly.

Mariah was quiet for a moment. Then she said, "When those guys in the jungle went after me, I might have killed them myself if I could have."

"Sure. Self-defense."

"No, it was more than that." *Should I really try to explain this?* she wondered. "I think I would have felt pleasure."

They were both silent for some time. Finally, Curt spoke. "Totally understandable," he said. "It's part of being human. We couldn't survive as a species if we had compunctions about killing in the heat of battle. We're probably hardwired to enjoy it, in an innate sort of way, when our own lives, or those of our loved ones, are threatened. What really matters is how we behave when lives are not on the line. That's the other side of being human. We're fundamentally generous and altruistic. At least most of us."

"Maybe so," said Mariah. "But I'm not sure that makes me feel any better. And I'm afraid I'm beginning to get cynical. I'm starting to look below the surface of things, half expecting to see evil inside."

"Take it from a charter member of the cynics club: you'd be at least half-right. But here's the thing. A lot of the time, what you see is what you get, and most of that is pretty good. You don't have to *expect* the worst, but you should be prepared for it."

Mariah shifted her position on the couch. Her shoulder brushed against Curt's and she felt a brief, sharp jolt, like when you touch someone after scuffing your feet on a carpet. She untucked her long legs and stretched them out in front of her. She was wearing white cotton shorts. "My legs were starting to fall asleep," she said. She watched Curt's eyes stray to her legs. He turned to her and smiled.

"You must be exhausted," he said. "I should let you get some sleep."

How could she persuade him to stay without seeming too forward? What did *too forward* even mean? She'd been finding excuses her whole life for not doing things she wanted to do. *And you've come close to dying three or four times in the last week*, she reminded herself. What could be riskier than that? "For some reason, I'm wide-awake," she said. "Maybe adrenaline. You don't have to go." They were now face-to-face, looking into each other's eyes. Curt leaned forward to kiss her. Their noses bumped, and Mariah immediately pulled back with a nervous laugh. "Sorry about that. My big beak."

"Actually, I like your nose," Curt said. "It looks kind of aristocratic. Not like this." Curt touched his misshapen nose.

Mariah laughed. "I think yours is cute. Macho in a way, but it also makes you look vulnerable, somehow."

Curt drew back in mock surprise. "So you think I'm macho and vulnerable," he said. He looked at Mariah for a few moments without speaking. Then he leaned forward and kissed her. This time their noses didn't bump. He kissed her again, gently, cupping her face in his hands, holding the kiss for several seconds. When the kiss ended, he kept his face close to hers and looked into her eyes. "That's another thing I like," he said. "Your eyes change color depending on the light."

Mariah wrapped her arms around Curt and kissed him, not softly this time but hard, her tongue between his lips. She moaned and began to cry with soft sobs, burying her head on his shoulder. "I'm sorry," she said. "It's been a hell of a couple of days."

"It's okay," Curt said. "I'm surprised you've held it together this long."

Mariah snuggled next to him, her head resting on his shoulder. *I could stay like this for a long, long time*, she thought. "What's your favorite memory?" she asked.

"Right now isn't bad."

"I mean . . . before. Like when you were a kid."

"I remember a picnic with my mother and sister," said Curt. "Before Lucy got sick. Beautiful late-spring day. My mom spread a blanket under a big oak tree by a pretty little brook. She made a chocolate cake for dessert. I brought my fishing rod. Caught a sunfish. I still remember that."

"You must have had a very happy family."

There was no reply from Curt.

Mariah raised her head and looked at him. "What?"

"It wasn't so happy. I didn't get along with my father."

"Oh," she said. "I'm sorry."

"Remember I told you about the dollhouse I made for my sister? After she died, I kept working on it. Just a few improvements, like a little dressing table and wardrobe. Kind of to honor her memory. And one day, I was doing the work in my bedroom, and my father walked in."

Mariah tried to picture the scene in her mind, guessing what might come next.

"He looked at what I was doing and got furious," Curt said. "Said I should be out playing football or climbing trees. Like other boys. I tried to argue—it's not like I didn't spend a lot of time outdoors. Sports, exploring with friends, tramping around. But my father just got angrier."

Mariah nestled her head back against his shoulder. He wrapped his arm around her and cleared his throat. "So he walked over to the dollhouse and started smashing it with his feet," he said. "Just destroyed it. I tried to stop him, but he pushed me away. I started crying and he hit me."

Mariah sat up and looked at Curt with shock, with sympathy, with anger at an insensitive, brutal father. "What a bastard," she said.

"He came up with a halfhearted apology later," said Curt, "but it was never the same between us. I could tell he thought I was a wimp."

Mariah shook her head. "What about your mother?" she said.

"My parents were really broken up about Lucy's death," said Curt. "She obviously felt like she needed to give him her full support. But my father made me feel that Lucy was the only child he really cared about. It got so I couldn't take it anymore. So I ran away." He paused.

Mariah waited for him to continue, reluctant to say anything that would interrupt him.

Finally, he spoke again. "I was fifteen," he said. "Started

hitchhiking. A young couple picked me up. Drove me all the way to L.A. I lived on the streets there for a while before a social worker noticed me. She found me a place to stay, entered me in school, and involved me with the local Boys' Club. Eventually she found me some foster parents. Older couple. Nice people. The husband was a biology professor at UCLA. Got me interested in science. I really got into my studies, and two years later I graduated near the top of my high school class. Then I got a full scholarship to UCLA, where I majored in microbiology." He smiled at Mariah. "There, now you know my whole life story."

"I doubt that," said Mariah, smiling. "Did you ever see your parents again?"

"Just my mother. Once," said Curt. "I was in my midtwenties. She was still living in Massachusetts—that's where I grew up. I asked her why she let my father treat me like that, but she didn't have an answer."

"You never saw your father again?"

Curt shook his head. "A few years after I got to L.A., I learned he'd died of cancer."

For a long time, they quietly sat together on the couch, Curt's arm around Mariah, her head on his shoulder. Mariah thought about all that Curt had told her, how lonely his childhood must have been. She was glad he'd confided in her and took it as a sign of his trust in her. But there was still so much more she wanted to know. She was hesitant to keep questioning him because he might take it as pushiness, might retreat back into himself. But she sensed that this was a rare moment. If he was ever going to truly open up to her, it would be now. But she'd have to choose her words carefully.

"You told me you'd never married because the right one never came along," she said.

Curt leaned back and looked at her with what seemed like sadness in his eyes. "I just wasn't too good at relationships with women," he said. "Seemed to connect with the wrong ones. Friend of mine used to say I was attracted to damaged goods."

"You think that's true?" asked Mariah. Did he think *she* fell into that category?

"I mean, we all have issues," said Curt. "But it's possible I was drawn to that. Maybe it had something to do with Lucy's death. Some kind of rescue syndrome. But to be honest, I think it had more to do with being afraid to make a commitment."

"After what you went through with your family."

"Maybe," he said. "I did come close to getting married once. But it was because we had a kid together. A boy. I was about twenty at the time. She was a year younger. We tried to make it work. Lived together for a couple of years, but I was in college full-time, working odd jobs nights, weekends, breaks. Between time in the library and trying to support the three of us, I wasn't home much. She got fed up and walked out one day while I was at classes. Took our son. Didn't even leave a note."

"Ever find them?" Mariah asked.

"Never," said Curt. "She'd been pretty private about her previous life. Basically, all I knew was that she'd grown up in Hawaii. That's one of the places I tried to track her down. But no luck." He leaned back in the couch and looked up at the ceiling. "It's been over twenty years now. Maybe just as well. I probably would have been a lousy father. Just like my own dad."

"I would have given anything to have had my parents when I was growing up," Mariah said. "Warts and all. And as for being a bad father yourself, you don't know that."

"Maybe you're right," Curt said. "I was pretty lonely after I left home. I wondered if I should have stayed, accepted my father's flaws, worked through it all. I forgive him now. He was really a better man, all in all, than a lot of others I've met in my life." He turned and kissed her gently on the lips. "Thank you for listening to all this," he said, stroking her cheek.

Mariah kissed him back, at first softly, then harder. She trembled slightly as Curt stood, clasped her hands, and eased her to her feet. She let him unbutton her blouse and run his fingers down her shoulders and across her chest, touching her tattoo. She felt small goose bumps spread across her skin as he reached back and unfastened her bra. She gently pushed him away, shrugged it off, and tossed it onto a chair. She slid down her shorts, stepped out of them, took his hand, and led him toward the bed.

"Martial law."

"Excuse me, Mr. President?"

The president looked directly at his homeland security secretary. "I said martial law. Deploy all the Guard troops you need. Dusk-to-dawn curfews. That includes Philadelphia. The Guard can distribute food and supplies to designated locations at night." The president wearily shook his head. "And we need to beef up security at all the nation's banks. More Guard troops. We have no choice. The alternative is total anarchy."

From his chair in the Oval Office, Alphonso Cruickshank watched for the DHS secretary's reaction. He knew the man to be experienced and levelheaded, and didn't expect that he'd argue. Still, he could see that the secretary was struggling to repress emotion from his face. Cruickshank knew that the president was making the right call after what had happened with the food trucks in Philadelphia and the Chicago bank. But the chief of staff had no illusions about the consequences. Some citizens would likely resist, perhaps violently.

The DHS secretary was speaking again, and Cruickshank was not surprised to hear him channeling his own concerns. "We'll have to expect some pushback, Mr. President."

"Your point?" asked the president.

"We'll have more armed confrontations. Certainly in the inner-city areas. Maybe even the suburbs. Distrust of the government's pretty strong right now. Combine that with panic and you have a toxic mix."

"I don't have to tell you how to handle that," replied the president in a soft but firm voice. "We've already had clashes. Hopefully, the Guard's learning how to work better with the citizens. Make sure Defense and the governor are right on top of this. That the Guard commanders have some experience. And that they don't take no for an answer."

"Yes, sir. First sign of violence, we confiscate firearms. House-to-house searches. We may even need mass detention centers."

Cruickshank saw the president nod. *The country might as well be at war,* he thought.

CHAPTER TWENTY-FIVE

At six o'clock the next morning, Bill Cothran, hands on his hips, once again faced the small group—Mariah, Curt, Alvarez, the U.S. Navy commander, the Filipino army colonel, and the civilian from the U.S. embassy. Mariah had taken a seat next to Curt. It looked to her as if Cothran hadn't slept. Or Curt. He had returned to his room sometime in the middle of the night after she had assured him she wouldn't mind. She'd slept deeply and dreamlessly and only woke up when Curt knocked on her door to tell her that Cothran wanted to see them right away. He hadn't told her why. Now, at the meeting, Curt seemed distracted and a little bit anxious. Something must be up.

"I've got some bad news," Cothran said. "Our captive escaped."

Mariah gasped. "What happened?"

"A guard claimed that a couple of guys overpowered him in the night and took the keys. Had a nasty bump on the head to show for it and was unconscious when his relief reported at 0400. We've got to assume that whoever released the guy has the virus. The microbiology team from Manila couldn't find any virus stocks in the jungle lab. Could be that our Omar fugitive is involved. Still no sign of that guy."

"Think they'll try to hook up with the Abu Sayyaf guerrillas?" Mariah asked. "Near that jungle hideout?"

"They'll know we'll be keeping a close eye on that group," said Cothran. "My guess is they'll try to leave the country. Doubt they'll risk a flight. They'll assume we're watching all the airports in the Philippines. They'll probably try to exit by the back door." He walked over to a map on the wall, pointed to the northern tip of a large island west of the Philippines, and ran his finger along the waters to the east of the island. "Through Sabah—Malaysian Borneo. A key smuggling route to and from the Philippines and a watery highway for contraband. Not to mention terrorists."

Mariah scrutinized the map. "Sabah's not far from Jolo," she said.

Alvarez nodded. "Even closer to western Sulu." He pointed to a group of islands in the western Philippines. "They'll probably try to cross by boat from this area. We do have some assets there, but there's a lot of ocean to watch."

"If they get to Borneo with the virus, how hard would it be to intercept them then?" Curt asked.

"Damn near impossible," said Cothran. "They could easily make it into Indonesia. And there you're talking hundreds of small islands. Thousands of boats. A lot of regional airports."

"September eleventh is only a few days away," said Curt. "Doubt that they're targeting Indonesia. Any way to put a hold on international flights out of that country?"

"We thought of that," said Cothran. "We approached the Indonesian government about grounding flights out of Jakarta. They refused. I don't blame them. We couldn't give them any specifics—only that we suspected that terrorists might be trying to board flights. And it's not even guaranteed that they'd fly out of Jakarta. A bunch of airports in Indonesia—even Borneo—have flights to other Southeast Asia destinations. Or they could cross the Straits of Malacca on the water. It would be a quick trip in a high-powered smuggling boat. We'll have people at all the obvious departure points watching closely, but we're talking a lot of islands, airports, harbors. At this point, our best option is to try to keep them from getting to Borneo in the first place."

"How do we do that?" asked Curt. "You said yourself there's a lot of ocean to watch."

Alvarez let his finger rest on a small island just east of Borneo. "Right," he said, "but the quickest navigable route goes past this island—Sibutu. You can see how close it is to Sabah. You guys might be able to intercept them in that area."

Mariah saw that Cothran was looking directly at Curt and her. "No time to mobilize the task force," he was saying. "And we'll need your microbiology expertise."

Mariah's first reaction was that finally, someone wasn't telling her that she'd have to stay behind because a mission might be dangerous. She knew Curt wouldn't object to her going. And she sure wouldn't let him go without her. But everyone else always seemed to want to protect her. On the other hand, she admitted to herself that she was exhausted from everything that had happened over the past few days. She'd do all she could to overcome that exhaustion, but she hoped that she'd be able to pull her weight and deal with the stress that had been eating at her. The last thing she wanted was to hamper Curt or jeopardize the mission.

As she struggled with her feelings there was a knock on the conference room door.

Cothran rose, with a smile on his face, and headed toward the door. "Looks like your teammate is here," he said. He opened the door and Angus Friedman walked through.

Mariah watched as Curt quickly stood and Angus rushed over, almost running, arms outstretched. Without speaking, the two men hugged each other.

Cothran moved next to Mariah and spoke quietly. "Curt's his father," he said. "Angus has known it for a while, was planning to tell Curt, but didn't get the chance before he was captured. So I told Curt just before the meeting this morning. Turns out he'd already suspected it."

Mariah tried to hold back tears, then gave in, letting them flow. She could see that Angus was crying too. Now Curt had his hands on his son's shoulders and was looking at him as if seeing him for the first time, saying something in a low voice.

Cothran finally cleared his throat. "Don't want to interrupt," he said, "but we've got a tight schedule."

"Could we just hear a little about what Angus has been through?" asked Curt.

"We'll be thoroughly debriefing him later," said Cothran. "But I'll let Angus give you a quick overview."

Angus nodded and began to speak, directing his remarks mostly to his father. "My fault completely," he said. "I went out for a walk after dinner that night in Manila. Wasn't paying attention and got kidnapped. The guys who caught me turned me over to another group. That's when it got a little rough. Bottom line is, they broke me." He paused and looked down at the floor. Everyone waited for him to continue.

"They know who I work for," Angus finally said. "They know about our mission." He raised his head and looked at Curt. "And, Dad, they know about you and me." He lowered his head again.

Curt moved toward Angus, placed his hands back on his shoulders, and looked directly at him. "It's okay," he said. "The important thing is you're safe now."

After several moments, Cothran spoke again. "Angus will accompany us to Sibutu," he said. "I'll fly us down. We need to take off quickly. Can you all be ready to leave in a half hour?"

That afternoon a single-engine, four-passenger Beechcraft Bonanza banked over the island of Sibutu, leveled off, and homed in on a grassy runway surrounded by palm trees. Cothran was piloting the plane. On their way to Sibutu, they'd explored the southern reaches of the Sulu Sea, looking for suspicious watercraft, but they'd only seen local fishing boats.

Cothran gripped the wheel in both hands and focused on the landing surface. "Be ready for a bumpy landing," he said to the others. "I'm not sure how long it's been since a plane has come in here."

Mariah cinched up her seat belt. Curt had praised Cothran's flying abilities as they'd walked back to their huts together to pack their duffels. He'd told her that the plane belonged to the task force in Jolo and that they used it for scouting missions, which meant it should be well maintained. Plus, Cothran had raved about the plane's performance and three-hundred-horse-power engine. But the runway, bordered all around by palm trees, looked pretty damn small to her. She glanced back at Angus, who was sitting just behind her, clutching the arms of his seat. He caught her eye and smiled.

"I think we'd have been better off with a helicopter," he said, motioning down toward the landing strip. "But at least it's a short taxi to the terminal."

"I don't see any terminal," said Mariah. She turned to the front and watched the approach.

The plane skimmed over the tops of the trees and dropped quickly toward the runway. Just before the wheels touched down, Mariah heard the engine rev up, and the plane bounced hard along the rough coral surface. Clenching her teeth to keep from biting her tongue, she focused on the line of palm trees on the far end of the airstrip.

The Beechcraft rapidly decelerated and came to a halt mere feet from the end of the runway. When Mariah finally unclenched her muscles and looked around, Cothran was calmly taxiing toward a small building on the edge of the field where a man in a bush hat was waving. They came to a stop and disembarked. The man approached, hand outstretched. "Welcome to Sibutu," he said. "Ryan Maloney. Kind of the jack of all trades around here."

They all shook the man's hand and introduced themselves.

"Kennedy, huh?" said Maloney, sizing Curt up. "Good Irish name. You've probably got some priests in your ancestry. Or maybe drunks. Most likely both." And at this he erupted into laughter, a loud bray that elicited chuckles from the others. "I can say that," he said. "I'm an ex-priest myself. Caretaker here now. Here, let me help you with your bags."

Maloney led the way to a battered jeep. They piled in, and he drove toward a complex of buildings several hundred yards from the runway.

"So what's the deal with this place?" asked Angus. "A school, right?"

Maloney nodded. "School's been here for decades," he said. "The original plan was that it would help convert the islanders to Catholicism. As you've probably heard, most of the people down here are Muslims—or animists. We didn't convert too many. These days we focus on offering a well-rounded education. And we keep pretty low-key about religion."

"Catholics are targets now, right?" said Angus.

"At least in some circles," said Maloney. "You might have heard that a priest in Sibutu was murdered by Abu Sayyaf a few years back." He stopped the jeep next to a long, one-story wooden building that looked like army barracks. "Here's where you'll be staying." He pointed to an adjacent building. "Mess hall. Dinner's at six. There's drinks and snacks there if you want something now."

They walked up a short flight of steps to a covered porch. Maloney opened a door, revealing a clean but Spartan room containing a bed, simple dresser, wooden straight-backed chair, small plain table, and a wardrobe in one corner. "Bathroom's over there," he said, pointing toward a small door at the far end of the room. "There are several rooms in this building. All made up for guests. Sort them out however you'd like."

When their host left, Cothran turned to the others. "Character, huh?"

"Is he connected to the task force?" asked Mariah.

"Sort of. He's lived in this part of Sulu since the eighties. It's kind of a backwater with very few Westerners, but it's strategically important. And of course, the area's an Abu Sayyaf stronghold. After 9/11, the CIA tapped him to keep his eyes open and report what he saw. He agreed. Believes that fundamentalist Islamic fanaticism is a global threat to Christianity."

"So he's going to work with us?" asked Angus.

"Indirectly," said Cothran. "He's loaning us an inflatable boat. Good engine—pretty fast. Actually, we bought it for him." He glanced at his watch. "Let's plan to meet for dinner at six p.m. and then get some sleep. We'll head out early tomorrow—to a small island with a good view."

CHAPTER TWENTY-SIX

In the predawn darkness, Mariah sat cross-legged on the beach of an uninhabited palm-treed island. Curt, Angus, and Cothran sat beside her, binoculars to their eyes. They'd arrived an hour earlier after a rough ride in choppy seas on Maloney's motorized inflatable boat. From their vantage point they could see the coast of Malaysian Borneo, a few miles to the west. Cothran had picked this spot, reasoning that the old smuggling route ran by this island. Because they were on the lee side, he'd said, chances were that any boat making the passage would pass by this shore.

There was a fresh, chilly breeze and Mariah was glad she'd worn a Windbreaker. She saw that Angus was wearing a fleece vest and that Curt had on the task force hat that Alvarez had given him. She stretched out her legs in the sand to keep her feet from going to sleep. Periodically, she scanned the horizon with her binoculars. Curt had taught her to take frequent breaks when using them and to never stare at one place for long, but she didn't expect to see anything yet. Cothran had said that any boat trying to avoid detection wouldn't use lights, and that they'd have better luck when the sun started to come up.

"Heard you were involved with Machupo," Mariah said to Cothran, partly to keep from dozing off and partly because she loved to talk about epidemiology.

Cothran nodded. "In Ecuador in the nineties," he said. "Know much about the virus?"

"Bolivian hemorrhagic fever," said Mariah.

"Right. Killed a fifth of the Achuar tribal people in one area before we could contain it."

"Nasty disease," said Mariah.

Cothran nodded again. "Patients bleed out all over—even through the pores of their skin." He scanned the horizon again with his binoculars. "Of course, Machupo was well known from Bolivia," he said. "Carried by the vesper mouse. Then CDC started hearing about a similar disease in Ecuador. They sent me down to check it out, and I confirmed Machupo. Never known from there before and vesper mice don't live in that area. We never found a local animal host. Best guess is a visitor brought it in. And it's easily spread from person to person. When it comes to contagious diseases, it's a pretty small world."

Mariah knew what he meant, had thought the same thing many times during her work back home at the Barn. The most remote places on earth were now readily accessible to visitors from far away, and those visitors didn't arrive alone. They brought diseases—plagues and poxes previously unknown in remote areas and for which the local populations had no natural immunity. The result was often catastrophic. Almost overnight an indigenous group—of people or animals—that, over millennia, had adapted to and successfully coexisted in a seemingly hostile environment of predators and pathogens, could be virtually wiped out. But Mariah also realized that at the same time, many of the most dangerous emerging diseases in the world had their origins in isolated, sparsely populated areas like the surroundings of a distant jungle village. The few human beings who did live in such places often did so without apparent susceptibility to the deadly viruses that lurked around them, viruses that resided in sometimes unknown species that inhabited the deepest recesses of rain forests or caves. Then disturbance from the outside, in the form of travelers or settlers from faraway places, could unleash these dangerous pathogens and provide an abundant and vulnerable new host in which they could explosively replicate. When the visitors returned to their homelands they brought the new diseases with them, diseases for which their own countrymen had no defenses. These were the variables that powered the work of people like Cothran. Mariah felt like she understood him. She was glad he was on their team.

The sky was lightening, and just as she lifted her binoculars to her eyes Angus pointed at the horizon.

"Something there," he said.

Mariah zeroed in through her lenses. A dark object, moving slowly on the lagoon's whitecapped water. A small white triangle projecting above it. "Looks like a sailboat," she said.

"A vinta," said Cothran, peering through his own binoculars. "Small outrigger canoe. Carrying Badjaos—Sea Gypsies. They spend their entire lives on those boats. Tough life."

"So they never go ashore?" asked Angus.

"They believe that if they even set foot on land, they'll get sick and die. Badjaos can put up with some pretty horrendous conditions at sea. But lately some of them have started to leave their boats." Cothran pointed to a small wooden shack on pilings on the outer reef. "That may be one of their huts," he said.

Mariah focused her binoculars on the structure. "It looks pretty well built," she said. "I think I see bamboo siding and some serious posts beneath it. Are they usually so sturdy-looking?"

Cothran stared through his binoculars. "You're right," he said. "No way that's a Badjao hut. Too well built. Listen."

Mariah heard the *putt-putt-putt* of a boat engine echoing

across the lagoon. Seconds later, a long, narrow outrigger canoe came into view.

"Pamboat," said Cothran.

"I read about those things," said Angus. "Main means of transportation around here. They don't look too seaworthy to me."

"You'd be surprised," said Cothran. "They're pretty stable with those outriggers."

Mariah watched closely as the pamboat headed toward the hut. She made out only one person, the boat operator, a short, round man wearing an old T-shirt and ball cap. But then she saw a second person emerge from the hut, dressed in a light jacket and slacks. He was holding a rectangular black object that looked like a briefcase and he seemed to be waving at the boat. The man and his bag looked out of place in the surroundings.

"Looks like our fugitive. Omar," said Cothran, staring through his binoculars. "Guy in the boat must be a local. Probably hired to take Omar to Sabah."

Mariah realized they'd have to act fast. In minutes, the boat would rendezvous at the hut and Omar would slip aboard. Not long afterward, he'd be in Sabah and it would be virtually impossible to find him again before it was too late. She watched Cothran pull a handheld radio from the side pocket of his jacket, extend the antenna, press the talk button, and speak quietly into the transceiver.

"Helicopter's temporarily grounded," said the garbled voice on the other end. "Took a bit of a beating in a storm on the flight back from Manila. We're repairing it, but it'll be a few more hours."

"What about a boat?" said Cothran.

"If we sent one from Jolo, they wouldn't get there until tonight. Your best bet is to wait for the helo."

"Roger, wait one," replied Cothran. He turned to the others. "Guess you heard that."

Angus had risen to his feet. "So it's up to us," he said. "Let's get moving."

"Hold on a sec," said Cothran. He spoke again into the radio. "We can't wait," he said. "We'll proceed on our own. I'll keep in touch." Without waiting for a reply, he turned to the others on the beach. "Angus is right," he said. "We need to move quickly." As they all stood and moved toward the inflatable, Mariah pointed to the hut where the man on the hut platform descended a short ladder and stepped into the arriving boat, case clutched in his right hand. The boat took off and powered toward the reef entrance.

"That's no ordinary pamboat engine," said Cothran. "They're moving out. In calm seas they could be in Sabah in less than an hour. But it's pretty rough outside the reef. That'll hold 'em up some." He turned to Kennedy. "Look, you and Angus go after them. With just the two of you, you'll have a better chance of catching them. More people would slow the boat down."

Here we go again, thought Mariah to herself. *Some guy trying to protect me, separate me from the action.* "We're a team," she said. "We go together."

"Well, we can't all go," said Cothran. "I'll wait here and keep an eye on you through the binoculars. Watch for other visitors." He stood and began tugging at the inflatable, a fifteen-footer with three seats and a forty-horsepower outboard motor. "Still have your weapon?" he asked Kennedy.

Kennedy nodded and they all helped Cothran launch the boat. When it was floating, Kennedy jumped in and started the outboard. Mariah climbed aboard and Angus pushed the inflatable into deeper water before hopping on board himself.

Curt put the engine in forward gear and turned back to Cothran as the boat slowly moved away from the shore. "We should be back to pick you up in a couple of hours—with Omar," he said.

Cothran nodded and pointed toward the bow of the inflatable. "Not that you'll need it, but there's a survival kit up forward. Good luck."

The inflatable moved out of the lagoon, passed through the reef entrance, and entered the open ocean. Even though the waters were choppier now, Curt brought the boat up onto a plane and they skimmed over the surface of most of the waves. Occasionally one broke over them, causing the inflatable to shudder and nearly stall, and drenching them in a cascade of cold water. They cleared the end of the island. Mariah made out the pamboat several hundred yards ahead. She saw that the narrow craft was struggling in the rough waters, pitching up and down, and periodically submerging its bow. Curt quickly closed the distance. He motioned for Mariah to take the helm and positioned himself on the middle seat. Angus knelt on the floorboards behind the forward seat and grasped the seat with both hands.

Mariah struggled to steer the boat. Every time a wave hit them the tiller would jerk to one side. But by experimenting, she found that if she loosened her grip she could maintain better control. They drew closer to the pamboat. In the distance beyond, she could see a large landmass. "Borneo?" she yelled to Curt, pointing ahead.

Shielding his eyes with a cupped hand, he looked where she was pointing and nodded. "Has to be," he said. "Keep following them."

Mariah could see that Omar was now steering the pamboat and the other man was standing, facing aft, legs widely spaced to maintain balance in the rough seas. He was raising something to his right shoulder. It looked like a long tube.

"RPG!" Curt shouted. "Grenade launcher. Turn sharp left."

As Mariah pushed the tiller over, she saw a bright flash. There was a whooshing noise overhead followed by a splash well astern.

"Zigzag course!" Curt yelled. He knelt at the bow of the boat, gripping a large black pistol in both hands. Mariah recognized it as the gun that he had carried during the night raid on the Abu Sayyaf camp.

Another flash from the grenade launcher was followed by a large splash just ahead. "Hold on!" yelled Curt as the wave struck the small boat, causing its bow to rear up. Mariah fell backward, striking her shoulder on the boat's wooden transom. As Angus moved toward her to help, she regained control of the tiller and the boat accelerated forward. She thought about putting on a life jacket but didn't want to interrupt her steering. She changed direction frequently, varying the times between course changes. The grenade launcher was still pointed at them and the pamboat was headed directly toward the landmass. She realized she'd closed the distance to a hundred feet or so.

Curt fired a short burst from his Beretta. The RPG operator tried to move but, burdened by the grenade launcher, lost his balance. He teetered for a moment at the pamboat's rail and tumbled over the side. Still steering, Omar turned, a pistol in his hand, and fired off a volley of shots as the boat crashed into a wave. Mariah, Angus, and Curt ducked below the inflatable's pontoons. The shots went wide. Omar turned again and faced forward.

Mariah struggled to steer as the inflatable pounded into short, steep waves as it closed fast on the coastline. The next thirty seconds or so registered in her mind like a kaleidoscopic sequence of bright, disjointed images. A foaming mass of spume dead ahead, waves breaking onto a stretch of fringing coral reef exposed by a low tide. A narrow channel between the reef and the landmass. The pamboat now only yards ahead, moving quickly toward the reef. Omar standing, then rolling over the side, clutching the case. The pamboat hitting the reef bow first, driving half of its length onto the exposed coral before coming to a stop.

Mariah saw Omar struggle to his feet and splash through the surf. A breaking wave knocked him down and he disappeared in the froth. Seconds later, he emerged, briefcase still in his hand, and stumbled onto the reef. He moved crablike across the jagged surface, head down against the breeze, lurching toward the channel on the far side of the reef.

Curt took the tiller from Mariah and eased the inflatable onto the edge of the reef, timing his landing between breaking waves. He stood and yelled, "Omar!"

The man stopped and turned. He set the case on the coral, pulled his gun from his belt, and pointed it toward the inflatable. A staccato burst of loud popping noises. Curt grabbed his right arm, toppled out of the inflatable, and fell heavily onto the coral. Omar picked up the case and moved toward the trees. Angus vaulted out of the boat and began running after him. "Drop the case!" he yelled. Omar looked over his shoulder, started to raise his weapon, but then accelerated his pace without firing.

Mariah knelt over Curt's still form and pressed her face to his. He was unconscious but breathing. Blood was gushing from his left bicep and staining the reef. Working quickly, she tore a strip from his T-shirt and tightly bound the arm just above the bullet hole. The wound didn't look serious, but he seemed to be losing a lot of blood. With the tourniquet in place, the blood flow slowed to a trickle. She washed the wound with seawater, ripped another strip off the T-shirt, rinsed it in the ocean, and bandaged the arm.

Curt was now awake and trying to say something. She bent closer to him.

"Go after him," Curt said. "Help Angus. He's not even armed." He pressed the Beretta into her hand. "I'll be okay," he said.

Mariah knew she had no choice. Omar was closing in on the narrow channel that separated the reef from the mainland. *How deep is it?* she wondered. If he could wade across, they might lose him forever. She reluctantly took the gun, hoping that she wouldn't have to use it.

After a final check on Curt, Mariah moved quickly across the razor-sharp coral. Even with the case in one hand and the gun in the other, Omar was outpacing both Angus and her. *This guy's in good shape*, Mariah thought. She figured that the distance between her and Omar was about a hundred yards. *What's a Beretta's range?* she asked herself. "Stop!" she shouted, pointing the gun in front of her. She was gratified to see that Angus moved to the side, giving her a clear line of fire. She hoped Omar wouldn't call her bluff and fire first.

Omar turned, faced his pursuers, and held the case up. "There's a detonator in here," he yelled, in English that was only slightly accented. "If I trigger it, the case will explode and that will release the virus. This wind will carry it a long way. You don't want to take that chance."

Angus and Mariah stopped in their tracks. Mariah hesitated. *Virus!* And did he really have a detonator? Would he be foolish enough to use it? Even if he did, what effect would it have in this remote location? She doubted the virus could survive in seawater. But if she let him go, the consequences could be far worse. She began to move slowly toward him, gun at her side.

Still holding the case aloft, Omar aimed his own gun and fired.

Mariah dove down, and her torso slammed against the spiny surface of the reef. Adrenaline kept the pain at bay, but she knew, could feel, that the coral had pierced and scraped her skin in several places. She looked up. Omar was moving away again. She quickly rose and ran up to Angus, who had also thrown himself on to the reef surface and was now scrambling to his feet. They both sprinted after Omar. When she thought they'd closed the distance enough, she knelt on the coral and raised the Beretta again. She tried to take careful aim but a gusty breeze and her anxiety made it impossible to hold the gun steady. She held the pistol in both hands as she'd seen Curt do, released the safety, and pulled the trigger. A half-dozen shots erupted as her arms jerked upward; the gun was still on semiautomatic setting. She cursed. Why had she never learned to use a firearm?

Omar was now yards away from the channel, with Angus in close pursuit. Seconds later, he reached it and plunged in, holding the case over his head. Angus was just steps behind.

Mariah quickly realized that Omar was in trouble. A swift current was funneling through the channel. Omar was immediately swept off his feet. As he lost his footing the case flew out of his hand, crashed to the reef on her side of the channel, and burst open. Mariah yelled to Angus to stop, but it was too late. He'd already entered the water and the current had caught him too.

Helpless, Mariah watched as Omar and Angus sluiced through the channel in a whirl of flailing arms. Seconds later, she lost sight of them.

Mariah was devastated. Angus had just returned to them, seemingly back from the dead. Now he was lost again. This would absolutely kill Curt. She walked to the edge of the reef and peered down the channel toward the open sea. Nothing. She sat on the rough reef surface and began sobbing.

After several moments, she wiped her eyes and forced herself to control her emotions. Curt needed attention. She had to get back to him. Then she saw the open case lying on the coral. She carefully approached it. It was made of hard plastic and was lined with Styrofoam. Insets in the padding held three bottles. She read the label on one: *Tanduay Rhum*. It was the name of the rum company on a billboard she'd seen in Manila. Surely Omar wasn't smuggling mere booze out of the Philippines, she thought.

Mariah examined the bottles, taking care not to touch any

of them. Each had a volume of one liter and all appeared to be intact. She heard a faint voice, carried toward her by the wind. *Curt?* Turning back toward where she'd left him, she saw that a man was standing over Curt's prone body. She moved toward the man, focusing on Curt's still form, hoping that the man was from the task force. As she closed to within a few yards she saw that the man was soaking wet and that he looked like the RPG operator in the pamboat. He quickly approached her. Before Mariah could react, he grabbed her by the shoulders, threw her facedown on the reef, and pinned her hands behind her back.

CHAPTER TWENTY-SEVEN

Dr. Emily Rausch collapsed into a chair in her Pennsylvania Hospital office, buried her face in her hands, and choked back a sob. The hospital had just lost its tenth medical staffer to Kandahar, and this death had been by far the worst: the chief nurse in pediatrics, an RN Emily had worked with closely at the hospital for twenty-two years, a woman Emily had counted among her closest friends.

Emily pressed her fingers against her temples and stared absently at her desk. The hospital was severely understaffed, and not just because of sickness and death. It was proving impossible to recruit new doctors and nurses. All those within or near the quarantine zone, which had now been expanded to include the western suburbs of Philadelphia, were already hard at work at the three area hospitals designated to treat Kandahar victims. And almost no one outside the area would willingly take the risk of working with infected patients. The White House had assured her that active-duty military medics would soon arrive to fill the void, but that contingent seemed to have been tied up in the bureaucracy. Already her personnel were putting in harrowing 130-hour weeks. They were seeing dozens of new cases daily and more than three fourths of the patients were dying. There seemed to be no end in sight. And then there were the bodies. The hospital morgue was full and they were running out of space—and body bags—to store the corpses.

The desk phone rang. Emily wearily reached for the receiver. She'd been expecting the call. She identified herself and listened quietly for several seconds. The phone began to tremble in her hand and the blood drained from her face. Keeping her voice steady, she told the caller that she understood and placed the phone back on the receiver.

The person who had called was from the Department of Homeland Security. The authorities, he'd said, were concerned about the accumulation of infected corpses harboring a lethal stew of Kandahar virus. The bodies had to be disposed of— quickly. They would have to be cremated, en masse. The caller had explained to Emily that a team of specially trained soldiers would arrive later today. Public relations personnel from the department would contact loved ones. The operation had been approved by the White House, said the caller. It was unfortunate, but there was no choice.

Mariah was lashed to a chair, her ankles bound together and her wrists tied behind her back. Sunlight was leaking through gaps in the bamboo walls, illuminating the walls and a thatched ceiling. She heard the cry of a seabird and the distant sound of a plane high overhead. She twisted around and again called softly to Curt, who was tied up in another chair that was lashed to hers. No answer. *Was he still unconscious? Worse?* Behind her, a door squeaked and then slammed shut.

"Well, well. Fancy seeing you here," said a voice that was at once familiar to Mariah and baffling. Where had she heard it before? She'd heard it somewhere . . . often.

Just as the man rounded her chair Mariah's brain recognized the voice, and her body began to struggle almost before she could comprehend what she was thinking. The voice was that of Frank Hoffman, and sure enough, Hoffman was now standing in front of her, watching her buck uselessly against her restraints.

"Calm down," he said coldly.

Mariah's mind was racing. "What's happened to Curt? What the hell's going on here?" She almost ended the questions with "sir," by instinct, but caught herself just in time.

"So many questions," said Hoffman, with a cursory shake of his head. "If you must know, we're in a hut. On a reef. A barrier reef, to be precise. If you don't know what that is, it's a coral reef that runs along a shoreline and is separated from the land by a lagoon. So you can't just walk out of here." He started to laugh, harshly, but the laugh quickly turned into a hacking cough. When he'd finally settled himself he spoke again. "And you asked about Kennedy. He's still asleep. At least for now. Any more questions?"

Mariah tried to size up the man standing in front of her. There was that typical phrasing, clinical and precise, just like the man. But Mariah couldn't reconcile the physical appearance of the person standing in front of her with the stern, reserved, no-nonsense boss she'd seen on a daily basis for the past half-dozen years. The Frank Hoffman she knew from the Barn was professional to the point of coldness. He rarely laughed. He rarely showed any emotion whatsoever. Now, studying the face of this new version of Hoffman, Mariah saw gleaming, blood-shot eyes and a frozen half smile. *God*, she thought. *The man looks unhinged.* What was he doing here? What had happened to him? Her gaze fell to a large pistol tucked into his waistband. Was he going to kill them? *Keep him talking*, she thought, *and try not to antagonize him.*

"Why are you here, Frank?" she asked. Maybe using his

first name would connect with something in the old Frank Hoffman.

"Too many questions!" barked Hoffman, clenching his fists and then gradually relaxing them. "Right now I've got a job for you." He pointed toward the far side of the hut. "See that case on the table? One of the bottles inside is cracked. You'll find an empty bottle on the table. I need you to transfer the contents of the cracked bottle into the empty one." He bent down and began to release Mariah's bonds.

Mariah stared at the table, at the briefcase, the one that Omar had been carrying, with rum bottles that she knew didn't contain rum. Was he really going to make her handle the virus? No protection. Certain exposure. She looked back at Hoffman, at his determined, manic expression. *He doesn't care*, she suddenly realized. *He doesn't care if I die. No matter what I do, he's not going to let me live.*

Knowing this, facing up to it, gave her a strange feeling of liberation, a sense that it didn't matter how she handled the situation. She was free to take all the risk in the world because in a way she had nothing to lose. She stared hard at Hoffman. "Go to hell," she said, slowly and evenly, her eyes fixed on his.

Hoffman drew his arm back and slapped her, hard, across her right cheek.

At first Mariah forced herself not to cry out, to ignore the stinging pain, to hide her fear. She didn't want to give Hoffman the satisfaction of seeing her hurt. But the slap also awoke something within her. A burning rage and a desire to fight, with everything she had. And to win. But first she had to get free, and Hoffman had just given her an opening.

She started to whimper. "Please don't hurt me," she said, her eyes still on his. "I'll do what you want. I'll transfer the virus." She could tell by the startled expression on his face that he was surprised that she knew that the bottles contained virus, and that gave her more hope. If the new Frank Hoffman betrayed his feelings that easily, maybe she could get him to reveal more. She decided to be direct.

"What are you planning to do with it, Frank?" she asked.

"Frank? Quit calling me Frank! Call me by my proper name. *Doctor Vector*." At that, he broke into a fit of coughing. When he finally settled down, he reached into a pocket, pulled out a bottle of pills, and popped a couple into his mouth.

Who the hell was Doctor Vector? Mariah forced herself not to roll her eyes. Hoffman must be totally deluded. And sick as well. Looked like he'd lost quite a bit of weight since she'd last seen him at the Barn. Pasty-faced. Red-rimmed eyes. And a nasty cough. His defenses would be down. Or so she hoped. She'd keep asking questions. "Why should I call you Doctor Vector?" she asked.

"Shut up," barked Hoffman as he fumbled with the line that bound her to the chair. He straightened up, suppressed another cough, and pointed again at the table. "I'm waiting," he said.

She was now free. She stood and faced Hoffman. The gun was in his hand, pointed at her face. His finger was on the trigger. His eyes were no longer gleaming; they now looked more like what she remembered from the Barn. Cold, expressionless. She turned and walked toward the table, her mind racing. *Think like a scientist*, she told herself. That meant looking at the evidence, seeing connections, drawing conclusions, foreseeing possible outcomes. *Start with the evidence.* The virus had gone from the Barn to a remote lab in the Philippines where they'd scaled it up. Omar had been smuggling it into Borneo. Omar must work for Hoffman, a.k.a. Doctor Vector. Omar was apparently Pakistani, home to many Islamic extremists. Abu Sayyaf, a Muslim terrorist organization, was linked to al-Qaeda, also a Muslim terrorist organization. The date on the document in the safe: 9/11. Looked like they were planning a virus release on that date. But where? And who was behind it?

She needed to stall for time. She looked directly at Hoffman. "Can't I have some protective gear?" she asked, making her voice sound plaintive, scared. "At least a pair of gloves."

Hoffman waved his gun at her. "Get moving!" he yelled, then broke into another fit of coughing.

Mariah waited as Hoffman bent over double with his racking cough, somehow keeping his gun loosely trained on her. When he finally straightened up, she was even more shocked at his appearance. His eyes were now so bloodshot that they looked like swollen red disks. Worse, blood was running from his nose and dripping off his chin onto his long-sleeved T-shirt.

Hoffman pulled a stained handkerchief from his pocket and blotted his face. "What are you looking at?" he wheezed as he gripped the gun in both hands and aimed it at Mariah's head. "Move!"

Mariah knew she had no choice, and now she knew something else. Hoffman's illness was no bad cold or flu. The symptoms were obvious. The bloodshot eyes, the hacking cough, the bleeding from his nose, the aggressive behavior. The man had contracted Kandahar virus. And, if she wasn't careful, she'd end up being exposed herself. She had to take precautions, even if it might rile up her former boss even more.

Slowly backing away from Hoffman, she grabbed the hem of her blouse and tore the bottom into three strips. Making a double thickness, she placed one part around her nose and mouth and tied it behind her head. *Not much help*, she thought, *but better than nothing*. She wrapped the other pieces around her hands. The delay had given her more time to think.

She was pretty confident about the *who* part of the virus release. Hoffman—she was finding it hard to think of him as Doctor Vector—had to be the ringleader. He wasn't the type to defer to someone else's authority. Unless he was somehow being blackmailed, or had been hired by terrorists, but that seemed unlikely. Since the death of his wife, the only person in the world he'd seemed to care about, he had no one to live for. And what would he do with more money? His work was his life now.

The *where* and *why* questions were more vexing. They certainly wouldn't release the virus in Borneo, she thought. Not enough bang for the buck. Somewhere else in Southeast Asia? She reviewed Hoffman's career history in her mind. From what she knew, he'd never served in Asia, not even in Afghanistan, so she didn't think he had an ax to grind in this part of the world.

She forced herself to slow her thinking. *Focus on motive*, she told herself. *Hoffman's motive. Think. What drives him?* She ticked off what she knew. His work ethic. Super-patriotism. His devotion to his wife. Her death, and how she'd died. He'd have every reason to go after Islamic extremists, but instead he'd enlisted their help. It didn't add up.

She sifted through her memory. Something was nagging at her, something she should have remembered, something important. She looked over at Curt. He'd be able to help her remember. But he was still out cold, head slumped on his chest, breathing softly through his nose.

Now Hoffman was striding up to her, pressing the gun against her head. "I said move!" he said, pushing her roughly toward the table. Then he backed away toward the open door of the hut and positioned himself in the doorway, as if to block any effort on her part to escape. "Make it quick," he said. "And be sure you seal that bottle well. Use the silicone on the table."

Even if she wanted to escape—which she surely did—where could she go? thought Mariah. At this point, her best bet was to keep Hoffman talking, to try to get him to disclose more, perhaps help her to remember that important thing that was still nagging at her. She decided to play on his pride.

"Obviously you're aware that your boss is dead," she said as she edged slowly toward the table. "Omar."

"Omar!" cried Hoffman. "He's just a tool."

Mariah saw a fleeting look of regret on Hoffman's face. *He realizes he revealed too much*, she thought. *Keep him talking, play on that ego.* "Well, he was clever enough to figure out how to smuggle the virus out of the U.S. and bring it all the way to the southern Philippines," she said. "Not to mention set up a lab down here and recruit a bunch of terrorists." At this, she saw Hoffman's face redden, but this time he managed to keep his mouth shut.

She decided to try a bluff. "We captured a guy in Jolo," she said. "We know about the plan to release the virus on 9/11. He didn't say where, but it's a safe bet it'll be in a major U.S. city." She watched Hoffman's face closely, saw his mouth start to open then clamp shut. "Funny, I'd never have taken you for a terrorist," she said. "You're too dedicated to your work. And too much of a patriot, I thought."

"I am a patriot," he sputtered. "Proud of it. The U.S. is the greatest nation on earth. Or was."

"Was?" Mariah feigned confusion.

"Yes, was. We're losing our way of life. And the government's just sitting back and letting it happen!"

"So that's a reason to attack your own country?" said Mariah.

Hoffman stared at her. His mouth started to open, then closed, as if he had decided to shut off a response. Finally, he said, "Figure it out. You're not stupid."

Just how was she supposed to *figure it out*? She needed more information. "I doubt that virus is still viable," she said. "You've brought it all the way from the Barn. Unless you've kept it frozen, it's probably inactivated by now."

"You take me for an idiot?" said Hoffman. "You think I don't know that I need to use a cell culture?" At this, he broke into a cackling laugh that soon devolved into another fit of coughing.

"But even a cell culture needs to be maintained at a stable temperature," said Mariah. "Hardly the conditions in the southern Philippines."

"Obviously, you didn't look closely at that briefcase," said Hoffman. "Besides, I have a Plan B."

"And what would that be?" asked Mariah.

"Enough!" yelled Hoffman. "We're wasting time!" His face took on a stony expression again. He waved the gun at Mariah. "Now move."

"And if I don't?" said Mariah. She desperately wanted to stall for more time, to get Hoffman to keep talking.

With a sound between a snort and a snarl, he steadied the gun and fired.

As he waited for Curt and the others on the small island where he'd said good-bye to them that morning, Bill Cothran was frantic. It was already midafternoon and there'd been no sign of them. He'd watched them for as long as he could, but he'd lost them when their boat had rounded the island. They should have been back by now. Had something gone wrong?

For the umpteenth time, he raised his binoculars to his eyes and scanned the ocean. Nothing. Not even an indigenous boat. Despite his efforts to stay optimistic, he ran through a variety of scenarios, none of them positive. An accident. A losing battle at sea. Capture. Worse. And without a boat of his own, he had no way of searching for them.

He began to second-guess himself. He should have gone with them. But almost immediately he knew that would have been unnecessary, even foolish. Curt was at least as capable as he himself was of handling anything that came up. And four persons in that inflatable would have slowed it down way too much.

In a few hours, it would be dark. It was time to call the task force again. He'd kept in regular touch with them since the inflatable's departure. He glanced at his watch. Based on his last contact with the task force, the helicopter should be ready to go by now. It was time to initiate a search.

Mariah screamed—she couldn't help herself—as the noise of the shot boomed in the hut. For several seconds, she heard nothing more; then, as her hearing gradually came back, she was aware of a high-pitched ringing in her ears. She expected to feel pain but nothing seemed to hurt. She looked down at her feet, where Hoffman had pointed the gun. No blood, but a fist-sized hole in the floor of the hut. She was sure that if he'd wanted to hit her, he could have. He was just trying to scare her.

Knowing that Hoffman was deadly serious, she moved to the table, unlatched the case, and opened it. The three bottles were inside, secure in their Styrofoam inserts. She could see a small crack in one of them, but didn't see any signs of leaking. The other two bottles appeared to be unblemished. She slowly pulled an undamaged bottle from the case, hoping Hoffman would assume it was the cracked one. With her back to him, she set it upright on the table and pretended to be fumbling with the cap. She thought about what she'd learned so far. Clearly he was planning a virus release, but she still didn't know where.

Suddenly she remembered the thing that had been nagging at her. A discovery, back in the task force headquarters, in the safe on the table. An envelope full of currency. Euros and British sterling. Someone was going to Europe. Was Hoffman planning an attack there? England and the continent? And if so, why?

She needed more time to think. She shifted her position slightly to better screen her actions from Hoffman. She grabbed the empty bottle and turned around, holding it in front of her, her cloth-covered hands wrapped around it so that he couldn't see the contents. She turned and began to walk rapidly toward him. "This bottle's leaking badly," she said.

"You think you're scaring me?" said Hoffman. "Get back. I *will* shoot." He began to cough again.

Mariah kept walking.

"I'm warning you," gasped Hoffman between coughs. He gestured with the gun.

Mariah paused and waited. Soon Hoffman was no longer able to control his coughing. Blood was running from his nose and mouth. He bent over at the waist. Mariah stood still, swinging the bottle to and fro in her cupped hands, thinking, thinking. She went back to motive. *Hoffman has to hate Muslims*, she thought. They'd killed his wife. So why attack Europe? And why use Muslim terrorists to help him?

She tried to put herself into his mind. What was it he'd said? The government sitting back and letting it happen. What was *it*? She remembered something that Hoffman had said at a meeting back at the Barn, a year or so ago, that Western nations were coddling Muslims, that sharia law was taking root in European cities, and that it wouldn't be long before it happened in the United States as well. At the time she'd attributed his remarks to his super-patriotism. She'd heard such talk before from right-wing Americans. But after Curt had filled in some of the details of what had happened to Hoffman's wife, she began to see a bigger picture, a picture involving revenge. A terrible thought flashed through her mind. Was Hoffman scheming to launch a devastating attack in Western cities and make it look like Muslims were behind it? Was he *framing* Muslims? Did he figure that this would result in a massive counterattack against Muslim nations? A deranged, horrific plan. *But the man is crazy*, she thought.

She began to advance again toward Hoffman, who was still racked with coughing. She raised the bottle over her head.

Hoffman straightened up. Mariah deliberately looked over his shoulder through the open door, affecting surprise in her face. "What took you so long?" she yelled. Hoffman started to turn. *Now!* Mariah took a couple of rapid steps forward and swung the empty bottle down on the wrist of Hoffman's outstretched arm, the arm holding the gun. The pistol clattered to the floor. The force of the blow drove Hoffman back. He teetered on the edge of the porch, struggled to maintain his balance, and pitched over the side. Mariah heard some solid part of him—his head, she thought, wincing—clip the ladder and then a flat smack as he splashed into the lagoon below. Mariah moved to the edge of the porch and looked down. Hoffman floated below, motionless, blood pulsing from his temple, staining the seawater around him a reddish brown. The current began to sweep his body away. Mariah saw that the hut was anchored by sturdy posts to a coral reef, and that the water depth of the reef was very shallow. A narrow channel ran through the reef, and as Hoffman had said, a broad lagoon separated the reef from a landmass, which Mariah assumed was an island.

Trembling, she picked up the gun, placed it on the table, and walked over to Curt.

CHAPTER TWENTY-EIGHT

A man stood on a walkway above the south bank of the Thames River and gazed at the London Eye, a gigantic Ferris wheel with enclosed passenger capsules. It offered the best views in the city, the man knew. And the best vantage point for all manner of other tasks too.

He secured a waxed cotton hat more tightly on his head and turned up the collar of his raincoat against the chilly drizzle. He was glad it was raining. The weather was keeping most of the tourists away and he could carry out his reconnaissance without arousing suspicion. Not that he would normally look out of place. He'd lived in London for nearly twenty years and had learned to dress like a well-heeled Englishman, right down to the tan Burberry Westminster trench. Just what was needed to be a covert member of a sleeper cell.

He pulled a cell phone from his pocket and surreptitiously snapped a series of photos—of the cityscape up and down the river, and of the Eye and the ticket office. The office was open but only a few hardy tourists were buying tickets, and there was a notable absence of security in the area, not even a patrolling bobby. But he knew that in better weather, with larger crowds, there would be a police presence. He watched as the capsules discharged and embarked passengers, using the camera's zoom function to zero in on the operation of the capsule doors. He timed how long it took for a capsule to load new occupants and to rotate from ground level to the top of its arc. He slowly walked along the concrete path beside the river, counting his steps, noting where openings in the riverside barrier led to steps down to the water. He made a few notes on a small pad, glanced at his watch, and briskly made his way back toward the Waterloo tube station. His contact was expecting a report within the hour.

Mariah leaned over Curt and spoke to him softly but got no response. She released the ropes that bound him to the chair and gave his shoulder a gentle shake. "Come on," she said, trying to keep the panic out of her voice. "Wake up. Please." She heard him moan and then saw his eyes flutter open. "Shhh. Be quiet," she told him. She found a flask of water, uncapped it, and held it to his lips.

Curt took several swallows, gave a slight shake of his head, and looked around the hut. "What's going on?" he asked. "What's this place?" He started to rise from the chair.

Mariah gently placed a hand on his shoulder and eased him back down. "Take it easy. You've been out for a while." She picked up his ball cap from the floor beside the chair and handed it to him.

As Curt settled back in the chair Mariah triaged her thoughts. She willed herself to tell Curt about Angus, even though she knew that would hurt him more than anything else in the world. But he had to know. And she had to remain strong.

"Angus is gone," she said. She wanted to look away, to avoid seeing the hurt. But she kept his eyes on his, moved closer to comfort him.

For several seconds Curt said nothing, his eyes moving back and forth from Mariah to somewhere on the far wall, his face an expressionless mask. Finally, he said, "What happened?"

Mariah told him about the chase on the reef and the current funneling through the channel. She watched him closely. His face remained impassive, but he was now looking straight down toward the floor. She had come to know him well enough to realize that his avoidance of her gaze was a sign that he was struggling to contain his emotions. He wouldn't look back at her until he was under control again.

Finally, he looked up. "How did we get here?' he asked.

"After Angus and Omar were swept away, I was able to rescue the briefcase. Three containers of the virus inside. Disguised as bottles of rum. I was working my way back to you when the guy who'd fallen out of the pamboat showed up and overpowered me. He tied us up and brought us here. Must have drugged you or something. You've been out for a while." Mariah paused and looked intently at Curt. "And Hoffman—who is also Doctor Vector—was guarding us."

"Hoffman, Doctor Vector?" said Curt, confused.

Mariah nodded. "I was as shocked as you are," she said. "Claims Vector is his real name. The guy's totally crazy. Plus sick as hell. All the symptoms of Kandahar. I was able to get out of him that he was planning to release the virus in a city. Probably Europe. I'll explain more later. Right now we need to get out of here before someone comes looking for him."

"So where is Hoffman now?" asked Curt.

"I—he's gone," said Mariah. She turned away and tried to stave off a bout of trembling. "One of those bottles is cracked," she said, pointing to the table in the hut. "Hoffman thought it was leaking, but it's not. He tried to get me to transfer the contents to an empty bottle, but I hit him with it." She pointed to the veranda. "He fell off the porch and hit his head. He's gone now." She realized the trembling had begun again and made an effort to steady herself.

Curt rose from the chair, walked unsteadily to the porch, and looked out. "No sign of him," he said. "Must have floated away. Current's pretty strong." He glanced at the table. "His gun?" he asked.

Mariah nodded. "Knocked it out of his hand with the bottle."

Curt shook his head. He walked up to her, looked into her eyes, and wrapped his arms around her. He didn't speak.

Mariah buried her head in Curt's shoulder and sobbed quietly for several seconds. "Thank God it's over and you're okay," she said, knowing that there was no way he could be okay after losing his son again—this time for good. She pulled away and looked intently at him. "I'm so sorry about Angus." When Curt didn't respond, she said, "We've got to get going. The guy who brought us here could come back anytime."

Curt walked back to the door and looked back out at the lagoon. "No sign of a boat," he said. "I can see an island, maybe a mile or so away. Wonder if it's inhabited." He turned toward Mariah. "We could try swimming."

Then, from behind Curt, Mariah heard the clumping of footsteps ascending the wooden ladder. The hair on the back of her neck stood on end. A second later, Frank Hoffman's bloodied head appeared at the edge of the porch. Because she was closer to the table than Curt was, Mariah grabbed the gun, clutched it in both hands, and pointed it at Hoffman, who looked both crazed and utterly determined.

Calm down, she told herself urgently. *Steady your hands. Aim carefully, Mariah. Don't miss.*

Hoffman lurched through the doorway, blood oozing from his scalp, his mouth twisted into a snarl, staring at the gun in Mariah's hands. "Kill me, and Kennedy will never see his son again," he said. At this, both Mariah and Curt froze. Hoffman stood triumphantly, hands on his hips. "I see I've got *your* attention," he said to Curt.

Mariah quickly answered. "What are you talking about?" she said.

"Angus Friedman. We know he's Kennedy's son. He spilled his guts after we captured him in Manila."

"Even if that was true—which it's not," said Mariah, "Friedman was killed on the reef. With Omar."

Hoffman's lips were pressed together in a thin smile. He slowly shook his head. "We rescued them both," he said. "If you want Friedman to live, put the gun down on the floor. Slowly. Then push it over to me." He suppressed a rising cough.

"Don't listen to him, Mariah," said Curt. "He's bluffing. Give me the gun."

Mariah's mind raced. What would Curt do to Hoffman? What would the other terrorists do to Angus if Hoffman didn't return? She was pretty sure Curt would never see his son again in that case. She couldn't let that happen. The best thing to do now was to buy some time. She turned to Hoffman. "If I give you the gun, can you guarantee that Friedman will live?" she asked. "And us?"

Hoffman was silent. Mariah hoped he was thinking back to a few minutes ago, when she'd attacked him with the empty bottle. Would that have been enough to convince him that she wouldn't hesitate to use the gun?

"I can do that," he said finally.

"Why should we believe you?" asked Mariah.

"Easy." Hoffman pulled a portable radio from his trousers pocket, turned it on, and depressed the talk switch. "Transporter, this is Vector. Meet me at the hut as soon as you can. If anything has happened to me by the time you get here, pass the word to kill the kid." He turned to Curt and Mariah. "My guys will be here shortly. With Friedman. You give me the gun, we tie the three of you up when they get here, and we'll be long gone before anyone finds you. Friedman lives, you live, everyone wins."

"Except for most of the population of a Western city," said Curt. "Don't do it, Mariah. It's one life against thousands, maybe millions."

Curt had spoken forcefully, but Mariah now knew him well enough to pick up a note of uncertainty in his voice. She considered what he'd said. In his professional capacity, he had to say it. Based on the math alone, there really was no choice. But Angus was his son, a son he'd thought he'd lost again, for the second time since they were reunited. She tried to see the situation from his point of view. She'd never have the courage to sacrifice her own child even to save countless others. She forced herself to concentrate, to think objectively, professionally. Could she and Curt somehow get away, stop the plot, *and* free Angus before it was too late? She leaned down to place the gun on the floor. "We have to do this, Curt," she said. She slid the gun toward Hoffman. Curt didn't object. Was he trusting her to find a way out of this? Had he come up with an idea of his own? Or had his love for his son overwhelmed his professional training?

"Smart woman," said Hoffman, retrieving the gun. "Now get on the floor. Opposite sides of the hut."

For several minutes, Curt and Mariah sat in silence, with Hoffman's gun trained on them. Mariah watched him for signs of wooziness and was mystified as he continued to show none. He'd smashed his head into a ladder rung in the midst of a free fall of about fifteen feet, blood was running from his nose, and he frequently broke into bouts of coughing. He was obviously dying from Kandahar. How was he still alive, let alone standing here, holding her and Curt hostage? A superstitious voice in the back of Mariah's mind wondered if there was something subhuman about Hoffman at this point, if his rage and bitterness had formed some sort of inexplicable shield around him. Regardless, he had to know he was close to death. And that made him especially dangerous, a man who had nothing left to lose, who could risk all to accomplish his evil task.

She heard the sound of an approaching outboard motor. Hoffman backed up through the door of the hut and motioned with his gun for Curt and Mariah to join him. Less than a minute later, an inflatable boat pulled alongside the hut. Three men were inside. One was stocky with a ragged T-shirt. The guy from the pamboat, thought Mariah. The one with the RPG. The other, thinner man wore a dark ball cap. *Omar*. And the third: *Angus!* All three appeared to have cuts and scrapes but otherwise seemed in surprisingly good shape after their tumbles in the reef surf.

"Up here, Abdullah," Hoffman barked to the man in the old T-shirt. "And bring Friedman."

"Wait," said Mariah. "People are already looking for us. It's not like this hut is well hidden. If you leave us here, someone's bound to find us pretty quickly. The authorities will figure out what happened and it won't take them long to track you down. You're better off taking us with you, hiding us somewhere less conspicuous." She couldn't yet see what advantage this would give them, but her goal was still to buy time. Would her argument work with Hoffman, or would he be suspicious? Hopefully he'd think her motive was to save their lives. She looked at Hoffman. He seemed to be considering what she'd said. Good sign.

With his pistol trained on her and Curt, Hoffman looked over his shoulder down to the boat. "Okay, leave the boy there," he said. "Get up here and tie these two up. They're coming with us."

In an office just off the main newsroom of the *Philadelphia Inquirer*, Tony Parnell sat at a small table with the paper's metro and managing editors and tried to keep his eyes from closing.

It was late in Philadelphia, close to 10 p.m., and the last few days had been exhausting. He'd moved his family to his sister's place over the weekend and had been working day and night on a tight deadline to complete his latest and most important update on the Kandahar epidemic. He'd finished the long piece a couple of hours earlier, double-checked his facts and sources, and submitted it to the metro editor, who'd made a few cuts then passed it on to a copy editor for final corrections.

The windowless room was uncomfortably warm and smelled of body odor and stale coffee. As Parnell struggled to stay awake, the managing editor slowly scanned the article draft. She finally looked up at him over the top of her glasses. "So you're saying they're turning the corner on this thing?" she asked.

Parnell nodded. "According to the health authorities, the number of new cases has peaked and is starting to go down. And they've ramped up the manufacture of ribavirin—that's the antiviral drug. Seems to work well in newly diagnosed patients."

The managing editor looked back down at the copy. "See they still don't have a vaccine," she said.

"They're on an emergency crash program," said Parnell. "They've made progress, but production's still a ways away. Maybe a month or two, according to my source at FDA, but I agreed not to put that in the article. The agency is usually pretty closemouthed about vaccine timetables until the trials are done. They don't want to raise false hopes."

"You seem pretty upbeat about the financial situation," added the managing editor.

"I don't know about upbeat," said Parnell. "But even with that run on the banks a few days ago, we seem to have avoided a complete meltdown. You have to give the president credit—and his treasury secretary. They've done all they can to calm the nation. But there's still a lot of panic out there."

"That's an understatement," said the managing editor. "It's

like the Wild West. A lot of people are taking the law into their own hands, or ignoring the law completely. Crime's way up. But you know that." She turned to the metro editor. "You've gone through this carefully?" she asked.

"Fact-checked everything. Copy editor made a few grammatical and spelling changes. It's good to go."

"Okay. Get it proofed and ready for the early edition," said the managing editor. "We'll run it as the lead."

Sandwiched between their captors, Curt and Mariah made their way down the ladder of the hut and boarded the inflatable. Curt recognized it as the one they'd borrowed from the ex-priest in Sibutu. With what he hoped was a reassuring smile, he nodded at Angus, who was seated in the bow, facing aft, his arms behind his back.

Hoffman motioned for Curt and Mariah to sit beside Angus while Abdullah sat on the inflatable's middle seat next to Hoffman, facing forward, a gun leveled at them. Omar placed the briefcase with the bottles in the stern, started the engine, cast off the mooring line, and steered the boat toward the reef opening.

Smart move on Mariah's part to talk Hoffman into bringing them along, thought Curt. Could they take advantage of it? Cothran had mentioned a survival kit in the inflatable, somewhere in the bow. Anything he could use? What was in those things? Flares. Waterproof matches. Fishhooks and line. Maybe a small solar still. Reflecting mirror. Patch kit. What else? A knife? There had to be a knife. Where exactly would the kit be? Maybe under the seat. Close to one of the pontoons. Which side? How would he reach it?

The inflatable hit a wave, and Curt saw that Mariah almost bounced off her seat. It was impossible to hold on with their hands tied. That gave him an idea. He waited.

The boat pounded into another wave. Curt fell backward dramatically, cursing for effect. As if struggling to regain his seat, he maneuvered his body toward his side of the boat. He groped under the seat, along the side. *Nothing.* Abdullah was now moving, reaching toward him. "I'm trying to get up," yelled Curt, twisting on the bottom of the boat, working his body backward toward the other side. *There!* His hands fastened around a plastic pouch. He lunged forward and made out the sound of Velcro releasing. Could the others hear it? Abdullah reacted quickly. With his free hand, he grabbed Curt by the front of his shirt and jerked him back onto the seat.

Curt sat quietly, pretending to catch his breath, waiting. His captors soon relaxed their attentiveness. Except Hoffman. He'd never taken his eyes off Curt. But neither he nor Abdullah could see Curt's hands. Curt felt along the outside of the pouch. Holding it with one hand, he carefully inched the zipper open with the other, reached inside the opening, and groped the contents. A folding pocketknife, exactly what he had been hoping for. He forced his face to give away nothing, no relief, no exultation, nothing. If he could just release the blade—there. He felt the edge. Plenty sharp. He began to carefully saw at the line around his wrists, pulling the knife away every time the boat hit a wave. The last thing he needed to do was stab himself.

Abdullah and Hoffman were scrutinizing him closely now, suspiciously. They must know something was up, thought Curt. He gave up all pretense and began sawing quickly. Just as Abdullah rose to his feet and started shrieking at him, Curt's hands broke free and he lunged toward the man, slashing at his gun hand with the knife, striking his wrist with the open blade, cutting deeply. The gun fell to the bottom of the boat. Curt dove with his knife in front of him. Abdullah tried to twist away, but the knife penetrated his shoulder. Blood sprayed into the boat, a horrific geyser. The momentum of Curt's attack caused

Abdullah to lose his balance. The back of his knees buckled against the pontoon and he tumbled into the ocean.

Hoffman, who'd seemed paralyzed during the few seconds Curt was attacking Abdullah, now broke into action. He reached toward the gun in the bottom of the boat and instead found Curt lunging toward him with the knife. Hoffman rolled away, the knife blade narrowly missing him.

There was a scream from the water. Curt turned and saw Abdullah struggling, arms flailing above the sea surface—and something else, moving just underwater. A fin cut through the surface, and a sleek, dark form raced toward Abdullah's body, which gave a slight shudder when the shark reached it. Curt heard more screams.

"Give me the knife!" yelled Hoffman in a labored gasp. "Now!"

Stupid! Kennedy scolded himself. He'd allowed himself to get distracted. Now Hoffman had the gun. Omar was still at the outboard. Hoffman leaned forward, his eyes bulging, and aimed the gun at Curt's head. Curt realized he had no choice and grudgingly handed over the knife.

"Okay. You guys are next," wheezed Hoffman. "Over the side."

Curt looked at the growing red stain in the water around Abdullah's shuddering form. He turned back to Hoffman. "Fuck you," he said.

The sound of a gunshot nearly deafened him. Was he hit? Nothing hurt. He looked at Mariah and Angus, and was relieved to see that they both seemed okay.

"The next shot goes into you," said Hoffman. "One way or another, you all go over the side. Alive or dead. Your choice." He began to cough, then caught himself and spat over the side.

"Leave them alone," said Curt. "I'll go. Just let them live. They're harmless." Without waiting for an answer, he rolled over the side. When he resurfaced after momentarily submerging, he heard Hoffman yelling and saw him point the gun toward

Mariah and Angus. Helpless to intervene, willing the sharks to keep their distance, Curt watched Mariah and his son stand shakily. *For God's sake, at least untie them*, he screamed silently. Then he saw Hoffman give Mariah a hard push and watched as she toppled over the side. Without delay, Angus jumped in after her.

Curt quickly swam to them, positioning himself to screen their view of the sharks, which continued to feed on Abdullah's corpse mere yards away. There were no more sounds from Abdullah now, but what was left of his body continued to jerk and bob as the sharks barreled against it, tearing off chunks of flesh. Curt knew the sharks would sense them soon. How long did they have? He heard a shout from the boat. Hoffman was yelling to Omar to take off, that their captives were now just shark bait. Curt figured that Hoffman was deranged enough to prefer that they die horrifically rather than waste bullets on them. He heard the outboard motor rev up and saw the boat begin to move away. Curt quickly moved behind Mariah and Angus and untied them. "Swim," he said. "As fast as you can. Move."

"What about your arm?" asked Mariah.

"I have two," said Curt.

"We shouldn't have that far to go," said Mariah. "Those guys dumped us out not that far away from the hut." Treading water, she raised her head as far as she could. "I see it!" she said, pointing. "Maybe a mile away."

Curt didn't doubt her. Perched above the barrier reef on its high posts, the hut should be visible for at least a mile, even from the sea surface. But it was a hazy day, and try as he might, he couldn't make it out.

Then Angus spoke. "I see it too."

Mariah began to swim, in a slow crawl. She looked back over her shoulder. Just follow behind me," she said. "We'll rest whenever you need to."

Curt was happy to have Mariah lead the way. He remembered that she'd told him that she'd been a swimmer in high school, and that that was one of the reasons she wanted to qualify in scuba. He swam behind her, alongside Angus, doing a sidestroke with his good arm, the other pressed to his side, his legs scissoring back and forth with a steady motion. Thankfully, the swells had died down and there was little wind. Their biggest challenge would be making it to the hut before dark. Assuming the waves didn't bash them to pieces on the coral, they should be able to rest there until morning, and then make their way across the lagoon, which he hoped was shallow, to the island he'd seen from the hut. He willed himself, and the others, not to look back. The last time he'd glanced toward Abdullah's remains, there seemed to be fewer fins circling than there had been before. He didn't know where the other sharks had gone. He couldn't think about it.

After several minutes, Mariah signaled a halt. As they all rested, she asked them how they were doing.

"Could be better," said Angus. "Never was much of a swimmer, even living in Hawaii as a kid. And I banged up my shoulder earlier. But don't slow up for me. I won't be that far behind."

"We stay together," said Mariah firmly. "Steady, even pace. Use your legs. Watch me." She demonstrated a sidestroke and scissors kick.

They resumed swimming, taking frequent rest breaks. After an hour or so, they paused again to take stock. Curt could now see the hut, but it looked to be at least a half mile away and the sun was only a couple of degrees above the horizon. He figured there was no way they could make it to the hut before dark. His right shoulder and legs were burning. His left arm, the wounded one, was numb, useless, and he could see that it was bleeding again. He remembered something else: sharks were more active after sunset.

Curt glanced over at his companions. Mariah looked strong and neither was complaining, but Angus was gasping for breath and his face looked drawn and haggard. His mind began to gallop forward into darkness. Was this it? They'd survived gun battles, knife fights, a viral epidemic, he'd finally found two people he cared deeply about, one a long-lost son, and this was the end? He looked more closely at Mariah and saw fierce determination in her eyes. Her arm was wrapped around Angus and she was telling his son that they didn't have far to go. He began to swim again.

CHAPTER TWENTY-NINE

Bill Cothran leaned out of the open door of the UH-60 Black Hawk helicopter and peered at the sea surface a hundred feet below. Besides himself, the copter carried a crew of four: pilot, copilot, and two rescue swimmers. The sun had set an hour earlier and darkness was closing in fast. They'd been searching for two hours already, ever since he'd been picked up on the small island by the task force contingent.

Cothran figured they'd have less than a half hour to find Curt, Mariah, and Angus without artificial light. They'd been searching in semicircular arcs emanating from where the inflatable had left the beach early that morning, and there was still a lot of ocean to cover out to the farthest radius the boat could have reached in that time. It was like looking for a needle in a haystack. And after dark, finding something as small as an inflatable—or a body—would be all but impossible even with the single powerful searchlight installed on the helicopter.

One of the rescue swimmers shouted and pointed. Just ahead, on a shallow reef, Cothran could see a small structure. The helicopter swooped down. The structure materialized as a thatch-roofed hut on raised pilings. They moved in for a closer look.

261

At first, they saw no activity, no sign of life. As they debated whether to lower one of the swimmers to examine the hut more thoroughly, Cothran saw something floating near the shack. The pilot brought the copter down to a few yards above the sea surface. The floating object was a baseball cap.

It was well after dark. Though the night was clear, the moon had not yet risen and Curt could barely see his hands in front of his face. He wasn't even sure they were still swimming in the right direction. Adding to the problem, Angus was no longer capable of swimming on his own. With his good arm, Curt had been trying to help Mariah pull his son along, but it had been very slow going and he was exhausted. Then something bumped his leg.

Curt forced himself not to recoil, not to betray his fear about what might have hit him. But he knew they had a decision to make. Keep swimming in what might turn out to be entirely the wrong direction until, utterly spent, they slipped below the sea surface, one by one? Or save their strength and slowly tread water, waiting for daylight, easy prey for circling sharks? Should he share his thoughts with Mariah? But if he betrayed his uncertainty, what would it do to her morale—and Angus's?

Then Mariah spoke. "Rest break," she said, rolling onto her back and floating motionless in the now calm sea. She pointed toward the sky. "I've been checking that constellation. We're still moving in the right direction. Based on our swimming speed, I figure we should be at the hut in an hour or so."

Curt thought she was being overly optimistic. Even if they made it to the reef, how would they ever find the hut? But he was grateful for Mariah's swimming ability, for keeping their spirits up, and for her calming steadiness. Following her lead, he floated on his back, gulping in fresh drafts of cool marine air, his good arm propping up his son. Then he saw a bright light shining down on the water's surface.

Around 4:00 a.m. the following morning, a squad of three soldiers in camo fatigues, faces blackened, crouched in a tangle of twisted mangrove tree limbs and peered through night-vision binoculars at an inflatable dinghy approaching the shoreline of Sabah, Borneo. The boat carried two men. The sound of its engine echoed off the forest canopy, and soon it nosed against the muddy bank and came to a stop. A stocky man in the bow stepped out, carrying a case. His feet squelched in the thick mud. A thin man in the stern killed the engine, disembarked, and began to secure the boat to a tree.

Now, thought the squad leader, a young sergeant. He had the element of surprise. The intruders would be bogged down by the mud, slowing their reaction time. Their hands would be occupied by the bowline and case. Their weapons would probably be tucked away, in pockets or waistbands. And they'd take a few moments to locate him, even aided by the pale light of a waning gibbous moon filtering through the forest canopy. The sergeant had ordered his men to remain hidden in the trees, to keep their binoculars trained on the visitors, and to watch for sudden movements like a grab for a weapon. He stood, his pistol extended at arm's length, and yelled, "Hands up!"

In the faint moonlight he saw the bow man suddenly duck behind the hull of the inflatable, a reaction he hadn't anticipated. Now he could no longer see the man, couldn't even tell where to aim his .45.

The soldier's abrupt realization that he was about to be shot coincided exactly with his view of a bright muzzle flash at the boat. A microsecond later, he felt a searing pain in his side and a violent blow that spun him around and propelled him into a tree.

The other soldiers quickly returned fire. The stern man screamed and went down. Clutching the case and firing back over his shoulder, the bow man lurched out of the mud and darted into the forest as a hail of bullets shredded the leaves around him.

Ignoring his pain, the sergeant ordered his soldiers to disarm the downed man and pursue the other. While they were gone he checked his side. Minimal bleeding, superficial wound. What hurt more was his right shoulder, all out of kilter, probably dislocated when he'd hit the tree. He made himself as comfortable as possible, reloaded his weapon, and waited for his men to return. He could hear the wounded man moaning by the inflatable. Still alive. Maybe they could get some information out of him.

Minutes later, he heard noises coming through the forest. The other soldiers emerged. They had a briefcase with them, but no captive. They told the sergeant that they'd followed footsteps and broken limbs, then lost the trail at a stream bank. Chances were the fleeing man wouldn't get too far, they said. The jungle was all but impenetrable. They'd tend to their squad leader and then resume the pursuit.

In a small cabin near Pennsylvania's Allegheny National Forest, just south of the New York border, Sally Parnell sat across from her sister, Frederica, at a worn Formica table in the kitchen. Her seven-year-old son, Bobby, was upstairs, asleep. At least he was supposed to be asleep. The previous evening she'd checked on him well after his bedtime and had found him reading under the bedcovers. She'd scolded him, of course, but was secretly glad that he seemed to have inherited Tony's and her love of books.

She sipped from a cup of herbal tea and looked at her sister, saw worry in her eyes, and sensed that she wanted to say something. She knew Fredi well enough to predict that she wouldn't be able to contain her thoughts. "Okay, what is it?" she asked her.

"You know it's not safe, even here," her sister blurted out. Then she was silent, as if waiting for Sally to challenge her.

Sally wasn't surprised by the remark. Fredi had always had a streak of paranoia. Usually Sally would humor her instead of arguing. Her sister was a naturally skilled debater and at least as well read as Sally, though her reading tastes differed from her own preference for classical literature. Mysteries and thrillers, often with some kind of conspiracy theme. But Fredi seemed genuinely worried, which in turn worried Sally, because, of all the places she and Bobby could be right now, she couldn't imagine a safer one.

"What's not safe?" Sally asked.

"Look," said Fredi. "People are panicking. Rioting. Looting. Breaking into banks. There's no more law and order. The police and National Guard can't control the mobs. They've been concentrating resources on large towns and cities where they're overwhelmed. No way can they afford to send forces to protect people in rural areas. And don't kid yourself. It won't take long for the yahoos to realize they'd have easy pickings in areas like this. Not even any neighbors. We'd be sitting ducks."

Leave it to her sister to see the dark side of everything, Sally thought. She admitted to herself that Fredi might have a point if the cabin were closer to Philadelphia, where everything was going to hell. But way up here? "Come on, Fredi," she said. "We're two hundred miles from the quarantine zone."

"And what would *you* do if you were trying to escape the epidemic and all the crap that's come down with it? You'd get as far away as you could. Haven't you heard about the battles at the borders? Panicked Americans determined to get out of the country, Mexican and Canadian border agents just as determined not to let them through."

"You still haven't said why they'd come around here," said Sally, realizing that her voice sounded less confident than before, as if she was already conceding that her sister's logic wasn't as warped as she'd like to believe.

"Think about it," said Fredi. "You're trying to get away from a spreading, deadly disease, knowing that any day your town, your home, will fall into the quarantine zone, that even before that happens you'll probably be loaded onto a train and shipped off to some desert military installation. Commerce has broken down, banks are closed, you can't get money to buy necessities even if they were available, which in fact they're not anymore in much of southeastern Pennsylvania. You're prevented from leaving the country. The rest of the world isn't even accepting flights coming in from the U.S. So where would you go? Sparsely populated rural America, where you'd have less chance of catching the disease, where when you're forced to steal to survive, there's not going to be law enforcement around to stop you. Look at a map. If you're living near the epidemic, this part of Pennsylvania is the closest large, low-population rural area. Two hundred miles is nothing."

Fredi paused, thrust her head forward, and looked directly at Sally. "They've already had home invasions in the county," she said meaningfully.

Sally looked at her sister, who'd leaned back in the kitchen chair, silent again, shoulders slumped, as if the monologue had drained all her energy. Sally didn't say anything for some time. It was pretty clear that Fredi, who'd never married, had always lived alone, was losing it, which was understandable given her isolation up here in this lonely cabin, the current situation, and her characteristic paranoid tendencies. She figured Fredi had been closely following the increasingly dire news about the spreading epidemic, and she'd had no one to talk with about it and had obviously let her imagination run wild. Still, Sally wasn't quite ready to dismiss out of hand her sister's fears, especially if that news about the home invasions was accurate.

Finally, she asked Fredi, "So what would you propose we do?"

CHAPTER THIRTY

Doctor Vector moved deliberately to the waiting immigration agent at London's Heathrow Airport. He walked slowly, in part to appear calm and unhurried, in part to avoid breaking into a hacking cough, and mostly because of sheer exhaustion.

He handed a fake passport and a customs form to the official and waited, expressionless. After several seconds of scrutiny and a question about the purpose of the visit, the agent entered some data in a computer, stamped the passport, handed back the documents, and motioned to the next person in line.

Vector headed toward the exit. He knew that cameras were watching his every move, that, this being London, he would be under photographic surveillance nearly every minute he was in the city. It was only a matter of time before he was found. But he had one last thing to do before he died.

He carried only a small backpack and a plastic bag marked *Duty Free* that contained a bottle labeled *Tanduay Rhum, for Export.* Omar had come up with the idea of disguising the virus as liquor, and he'd had a contact inside the Kuala Lumpur duty-free shop who'd made the necessary arrangements to get the bottle aboard the plane. Vector's pack also held a large, two-layer plastic container. The top held a dwindling supply of ribavirin pills. The bottom layer held something else.

Doctor Vector rounded a corner and saw a sea of people waiting for arriving passengers. He shouldered his way through them, exited through a pair of glass doors, and paused at the edge of a roadside curb. The coughing was coming on again and he couldn't control it. For the better part of a minute, he hacked spasmodically into a handkerchief. When he finally stopped, the handkerchief was stained bright crimson. He tossed it into a nearby trash barrel and made a mental note to pick up a few packets of Kleenex, or whatever the British equivalent was. He flagged down a cab. Two more days, he told himself. He just needed to live two more days. Two days to lie low, to wait, to endlessly rehearse the plan in his mind, to visualize the satisfying outcome. He'd go over every detail in his mind and then review again, and again. He couldn't afford a single mistake.

"So you have some news?" said Curt as he, Mariah, and Angus met with Cothran at the task force headquarters in Jolo. They'd spent the last two days recuperating there, but were now mostly strong enough to continue the hunt. Earlier Cothran had told them that Omar had been killed in a task force ambush in Borneo, but that Hoffman had gotten away. He'd added that they'd recovered the briefcase but it looked like one bottle was missing.

Cothran nodded. "We sent Hoffman's photo to every major airport in Southeast Asia, the U.S., and Europe. Got a hit in London this morning, UK time. Gate agent remembered the guy was carrying a bag from duty free."

"Chances are that's the missing virus bottle," said Mariah. "Disguised as rum. He must have had inside help."

"Sounds logical," said Cothran. "The UK authorities found video of him leaving the airport and boarding a taxi. Picked up his image again near St. James's Park, then lost him. They're still looking. Posted copies of the photo everywhere and put his image on TV. And they're broadcasting an announcement asking the public to be alert for any suspicious activities."

"They should put out the info that the guy's sick," said Mariah. "People should be aware that he might be coughing. And they should keep their distance."

"Today's the ninth, London time," said Curt. "If he's planning a 9/11 release, he'll probably stay undercover until then. Let's hope the UK authorities are vigilant."

As she listened to Cothran, Mariah studied Angus. It was hard to believe that it was only a week ago that he'd been captured in Manila. But he did seem strong and confident. And it seemed like he couldn't take his eyes off Curt.

Doctor Vector sat in a dark far corner of the Ploughshare, a small pub in the Westminster section of London, near St. James's Park. He'd chosen this tavern in part because of its location, only minutes away from the Eye, but mostly because it was a bit off the beaten track, even for this bustling part of the city, and tended to have fewer visitors than a more popular pub like the Feathers. He'd weighed the advantages of going to a busier place, where he could get lost in the crowd, against the likelihood that law enforcement would be carefully watching the better-known establishments. Not that they wouldn't be watching everywhere, he thought, but other than a security camera outside the front door, he hadn't seen any signs of electronic surveillance here.

Still, he kept a close watch on the entrance as he picked at a shepherd's pie, his first meal since Borneo. He had no appetite. In fact, even the sight of food made him feel like gagging, but he knew he needed to eat, needed all the strength he could muster—at least for the next two days.

He'd scrutinized the building on the way in, noting where the exits were, rehearsing routes of escape. The kitchen door was right behind his booth. Before he'd entered, he'd located the external entrance to the kitchen, in an alley, where food was delivered and garbage removed. He'd need a rapid exit if he was discovered. He knew he couldn't move fast with this damnable sickness. But his preparation should allow him to slip out before any suspecting authorities could grab him.

As he chewed another mouthful of food, he saw the front door open. Two men stepped into the pub, both medium height, wearing Manchester United football jerseys. It was immediately obvious to Vector that these weren't football fans stopping by for a few pints while they watched the game on the pub telly. These guys were broad-shouldered and lean-waisted. One was square-jawed with a large head and a thick neck. The other was thinner with an aquiline face and nervous, darting eyes. Vector could make out slight bulges at their waists under their loose-fitting jerseys. The men didn't head to a vacant table. They paused in the doorway, their eyes flicking around the room. Vector quickly ruled out MI5 or MI6. Those agents wouldn't dress like these guys, wouldn't be so obvious, would know better than to stand right in the front door and scope out the room. The guys who just walked in were almost certainly undercover metropolitan police, no doubt tough enough but without the range of skills of MI5 and 6 agents. And that gave him a distinct advantage.

Vector quickly considered his options. He could remain at his table, head down, ball cap pulled low over his eyes, and hope they didn't notice or recognize him. He could create a distraction, yell "fire" maybe, and escape in the confusion. Or he could scoot out through the kitchen, with at least a head start. He had perhaps two seconds to make his decision.

He chose option three.

He swiveled in his booth, planted his feet, ducked low, and propelled himself through the swinging kitchen doors. The exit was to the left, just beyond the sinks. Dodging around a startled kitchen staffer, he raced to the door, threw himself against the crash bar, and rushed through the opening. He was in the alley. As he gasped for breath and tried to keep from coughing, he saw a large trash barrel and maneuvered it against the door, knowing it would only slow his pursuers momentarily, but, still, would give him more time to prepare.

The brief burst of activity had sapped nearly all of Vector's strength, and pain surged through his body like an electric current. He was under no illusions about being able to outrun the men. They'd catch him pretty quickly. If they were smart, like him, one would follow through the kitchen and the other would run around and block the alley exit, radioing ahead for backup. But he didn't think they were that smart. They'd be on him like two dumb hounds after a fox, thinking they had him, visualizing the accolades and promotions that would follow after the capture.

In his earlier inspection of the alley, Vector had seen a large Dumpster just outside the kitchen exit. Wheezing heavily, he quickly moved behind it, out of sight of anyone coming through the door. He crouched and waited in the shadows. He wasn't armed because it would have been impossible to get a gun aboard the flight from Malaysia, let alone through Heathrow, but he had a weapon, which was more than enough for his purposes: a thin, metal ballpoint pen, picked up at duty free in Kuala Lumpur.

He heard the sound of the door opening and the trash can scraping on the pavement. He positioned his feet, bent his head, and peered under the Dumpster. There were two pairs of legs on the other side of the trash bin, side by side, facing the far end of the alley, obviously looking for a fleeing man. It was a long alley, and when they didn't see him they'd likely conclude he was still in here somewhere. Chances were they'd check the Dumpster first, then look for other doorways in the alley. He waited, clutching the pen in his right hand, balanced on the balls of his feet, listening for any conversation that would betray the hounds' next move. He willed fresh energy into his body.

Their legs were moving now, toward the Dumpster. They were coming around the side to his right, where there was only a narrow space between the Dumpster and adjacent wall, where they'd have to go through the opening one at a time. Slowly, very slowly, Vector raised his head and noiselessly pivoted his feet to the right, still crouched, leaning slightly forward, the pen gripped tightly in his hand and now positioned so that its tip pointed straight up. His next moves would take virtually all of his remaining strength. He steeled himself for what he knew he had to do, rehearsed in his mind the close-in, hand-to-hand combat training he'd had years before, training you never really forgot, though you could get rusty without practice.

The thick-necked guy appeared first, head peering around the corner of the Dumpster, not seeing anything right away, then moving his whole body into the opening.

Vector sprang forward and upward, the pen held in front of him, his elbow locked and pressed against his side to assure maximum thrust. By the time he reached the policeman, he'd gained enough momentum to knock over a man twice his size. Ideally he would have aimed for an eye, but the dim light would have made it too easy to miss the target. The neck would be better.

He drove the pen into the policeman's jugular and simultaneously brought a knee up, hard and fast, into the man's groin. The man made a gurgling noise and toppled back into the man behind. Both went down. A jet of blood sprayed from the protruding pen. Vector raised his foot and brought a heavy boot down on the face of the second man, heard the sound of crunching bones. He balled his fist and delivered a powerful blow to the chest of the first man, right at the heart. The man wheezed and went silent. Vector turned back to the second man, wrapped his hands around his head, gripped hard, and gave the head a violent twist, first one way and then the other. He heard the sound of tearing cartilage, saw the man's eyes bulge out, and felt the neck go loose in his hands.

He bent low, checked for pulses. Nothing. Thirty seconds. That's all it had taken. As he gasped for breath and began coughing again, Vector allowed himself a brief moment of self-satisfaction. Obviously these guys hadn't known much about him, hadn't known who he was, what he was capable of. He stood, wiped his hands on his pants, and began to plan his next moves.

CHAPTER THIRTY-ONE

SEPTEMBER 9

Sally Parnell sat bolt upright in bed. She'd heard a noise, sounded like it was coming from downstairs. She remained motionless, slowed her breathing, listened. A gust of wind rattled the bedroom window and raindrops spattered the glass. Is that what she'd heard, what had awakened her? Just the storm?

She pushed a small button on her wristwatch, illuminating the dial: 4:10 a.m. She glanced over at the cot next to her. She could hear Bobby's soft snores. There was no noise from the adjacent bedroom, where Fredi was sleeping. She listened for a few more seconds. Wind and rain, Bobby's peaceful snoring. That was it. Nothing more. She lay back in her bed, settled her head on the pillow, and closed her eyes.

Heard the noise again.

Saw light outside the bedroom window. But it was way too early for sunrise.

She lay as still as possible. There was the sound again. Close. Not the wind or Bobby's snores. It was definitely coming from downstairs somewhere. Clunking footsteps, muffled voices. On the porch?

Then she heard the sound of breaking glass.

Two days earlier, Sally had finally agreed to her sister's plan, partly because Fredi had been so adamant, partly because she had a nagging feeling that Fredi might be right, but mostly because there really wasn't anything to lose by doing what her sister had urged, and it wasn't like Sally had anything else to do. So they'd prepared. Since she'd moved to the cabin, Fredi had become something of a survivalist and the place was already a minifortress, with battery-operated, motion-sensing outdoor spotlights, reinforced doors with triple-bolt locks, heavy wooden shutters on the inside of each downstairs window, even a safe room. Now they'd beefed up the defenses with various other protective measures—many of which Sally thought were over-the-top, but she didn't argue—and weapons ready at strategic locations. No firearms; Fredi didn't believe in guns. She said that if intruders found you with one, they'd be more likely to use their own. And no dog, which might have been the best defense of all. Too much trouble, her sister had said.

Fredi had also worked up a step-by-step protocol for what to do if they had unwelcome visitors, and she'd insisted on rehearsing it. As Sally threw back the covers and swung her legs over the side of the bed, she ran through the sequence in her mind. Step one was to make sure her sister was awake. She ducked low so that anyone looking up at the bedroom window wouldn't see her shadowy form.

Fredi was already up, fully dressed, clutching a canister of pepper spray. After a brief whispered conference, Sally returned to her room to focus on step two: her son. She moved to his bed and gently shook his shoulder. "Sweetheart. Wake up, Bobby," she whispered. He moaned and rolled over. She shook him harder.

"Wha . . . " he said.

Sally placed a gentle hand over his mouth, wanting to alarm him as little as possible. "Shhh," she said. "Time to go to the playroom." There was a secret place in the back of the bedroom closet, accessed through a heavy metal door hidden by hanging clothes.

When they'd practiced this earlier, Sally had told Bobby it was like a game. She'd had to tell the boy that some bad people might be coming to the house and that if they did, he was to hide in there until she told him it was safe to come out. The inside of the door was fitted with a heavy-duty dead bolt. There was a light in the room, some toys, bottled water, even a few snacks. There was a porta-potty and a comfortable foam mattress, blanket, and pillow. And there were books, lots of them, some of Bobby's favorites. She knew he was apprehensive, even scared, but he was a brave boy, and when he saw the space, and especially the books, she could tell he felt more at ease.

Crouching down, she led him into the closet and opened the inner door. She reviewed the secret knock with him, five rapid taps, a pause, then two more. Under no circumstances was he to open the door unless he heard that signal. She kissed him quickly on the cheek, not wanting to make it seem like more than a brief casual good-bye. "See you soon," she whispered. "Don't forget to lock the door when you get inside." She waited until he'd entered the space, closed the door behind him, and slid the bolt into place.

She quickly rejoined Fredi. "Got your cell phone?" her sister asked. "I can't get a signal on mine."

The cabin didn't have a landline and Sally had already learned that cell service here was spotty and affected by weather. She turned on her phone and waited. One bar. She pulled up her husband's number and touched the screen. She and her sister had previously agreed that they'd first call Tony if anything went wrong. As a reporter, he always kept his phone charged and handy and he'd ask the right questions, know who to call in an emergency, even 911, though first responders would take at least an hour to get to the cabin. It would be a six-hour drive for Tony.

Tony answered right away. "Someone's trying to break in,"

said Sally. There was silence on the other end. "Tony?" she said. "Can you hear me?" No answer. She looked at the phone, saw the word in the upper left where the bars should be: *Searching . . . Damn*. Sally knew she could get a steady signal outside, in a clearing up on the hill. But that wasn't an option now.

She heard the sound of crashing downstairs, and then splintering wood. She exchanged glances with Fredi, and together they ducked back into Fredi's room. They grabbed weapons there—an old wooden baseball bat for Sally and a fireplace poker for Fredi—and then began to creep down the stairs.

The fight in the alley had sapped nearly all of Doctor Vector's strength, strength that he desperately needed to recover before the big event, the day after tomorrow. After confirming that the two policemen were dead, he'd left the alley as quickly as possible and ducked into a stall in a public restroom at Waterloo Station. There he'd taken several minutes to collect himself, consult a large folding map of the city, and plan his next moves. He'd then made a few purchases from a shop on a nearby side street.

He was now back in a small flat on the third floor of a walk-up apartment building. Shortly after arriving in London, he'd rented the room from a stringy-haired, matronly woman who'd been content to simply take his cash and not ask questions.

Vector dumped his purchases out on the bed and sorted through them. Scissors, sunglasses, ball cap, small backpack, paperback novel, and a supply of energy bars. On his way to the pub earlier in the day, he'd seen that his likeness had been plastered all along the route. He had no time to effect a truly professional disguise; these items would have to do.

Thirty minutes later, he scrutinized his appearance in a small mirror. *Not bad*, he told himself. The cap and sunglasses were a big help. He checked his ribavirin supply. Enough for three more days, a day more than he needed. He shook a couple out, filled a water glass from the communal bathroom down the hall, and popped the pills into his mouth.

Just two more days, he told himself. Two more days before he would set off a spectacular series of events. Then he could join Karen, his devoted wife, the love of his life, secure in the knowledge that he'd avenged her awful death. He stretched out on the lumpy mattress, flicked on the bedside lamp, and reached for the paperback.

Sally and Fredi reached the bottom step and paused. The splintering noise was coming from the front living room window. Remembering the earlier breaking glass, Sally figured the intruders were trying to breach the shutters that were not really shutters at all, but strong barriers, solid oak affairs with a row of heavy dead bolts to hold them shut. They'd need an ax to break through those things, and that's what it sounded like they were using. How long before they were successful? Twenty, thirty minutes? But she and Fredi had another defense that would buy more time.

Without conversing, Sally and her sister crept to the large stone fireplace and removed a flat, thick steel plate that was covering the opening. They muscled the plate up against the wooden shutter, and secured it with prepositioned iron brackets that swiveled into place, firmly fastening it to the window frame.

Sally checked the time: 4:45. Still almost two hours before sunrise. Would the intruders leave when the sun came up? Could she and Fredi hold out until then?

They inspected the other windows on the first floor. All secure. No way of knowing how many intruders were out there or whether they would try multiple possible entry points. The ground floor had three rooms: large open living room, kitchen, and bath. All the rooms had windows with the heavy oak shutters. There was only one metal plate, but Sally hoped that if it successfully blocked the first window, the invaders would logically assume that all the windows were similarly reinforced. She and Fredi positioned themselves on chairs so that they had a view of the entire ground floor. Outside, the crashing, splintering noises continued, seemingly louder than ever.

Minutes later, Sally heard the dull clang of metal on metal. *They're through the shutter now*, she thought. Would they give up when they realized that the ax wouldn't work on the metal plate? She sat quietly, waiting, hearing loud voices, curses, the clanging sounds of the ax striking the metal plate. Then it grew quiet. She waited several minutes, hearing nothing more. She looked over at Fredi, caught her eye, communicated an unspoken question. She saw her sister shake her head and point to her wrist, then hold up her hands and flash her ten fingers twice. Twenty minutes.

They both sat as motionless as possible, heard no more noise from outside. Twenty minutes passed. Fredi was making no effort to move. Sally couldn't stop thinking about Bobby. *He must be going crazy up there*, she thought. Finally, after thirty minutes had passed, she stood and crept over to her sister. "I'm going to check on Bobby," she whispered.

"Okay," said Fredi. "Just be sure to look outside from the second-floor windows first. Make sure they've gone."

Sally nodded and ascended the stairs, two quiet steps at a time. Before entering her bedroom, she looked out the window on the opposite side of the house and was momentarily jarred by the darkness she saw outside. Earlier, the outside lights had been on. But they were motion-activated, she remembered now.

If it had been still enough outside for the lights to go out, the intruders must have left.

She entered the bedroom, flipped the light switch, and glanced toward the window.

A face was staring back at her.

CHAPTER THIRTY-TWO

SEPTEMBER 11

At midmorning, an excited throng of tourists filed into a passenger capsule of the London Eye. Doctor Vector was the last person to board. He wore a loose-fitting green parka. Long, blond hair curled from beneath his ball cap, which bore the logo of the Toronto Blue Jays. He had sunglasses on to hide his bloodshot eyes. Since the incident behind the restaurant, posters had been plastered all over the city, broadcasting his description but accompanied by a sketch that, to his relief, looked almost nothing like his current appearance.

After Vector had stepped through the capsule opening, the doors began to automatically slide shut. Just before they closed completely, he surreptitiously placed a short, hard plastic tube in the gap. When the doors were secure, the rubber gasketing on their edges held the tube in place. He then focused on controlling his breathing to avoid breaking into a cough. In addition to taking ribavirin that morning, he'd swallowed a large dose of cough suppressant.

He turned to look at the other passengers, who were pressed against the railing on the other side of the capsule, eagerly pointing out London landmarks. *Typical tourists*, he told himself. Expensive digital cameras and iPhones. Pressed up against the capsule windows, pointing and jabbering. Totally oblivious to the danger that would soon engulf them.

It took fifteen minutes for the capsule to reach its highest point. A perfect day for the task, thought Vector. Light breeze blowing from the east toward Buckingham Palace, which was a little over a mile away. And closer, in the same direction, were 10 Downing Street, Westminster Abbey, and historic St. James's Park, which would be clogged with visitors in the late summer. It was a cloudy day. He knew that would reduce ultraviolet radiation and increase the effectiveness of the agent. He looked around the capsule. The passengers had crowded together in one area to snap pictures of the palace.

Vector reached into a pocket in his parka and pulled out a twenty-ounce water bottle sealed inside a ziplock bag, which, if asked, he'd explain away by saying he'd had too many bad experiences with leaky water containers. From inside the parka he retrieved a plastic spray nozzle with a long, thin tube. He checked the other passengers again. They were all intent on the view below. From the bottom of the backpack he removed the plastic pillbox that he'd brought with him, all the way from Philadelphia, through Southeast Asia, and now to London. He'd checked on its contents earlier—the level below the ribavirin. His soldiers were holding up well, even though they'd gone several days without feeding. This was a female army, all gravid females, in desperate need of a blood meal. Well, they'd soon have one.

He unzipped the plastic bag and then carefully unscrewed the cap of the water bottle and placed it on the floor. He inserted the spray nozzle tube into the liquid, tightly screwed down the nozzle cap, and adjusted the nozzle setting to release a thin jet of liquid. When the liquid hit the air outside, it would disperse into millions of tiny droplets, each packed with virus particles. The nozzle was narrow enough to fit snugly into the plastic tube secured in the door opening. He began to conjure up images of television newscasters staring boldly into their cameras and telling their viewers that this attack had made September 11, 2001, look like a walk in the park, then forced the reverie out of his mind. He couldn't allow himself to be distracted—not even for a second.

He lifted the bottle to make the insertion. *Here we go*, he told himself. First the bottle contents, distributed over the city in a nice aerosolized mist. Next he'd quickly launch his soldiers through the plastic tube. It would take days before the first results showed. Then it would be too late to stop the rapidly spreading epidemic. He carefully fit the nozzle of the bottle into the plastic tubing and moved his thumb toward the plunger.

"What do you think you're doing!"

The interruption was so unexpected that Vector nearly dropped the bottle. He turned slowly to face a large, angry-looking woman with her hands on her hips. Could he bluff his way out of this? he asked himself. What difference did it make? He was going to die with the rest of them anyway. The act of securing the nozzle into the plastic bottle had probably already released some virus. He turned back toward the door.

A body slammed against him and toppled him to the floor. The bottle fell out of his hand and rolled away. The woman who'd questioned him was on top of him, calling out to the other passengers. Several more joined in. Using belts and shoelaces, they soon had Vector thoroughly restrained. By this time he was bleeding from his nose, had a bad cut on his chin, and had broken into a coughing fit. A young woman called 999—Britain's emergency number—on her cell phone. Consulting with the other passengers, she reported that they'd restrained a passenger on the Eye who'd tried to spray something over the city. They suspected a toxic substance. A gray-haired man gingerly picked up the spray bottle. Using a handkerchief to avoid direct contact, he dropped the bottle and handkerchief into Vector's plastic bag, and zipped it shut. Another man, wearing a "Britannia Rules" T-shirt, did his best to calm the other passengers until the Eye could complete its rotation to the ground.

The next day, Richard Blumenthal of CDC, and now acting director of the Barn, addressed Curt and Mariah at a small table in Hoffman's old office. "We're sure glad you two are all right," he said. "The country owes you an immense debt of gratitude."

Mariah saw Curt nod in acknowledgment, but she couldn't bring herself to do the same. She was tired, more tired than she'd ever been. And she was relieved. But all she could muster at this point was what she hoped seemed like composure. She'd sat close enough to Curt to be able to feel his warmth radiating through his shirt, and she had to will herself not to lean into him.

"London sure dodged a bullet," Blumenthal was saying. "Thanks to the passengers in the Eye. They stopped the release just in time, but some of the virus got out inside the capsule. Seven tourists are pretty sick."

"And Hoffman?" asked Mariah.

"Ah, yes. The notorious Doctor Vector. Close to death," said Blumenthal. "Kandahar. Seems that he already had it. He was treating himself with ribavirin, but just to delay the inevitable."

"He was already in bad shape when he showed up in the Philippines," said Mariah. "All the symptoms of Kandahar. He obviously had nothing to lose at that point. Basically he was a suicide bomber."

"One way to put it," said Blumenthal. "I have to admit, the guy had me totally fooled. I figured him for a super-patriot."

"It's not like anyone really knew him well," said Curt.

For several seconds, no one spoke. Then Blumenthal said, "Oh, there was something else."

Mariah and Curt looked questioningly at Blumenthal.

"He was carrying a plastic container. A large pillbox. Two layers. You've probably seen these things. They have partitions to arrange the pills by date. The top was holding a couple of pills. Ribavirin. Vector must have had just enough supply to last through 9/11."

"The bottom part?" asked Curt.

"That's where it gets interesting," said Blumenthal. "Ticks. A thousand or so in ten little capsules with perforated tops. All gravid females."

"My God," said Mariah. "He must have been planning to release those as well. He did talk about a backup plan in the hut. Plan B, I think he called it."

"You've got to hand it to him," said Blumenthal. "Pretty ingenious. We're assuming the ticks were infected with Kandahar. Fort Detrick's checking now."

Curt shook his head. "Hoffman must have had some entomology training. Renaissance man meets evil genius. Who knew?"

It all made sense, thought Mariah. Hoffman hadn't been totally relying on an aerosol release. He would have known that the virus might have been deactivated or weakened during its long journey from the Philippines to London. Or by atmospheric conditions after release from the Eye. She silently breathed a sigh of relief. It had been really close. Too close. After all that had been done to prevent the release, after all she and Curt had gone through, it had still almost happened. She shuddered inwardly, imagining what the consequences would have been if Hoffman had succeeded in London. She remembered her speculation about his intent and motive, to maybe release the virus in a Western city so that would trigger a massive U.S. response against the Islamic world. If the London attack had been successful, would the powers that be have listened to her, have paid any attention to her theory, and the logic and evidence behind it? And if they hadn't put stock in what she was telling them, would they have launched an immediate retaliatory strike of some kind? Against Pakistan or another Muslim nation? She liked to think they'd be more circumspect, spend time with the intelligence, carefully consider a range of options before acting. But she'd never know. She shifted her thoughts back to the States. "I understand we've got the outbreak under control here," she said.

"Looks like it," said Blumenthal. "We've contained the virus. No new cases since September ninth. Best guess is they'll lift the quarantine in the next couple of days."

"What about martial law?" asked Curt.

"No longer in effect."

"So," Mariah said hesitantly. "How bad did it get?"

"Pretty bad—but it could have been a lot worse. Over five thousand human cases and nearly four thousand deaths. Fortunately, no cases outside the final quarantine area, which encompassed a thirty-mile radius from Middle Valley. They had to destroy over a hundred thousand livestock animals and several thousand pets. And pretty much eliminate the wildlife in the quarantine zone."

Mariah shook her head. "How did the people handle it?"

"Once they understood the magnitude of the problem, saw the rioting, experienced the deaths of so many relatives and friends, most of them accepted the containment program and martial law," said Blumenthal. "The state and the feds are working on a compensation plan. But, as you might imagine, there's a lot of distrust of the authorities right now. And a bunch of lawsuits in the works. At one point, I was worried about a possible collapse of the government. But, if anything, federal authority seems to have gotten stronger. They're even talking about further restrictions on individual liberties. In the name of security, of course." Blumenthal looked back and forth between Curt and Mariah. "Seems we do have one thing to thank Hoffman for. It turns out he was very close to completing a vaccine for Kandahar. We found a prototype in his lab in the Barn, along with manufacturing details. We were able to take it to the final stage and make enough to inoculate most of the human population in the mid-Atlantic corridor. Of course FDA will first have to assure safety and efficacy. But we're doing all we can to fast-track the process."

"We're assuming that the virus strain hasn't mutated," said Mariah.

"That's right," said Blumenthal. "If it has mutated, the current vaccine may not be effective. But we think that's unlikely. Not enough time. And with the quarantine, animal culling, and tick eradication, we're pretty confident we wiped out the virus in Pennsylvania."

Curt and Mariah sat numbly. Mariah wondered if Curt was as exhausted as she was.

"Still a lot of unanswered questions," said Blumenthal when it was clear the other two had nothing else to way. "You'll take some time off now? You guys have sure earned it."

Curt nodded.

"Want to share where you'll be heading?"

"Someplace quiet," Curt said.

Mariah smiled.

That afternoon, a windowless cargo van sped down Route 95 just south of the Delaware-Maryland border. The van's driver hunched over the wheel, his teeth clenched tightly, his eyes focused on the road ahead. He'd been caught in traffic leaving Philadelphia and was running late. Doctor Vector had made his instructions clear back on September 1. The van's cargo, a large cooler, would be delivered today, September 12, in the nation's capital. Tens of thousands of demonstrators were massing on the Mall to protest what they believed was a slow response by the federal government to combat the spread of the Kandahar virus. For maximum effect, he needed to be at the Mall while the demonstration was still going on.

The driver rehearsed the plan in his mind as he sped down the interstate. He'd park the van as close to the Mall as possible, illegally if necessary, since the license plates were stolen and the authorities could never track the vehicle back to him. Not that it really mattered. He was prepared to give his life for the cause. He'd carry the cooler and a blanket to a grassy area near the demonstration. He'd be just another picnicker, lounging on the mall, watching the show. But the cooler didn't hold sandwiches and drinks. It contained ticks, thousands of them, in two dozen small plastic canisters. All he had to do was to uncap the canisters and release the insects. It would only take a couple of minutes. Doctor Vector had cryptically referred to this operation as Plan B. The driver hadn't asked questions other than to confirm the instructions. He knew better.

Minutes later, south of Elkton, Maryland, the driver saw a police cruiser parked by the side of the road. He hit the brakes. Too late. As he passed the cruiser he saw it pull out, blue lights flashing. He couldn't pull over. He was undocumented, didn't even have a driver's license. The cop would almost certainly search the van and find the cargo in the back end. He couldn't take that risk.

He pressed down on the accelerator. He could see the Susquehanna River bridge, just ahead. If he could put some distance between himself and the cop car, maybe he could make it across the bridge and take the Havre de Grace exit on the other side without being seen.

Halfway across the bridge, the van driver could see that the flashing blue lights were closing. He pressed the accelerator to the floor. *Damn!* A car just ahead, moving too slowly in the passing lane. He jerked the wheel to pass the car on the right, steered too close to the Jersey barrier at the edge of the bridge, and overcorrected. The van went into a skid. The driver took his foot off the accelerator, felt the vehicle begin to spin, and mouthed a silent prayer to Allah.

The rear end of the van slammed into the Jersey barrier, dislodging a large section of concrete. The van swayed unsteadily in the gap. The back end had torn open, and both rear wheels hung over the edge of the bridge. Then, with a slow screech of metal, the van began to slide. In slow motion, it toppled over and fell toward the water below. It landed upside down and began to float downstream toward Chesapeake Bay.

Tony Parnell cuddled next to his wife on the couch of their two-bedroom Philadelphia apartment and softly stroked her hair. Bobby was still sleeping, a good sign, because they'd been worried about nightmares. But seven-year-olds were pretty resilient, they'd assured each other, and with luck there'd be no lasting effects from the ordeal.

He wasn't so sure about Sally. She'd held it together pretty well so far, but the adrenaline would soon wear off. Based on her account of what had happened, she could be in for a rough stretch, psychologically. All in a rush, she'd told him about the noises in the night, the defenses, putting Bobby in the safe room, the attempt to break into the house, the face in the window. She'd stopped then, choked back a sob, squared her shoulders, and continued.

When she'd seen the face, she'd screamed and, without thinking, rushed to the window, swinging a baseball bat, smashing through the glass. She'd caught the guy square on the side of his head, watched him fall slowly backward, still clutching the extension ladder he'd climbed up on. The motion lights weren't working at that point—she'd figured the intruders had disabled them—but there was enough early dawn light for her to see the ground below. The guy on his back, pinned under the ladder. And three more men standing over him.

The men had then repositioned the ladder. One started climbing while the other two held the ladder firmly against the side of the house. The climber was moving awkwardly, leaning against the ladder as he slowly ascended, step-by-step. He was gripping the rungs with only one hand. She soon saw why. The other hand held a pistol.

There'd been a yell, behind her. She'd turned and seen Fredi standing there, shouting at her to get away from the window.

Then she'd heard the sound of sirens.

Parnell knew that he'd been responsible for the sirens. Before the cell-phone connection had broken that night, he'd heard Sally say that someone was trying to break in. He'd called 911, reported the intrusion, and given them the address and detailed directions. Obviously they'd arrived in the nick of time.

Afterward, when she was sure it was safe again, Sally had rushed to the safe room and given the secret knock. Several times. She was starting to panic all over again when the door finally opened. Bobby had slept through the whole thing.

CHAPTER THIRTY-THREE

At last, Mariah sat on the white sand beach, facing east as the sun began to rise over the Caribbean Sea. She first saw a smear of pinks and yellows and oranges above the long black band of the horizon. Then, as the dark layers of night peeled steadily back, creeping tendrils of blue began to stain the sky.

The ocean soon came into view, still smooth and glassy in the early morning. It first reflected the colors of the sky. But as the rising sun illuminated the sea the water took on an emerald hue, dark green in the distance, translucent up close. To Mariah, the ocean seemed to go on forever. She was learning that in the tropics, when the day is young and the weather is calm, the sea can seem as immense as the sky.

Sky and sea, blue and green. With the sun angling into the sky, Mariah could make out dark forms below the water's surface. Some were mounded and motionless, probably coral heads or algae-covered rocks. Others were large and moving. Mariah saw a dark-backed eagle ray flash white as it twisted after prey. Brightly colored reef fish shot through the water like bursts of rainbow shrapnel.

She rose and padded back to the snug, seaside bungalow

that she and Curt had rented for the week. Curt was just inside, already in his bathing suit, a towel slung over his shoulder, kneeling and rummaging through his duffel bag.

She stepped around him as he pulled a mask and snorkel from the bag. "Hey," she said, curling one foot beneath her and sitting on the edge of the bed.

"Hmm?" Curt said absently.

"I need to ask you something. I've been putting it off, but I can't wait anymore."

Now Curt stood up and looked at her, puzzled.

"When did you first figure out that Angus was your son?"

Curt took a deep breath. "Back when I first met him in Hawaii."

"Was it his eyes? Like yours?"

"Partly. But also his facial features."

"The strong jaw, right?"

"And something he got from his mother. The dark, curly hair."

Mariah nodded slowly, taking this in.

"So you suspected it too?" Curt asked.

Mariah nodded again. "When I saw his eyes. Like yours, even though his hair is dark. But I kind of dismissed it, wondered if it was just more common than I'd thought. And then there was his behavior at the hotel in Manila."

"He did seem kind of uptight," said Curt.

"More like disappointed," said Mariah. "Seemed to resent that I was there. Like he wanted to have some time alone with you. Then, when he disappeared, you seemed so devastated. More than I would have expected if it was just a professional colleague. I began to put two and two together." She looked searchingly at Curt. "So what will you do now?" she asked.

Curt returned Mariah's gaze. He paused for several seconds before answering. "To tell you the truth, I'm not sure," he finally said. "I only know that it will involve Angus . . . and you."

EPILOGUE

Two boys strolled along an empty beach, pant legs rolled up, shoes in their hands, splashing through the small waves that curled along the edge of the shore. One of the boys, a gangly kid of about twelve with a mop of curly red hair, bent over, picked something up at the water's edge, and cradled it in his hand. "Know what this is?" he asked his younger and shorter companion.

The smaller boy stared at a small, black, pillow-shaped object with spikes at both ends. "I dunno. Looks like a piece of plastic to me."

"Nope. It's a skate egg. My mother calls these mermaid's purses. The baby skate hatches out of them."

"What's a skate?" asked the younger boy.

"It's related to a shark and swims through the water with wings."

"Do they bite?"

"No, but their tails can sting you."

They continued down the beach. The older boy pointed out various shells, seaweeds, marine creatures, and pieces of flotsam and jetsam. He explained them all to his friend. For his age he knew a lot about marine biology and he enjoyed teaching others. He often came down to the beach alone to explore. His mother forbade him from doing this—she said he should always be accompanied by an adult. Plus, they were skipping school today. But his mom was at work now. She'd never know.

The younger boy saw it first—a large cooler lying on top of some seaweed at the high tide strand line. He pointed. "Let's check it out," he said. "Could be something valuable inside."

"I don't know," said the older boy. "It's probably somebody's lunch. Fell off a boat or something. It'll all be rotted and gross."

"It's sealed up," said the younger boy. "I'm gonna open it." He bent over the container and peeled away a layer of duct tape. Before opening the cooler's lid, he looked up at the older boy and saw that he was edging away. "Ha ha, you're a chicken." He swung the lid open. "Just some plastic containers," he said. "Wonder what's in them." He pulled one out and waved it at the older boy. The container was about four inches in diameter, three inches deep, and had a screw cap. Tiny holes perforated the cap. The plastic was opaque and the boy couldn't see inside. He started to twist the cap.

"Wait, maybe you'd better not open it," the older boy said.

"Why not?"

"I dunno. Maybe it's dangerous."

"You *are* a chicken." The younger boy felt good about calling the shots, being bolder than his friend for once. He unscrewed the cap. "Gross!" He quickly dropped the canister. "Bugs!"

The older boy looked down at the beach where the open container lay. Small black insects were scurrying over the sand. He'd seen these before. Plenty of times. "They're just ticks," he said. "They won't hurt you. Come on, let's go." But he wondered why a cooler full of ticks had washed up on the beach. Maybe he should tell someone—his mother perhaps. No, he couldn't do that. He'd just get into trouble.

GLOSSARY

Abu Sayyaf: Islamic separatist group based in the southern Philippines.

Acepromazine: Anxiety medication for dogs and cats.

Achuar tribe: Indigenous tribe in the rain forests of Ecuador.

Aerosols/aerosolize: Minute particles or liquid droplets suspended in the atmosphere. To aerosolize is the process of creating aerosols.

Aliquot: A precise portion of a larger volume of a chemical solution.

Amplify/amplification: Relating to microscopic pathogens, to substantially increase the population.

Animal model: Research animal, such as a lab mouse or monkey, used to test the virulence of a pathogen or the efficacy of a vaccine or therapy; obviates the need to directly expose human beings.

Animal Rights League: Fictitious animal protection organization.

Badjao: "Sea Gypsy" of Southeast Asia. Nomadic cultural group that spends its entire existence on the ocean.

Banyan tree: Large tropical fig tree that starts life as an epiphyte (a plant growing on another plant).

Barn, the: See *National Laboratory for Foreign Animal Diseases*.

Betel nut: Common name for the areca nut, a tropical palm nut that is frequently chewed as a stimulant.

Biohazard suit: Impermeable, whole-body garment worn to provide protection against dangerous chemical or biological agents. See also *hazmat suit*.

Biological Investigative Service: Fictitious branch of the Central Intelligence Agency; Curt Kennedy's employer.

Bioreactor: Apparatus used for large-scale production of bacteria, viruses, and vaccines.

Biosafety: The application of knowledge, techniques, and equipment to prevent personal, laboratory, or environmental exposure to potentially infectious agents or biohazards.

Biosafety cabinet: A local ventilation and air filtration device designed to protect the user or enclosed material from contamination.

Biosafety level: Level of biosafety protocols and facility design for working with specific infectious agents.

Biosecurity: Defined by the National Academy of Sciences as "security against the inadvertent, inappropriate, or intentional malicious or malevolent use of potentially dangerous biological agents or biotechnology." Originally applied to the protection of livestock and crops against infectious disease transmission.

Bioweapon: A living organism that has been deliberately adapted or developed to sicken or kill other living organisms.

Black Death: Devastating outbreak of bubonic plague, a bacterial disease transmitted by fleas on rodents that, in a Middle Ages pandemic, killed over a third of the population of Europe.

Black-legged tick: *Ixodes scapularis*, also known as the *deer tick*. Vector for Lyme disease.

Blue suit: Biohazard suit made of blue Tyvek material.

Breaking with: Coming down with an infectious disease.

BSL: Biosafety Level.

BSL-1: The lowest level of biosafety, applied when working with agents that do not normally cause human disease.

BSL-2: A level of biosafety considered appropriate for agents that can cause human disease but whose potential for transmission is limited.

BSL-3: A level of biosafety considered appropriate for agents that may be transmitted by the respiratory route and that can cause serious infection.

BSL-4: The highest level of biosafety. This level is used for the diagnosis/research of exotic agents, such as the Ebola virus, that pose a high risk of life-threatening disease, which may be transmitted by the aerosol route, and for which there is no vaccine or therapy.

Canine ehrlichiosis: A tick-borne hemorrhagic fever disease of dogs. Also known as canine rickettsiosis, canine hemorrhagic fever, tracker dog disease, canine typhus, and tropical canine pancytopenia.

CDC: Centers for Disease Control and Prevention. Atlanta, Georgia–based medical agency of the U.S. Department of Health and Human Services.

Cell culture: Process of growing cells in controlled laboratory conditions.

Confocal microscope: Imaging instrument using point illumination to improve the optical resolution of a specified area of a specimen.

Deer tick: See *black-legged tick*.

Dengue: An acute infectious tropical disease caused by a mosquito-borne virus. Also known as dengue fever and breakbone fever.

Deuce and a half: Two-and-a-half-ton military truck usually used to transport soldiers or equipment.

DHS: The U.S. Department of Homeland Security.

DOD: The U.S. Department of Defense.

Dugway Proving Ground: U.S. Army facility in a remote desert area of western Utah.

Ehrlichia canis: Scientific name for the rickettsial bacteria that causes canine ehrlichiosis.

Ehrlichiosis: See *canine ehrlichiosis*.

Fixative: In medicine: a medium such as a solution or spray that preserves specimens of tissues or cells.

Flow cytometer: Laser-based instrument used to analyze characteristics of particles, including cells, in a fluid.

Fluorometer: Instrument used to measure the fluorescent light spectra given off by a sample at different wavelengths.

Flying foxes: Large bats of the genus *Pteropus*, also known as fruit bats.

FMD: See *foot-and-mouth disease*.

Foot-and-mouth disease (FMD): Highly infectious viral illness that affects cloven-hoofed mammals like cows, sheep, and pigs.

Formalin: An aqueous solution of formaldehyde used as an antiseptic, disinfectant, or fixative.

Fort Detrick: Headquarters of the U.S. Army Medical Command in Frederick, Maryland, and location of U.S. Army Medical Research Institute for Infectious Diseases (USAMRIID).

GI Bill: Legislation that authorizes a wide range of benefits, including educational assistance, to military veterans.

Grippe: Old-fashioned name for influenza.

Growth chamber: Equipment used to grow biological organisms such as plants and insects under strictly controlled environmental conditions.

Hazmat suit: Impermeable, whole-body garment worn as personal protective equipment against biological and chemical hazards. See also *biohazard suit*.

Heifer: A young cow that has not yet given birth to a calf.

Hemorrhagic fever virus: Any of several arboviruses causing acute infectious human diseases, characterized by fever, prostration, vomiting, and hemorrhaging.

HEPA filter: High Efficiency Particulate Air filter for removing submicron-sized particles, including viruses, from the air.

High-pressure liquid chromatograph: Analytical chemistry instrument used to separate components in a mixture.

"Hot": Colloquial term for highly infectious.

Hot agent: Highly infectious pathogen.

Hot strain: Refers to a highly virulent subset of an infectious organism.

Hot virus: Highly infectious viral agent.

Image analysis/stereology inverted microscope: Microscope used for detailed analysis of images to determine the fine structure of objects, including cells.

Ixodes scapularis: See *black-legged tick*.

Jolo: Island in the province of Sulu in the southern Philippines. Also refers to the largest city on the island.

Kandahar hemorrhagic virus syndrome: Fictitious, tick-borne viral disease in this novel.

KIA: Killed in action.

Level 4: See *BSL-4*.

Long-tailed macaque monkey: Monkey species of the genus *Macaca*, indigenous to Southeast Asia, Borneo, and the Philippines. Also called crab-eating macaques.

Macaque: See *long-tailed macaque monkey*.

Machupo: Bolivian hemorrhagic fever, a rodent-borne viral disease of humans endemic in Bolivia.

Mass spectrometer: Analytical chemistry instrument that can measure the relative concentrations and masses of molecules and atoms.

Maximum containment laboratory: Enclosed space offering the highest level of biosecurity and biosafety.

MCL: See *maximum containment laboratory.*

Mercurochrome: Trade name for merbromin, a traditional, over-the-counter topical antiseptic. Because it contains mercury, the U.S. Food and Drug Administration removed it from the "generally recognized as safe" classification in 1998.

MI5: The security service of the United Kingdom, responsible for protecting the nation's citizens and interests against major threats to national security. Primarily focused on domestic threats.

MI6: The United Kingdom's Secret Intelligence Service, operating globally to gather information in support of national security, defense, foreign policy, and the economy. Primarily focused on foreign threats.

Micron: Unit of measurement equaling one millionth of a meter.

Mindanao: Large island and province in the southern Philippines.

Moon suit: Inflatable biohazard suit with external air supply.

Mount Dajo: Mountain on the island of Jolo, Sulu, Philippines.

Nanometer: Tiny unit of measurement; equal to one billionth of a meter.

National Laboratory for Foreign Animal Diseases: Fictitious animal health research facility operated by the U.S. Department of Agriculture in this novel. Also known as "the Barn."

Necropsy: Autopsy.

Negative air pressure: When considered from inside a container, the state when air pressure inside the container is lower than that of the outside.

Nipah/Nipah virus: A virus causing encephalitis that infects pigs and people.

Palawan: Island province in the western Philippines. Also refers to the largest island in the province.

Pamboat: Motorized outrigger canoe common in the southern Philippines.

Pathogen: Disease-causing agent, especially a virus or bacterium.

PCR: Polymerase chain reaction, a molecular technique that allows the production of a large quantity of a specific DNA. Commonly used for diagnosis of diseases.

PCR thermocycler: Instrument that uses the polymerase-chain-reaction process to amplify DNA and RNA samples for applications in genetics research.

PDA: Personal digital assistant, such as an iPhone.

Penn Hospital/Pennsylvania Hospital: Large private teaching hospital in Philadelphia, affiliated with the University of Pennsylvania.

Petechia: A small purplish spot on a body surface caused by a minute hemorrhage.

Plausible deniability: A posture whereby an otherwise accountable individual can credibly disavow knowledge of or responsibility for a culpable act.

Positive air pressure: When considered from inside a container, the state when air pressure inside the container is greater than that of the outside.

Purpura: A condition characterized by purplish patches on the skin or mucous membranes caused by hemorrhages.

Reston Ebolavirus: Hemorrhagic virus of macaque monkeys first evident in a monkey holding facility in Reston, Virginia. While fatal to monkeys, the disease has not yet affected humans. The disease was traced to macaque monkeys imported from the Philippines for research purposes.

Ribavirin: A synthetic, broad-spectrum antiviral drug.

Rickettsia/rickettsial bacteria: A genus of gram-negative bacteria that are carried as parasites by many ticks, fleas, and lice and cause diseases such as typhus and Rocky Mountain spotted fever.

RNA: Ribonucleic acid. A nucleic acid similar to DNA that forms on a DNA template and plays a role in protein synthesis and other cell activities.

RPG: Rocket Propelled Grenade (launcher).

Sabah: A Malaysian state in northern Borneo. Once part of the Sultanate of Brunei, later a British protectorate. Became part of Malaysia in 1963.

SEAL: Member of a U.S. Navy special warfare unit; stands for SEa, Air, Land.

SEM: Scanning electron microscope.

Sharps: Pointed or sharp objects or instruments used in biomedical work, such as scalpels and needles.

Sibutu: Island in Tawi-Tawi, the southernmost province of the Philippines. Sibutu is approximately ten miles east of Sabah, Malaysian Borneo.

Special ops: Abbreviation for special operations forces, composed of elite, highly trained active-duty and reserve/National Guard members of the U.S. military services and Department of Defense civilians, under the U.S. Special Operations Command. Includes Navy SEALs and Army Rangers.

Spectrophotometer: Instrument that measures the amount of light of specified wavelengths passing through a medium.

Straits of Malacca: Narrow sea passage between the island of Sumatra, Indonesia, and the Malay Peninsula. Connects the Pacific and Indian Oceans.

Sulu: Area, province, or archipelago in the southern Philippines consisting of numerous islands stretching from Mindanao to Borneo.

Symptomatic: Showing symptoms of a disease.

Synovial fluid: Viscous liquid that lubricates joints in mammals.

Tagalog: A member of a people native to the Philippines and inhabiting Manila and its adjacent provinces; also the language spoken by those people.

Tuba: A fermented palm wine. In the Philippines, it is manufactured from the sap of a coconut tree.

Umbilical: Cord connecting biohazard suit or hazmat suit to external air supply.

USAMRIID: U.S. Army Medical Research Institute for Infectious Diseases located at Fort Detrick in Frederick, Maryland.

USDA: U.S. Department of Agriculture.

USDA Wildlife Services: Program within the U.S. Department of Agriculture's Animal and Plant Health Inspection Service that manages wildlife conflicts to help people and animals to coexist.

Vector: A carrier that transmits a disease from one organism to another.

Vinta: Traditional sailing outrigger canoe of the southern Philippines.

Virion: A complete viral particle consisting of RNA or DNA surrounded by a protein shell and constituting the infective form of a virus.

Zoonotic disease/zoonosis: An infectious disease in animals that can be transmitted to humans.

ACKNOWLEDGMENTS

Many, many people had a hand in helping to shape this book and bring it to publication. My special gratitude goes to the following:

To my agent, Lauren Sharp, of Kuhn Projects, LLC. I cannot imagine a better agent. Her cheerful encouragement, unfailingly sound advice and judgment, and responsiveness were keys to significant improvements to the manuscript and a publication contract with a major publishing house. I also greatly appreciate the professionalism and support of the entire team at Kuhn.

To my editor, Matthew Benjamin, at Simon & Schuster. It has been a joy to work with Matthew. I am grateful for his enthusiasm for the novel, sharp insights, fresh ideas, and excellent suggestions. I particularly appreciate his quick responses to all inquiries and the fact that he does what he says he'll do, when he says he'll do it. My gratitude also to Lara Blackman and the top-notch editorial and production crew at Simon & Schuster.

To professional colleagues, whose expertise in agricultural and veterinary science and in biosecurity, biosafety, and biocontainment helped to ground-truth the novel's fictitious settings and premises. I am especially grateful to Dr. Rob Heckert, a veterinary scientist who formerly led USDA's animal health research program and has worked extensively in high-containment laboratories. Rob carefully read several drafts of the manuscript and made immensely valuable contributions. Jenny Withoff, another veterinary scientist, also graciously reviewed the manuscript and provided helpful feedback. Joe Kozlovac, a certified biosafety professional who has also worked in both the federal government and in academia, also provided valuable insights and suggestions.

To my supportive and helpful colleagues at the Georgetown University Medical Center's Department of Microbiology and Immunology, especially Richard Calderone and Len Rosenthal, and to the exceedingly bright and endlessly curious graduate students in my Agroterrorism course. I learn far more from them than they learn from me.

To the dedicated scientists and other professionals at the United States Department of Agriculture who work unstintingly in support of the nation's food and agriculture and who so willingly share their knowledge with others. I am especially grateful to Floyd Horn, former administrator of USDA's Agricultural Research Service. Floyd brought me into the agency and stimulated my interest in helping to protect the U.S. agriculture sector from deliberate attacks.

To many writing friends and associates who took the time to read the manuscript and offer valuable feedback and suggestions. I am profoundly grateful to Laura Oliver, a terrific writer, writing instructor, editor, and friend. Laura was a champion from the beginning and generously offered immensely valuable advice and perspective. I am also grateful to Susan Moger, another accomplished writer, writing instructor, and friend, and to Catherine Adams of Inkslinger Editing for their early reviews of the manuscript and excellent suggestions. While living in Annapolis, Maryland, I had the great fortune to join a writing group whose talented members not only were very helpful in offering substantive critiques of an initial draft of the novel, but who also became good friends. These include Charles Ota Heller, Karen Cain, and Marilyn Recknor. I also greatly appreciate the careful reading, constructive feedback, and strong encouragement from Mark Willen and Steve Berberich, members of the Novel Exchange Group of the Maryland Writers' Association.

To friends and immediate and extended family members who graciously and (I think) willingly read earlier drafts of the novel, offered very helpful, often surprising insights and suggestions, and/or comprised an enthusiastic support group. These include Charley and Pat Appleton; Cindy and Chris Delano; Vicki Duncan; Tally and John Garfield; Bill Mathers; Shane Merz; Tecla Murphy; Tom and Deborah Neal; Vern and Dorothy Penner; and Jim and Sharon Seymour; as well as my wife, Sue Parker; my mother, Ruth Parker; my siblings, Tony Parker, Steve Parker, and Ann Lonbay and her husband Jules; my sons and daughters-in-law, James and Tanya Parker and John and Lindsay Parker; and my cousin, Marion Myers.

And above all to my wife, Sue, who, at one time or another, has read or listened to virtually every word of every draft of the novel. She has done so with enthusiasm, a keen ear, incisive comments and suggestions, and, most important, with constant support and love. I owe her more than she can ever know.

ABOUT THE AUTHOR

Hank Parker is an adjunct professor at the Georgetown University Medical Center. He has been a U.S. Naval officer and deep-sea salvage diver; a seaweed farmer in the southern Philippines; a co-leader of an expedition that discovered and recovered remains of a Spanish Manila galleon; a research manager at the U.S. Department of Agriculture, where he helped lead programs to protect United States food and agriculture; a consultant on homeland security; and a professor of marine science. *Containment* is his first novel.